How to

Disappear

A novel in two parts

Rosanne Dingli

ISBN-13: 978-1514353424
ISBN-10: 1514353423

.

Yellow Teapot Books
Australia

Literary fiction

Designed and typeset by
Ding! Author Services
Cover art © Ravenna Bouckaert
Author portrait by Mark Flower

Also by Rosanne Dingli:

Death in Malta
According to Luke
Camera Obscura
The Hidden Auditorium
The White Lady of Marsaxlokk
Counting Churches – The Malta Stories
The Astronomer's Pig
The Bookbinder's Brother
The Red Volkswagen and other stories
Inverted Delusion
The Latin Cushion
All the Wrong Places (poetry)

More about this award-winning
Western Australian author
www.rosannedingli.com

How to

Disappear

Part One

1990-2009

One

Change

It fell heavily, that day – tumbling rain, spiralling, slanting, slapping onto heads. It streaked cheeks already damp with grief, it deadened human noises. No audible sniffing, just scrambling for scrunched-up tissues in a pocket smelling of orange peel.

'Don't cry.' Her voice, sharp and impatient. Her hand waving a creased hankie. 'Don't cry. He isn't your father.'

'What?'

'Don't mumble.'

Rain crashing onto headstones, sliding off marble tombs tilting in the damp. Trodden weeds sodden so the smell would, ever after, raise a memory of this. '*What?*'

'He wasn't your father. Don't grieve. Don't mourn like *that*.' She walked off, leaving without another word, passing through double gates whose badly-painted iron had peeled in weather so different. Sailing through, billowing bright raincoat, large umbrella and all.

Nothing else said for long breathless minutes. Raindrops and other stuff blown off the end of a numb nose dulled by the pain of winter.

Tea was good, taken at a corner table but by the service door, where noise from the kitchen – more noisy than the café, that afternoon – was loud conversation and crockery ringing, clattering, banging onto stainless steel. And the hiss of some glass-washing contraption, and the yeasty smell of a well-used oven.

'I said don't cry.'

Scalding tea, good, stronger than at home where there was no teapot, where teabags in mugs congregated on the draining board, and lost teaspoons came back to the kitchen after desultory imperfect searches through grey rooms.

'I was already pregnant when your dad ... when *Clint* came along, okay?'

'Already ...'

'You heard.' Strangely comforting, the rush of tea into a light green cup. She heard. Tears for a man not her father? But she missed him.

A break away to a toilet where others would crouch not to touch the seat, but to her was clean, cleaner than anything in her life. A break away from averted eyes, from talk of a pregnancy, of her conception. Unbearable. Mothers are not 'pregnant', mothers were 'before I had you'. Mothers were, 'when I was carrying your brother'.

Back at the table, to a plate of sandwiches already started. 'Ham and cheese, all right?'

'So Ian?'

'So Ian is much younger than you. Duh.'

'So ...'

'So I'm your mother – both of you. That's for sure. Ha! And that's what matters.' A wagged head, a damp hand reaching for another sandwich. 'Does *Ian* grieve? Ian's dead too.' Straight lipsticked mouth struggling full of cheese and ham.

'Mum, we don't know where he is or if he's dead.' Her own soft voice in a loud world.

Eye contact for an instant. Separate memories of that boyish freckled face, slitted eyes, shock of black hair so different, now that one thought of it, from her sandy ponytail. Separate understandings of temper, distance, rows, shouts, walking off into the night last April, and never coming back.

'Good as dead, is Ian.' A sniff, a nod, a fake smile at an inquiring waitress. Yes, another pot would be nice. 'The dead do not write, or phone, or send a card at Christmas. That's dead.'

More silence and deafening crockery, cutlery, laughter from a kitchen full of voices and sensations of warmth from more than just a yeasty oven.

'What are you now – fifteen? God.' More memories to crease the forehead.

'Seventeen ... very nearly eighteen.'

'Oh. God. God.'

'So why did we visit ...'

'... his grave? Why did I drag you out in this? Yeah – I wonder. The bastard!' Smile unmatched with sentiment, and one's heart clearly not decided. Or clear. 'The money, I think. I think it must be the money.'

'But we ...'

'Don't argue. Heaps of money. At least there's that. Having that sandwich or not?'

A soft fresh triangle of excellent bread, certainly not from the oven they could smell. Or perhaps yes, from there, then sliced thickly like this, spread with excellent butter, filled generously; real ham and yellow cheese with that delicious smell.

Smells, tastes, they somehow obliterated memories and started others. Cheese, good cheddar, would now always remind that Clint Winmarley was not her father.

'So who was?'

'Doesn't matter now.' Too old, too tired to slither

back into a sexually adventurous past. This slip of a girl – seventeen? Too young to be told of what happened behind the garages at Galveston Ave. 'Galveston.'

'That's his name?' Disbelief in eyes greyed, then made greener by light funnelled, slanted through a semi-circular windows: protractors full of clean coloured segments. Slices the hues of gems.

'Hah! No. Galveston Avenue was where we um ... met. Feels like a hundred years ago. I weighed a hundred pounds. Not for long, but.'

'What?'

'Saw him twice more and that was it – he was off to the mines or something. Or Mount Isa. How do I know? Or the peninsula. No idea.'

A realisation shot across the tablecloth. Grasping the edge of the round table like it was a life raft; a wobbly piece of driftwood in a life too wet with rain and promises wetly broken and wetly discarded, like teabags at home. A realisation coloured two faces, already glowing from the well-heated room and gusty hot draughts every time the kitchen door opened and slammed shut. He could still be alive.

'Good here, isn't it? More to eat?' Cakes in a glossy case eyed and eyed. The slip, slip, slip of a waitress's black skirt retreating and returning to a raised eyebrow, a raised hand. 'Two Eccles cakes ... no ... one Eccles cake and ...'

'I've had enough.'

'... and a slice of that chocolate tart. Looks very nice.' Returning to words left off minutes ago, when a couple at another table stood and left, just as the rain stopped, leaving a whiff of combined scents; sharp, clean, unusual scents never smelled at home. 'So Ian is a real Winmarley, see? And you ... you're not a real anything, are you?'

A hot flush, an eye on two cake plates; two forks shinier than any ever seen. 'I can't eat that. You'll have to.'

'I'll manage. Hah. I've always managed.'

'So ...' How insistent. Like the rain, that came again.

'So your father ... I mean, so Clint, bless his dear little dead heart, never knew, okay? He always thought you and your ginger hair were some throwback to his German great grandmother. On his mother's side!' Old tired laughter carried forward to the front of the café, and back to the kitchen door, and sideways to glass-enclosed cakes, and up to two straight lines of chandeliers. Fake crystal droplets. Kept so clean up there? A fleeting image of tall ladder, busy fingers, damp cloth, balanced bucket of hot soapy water ... came and went, and came again. 'What he couldn't figure was why you always have your nose in a book.'

She knew her mother would eventually get to her strange habits. Neither she nor Clint read anything – the only books in the house were in her small room.

'Let's get going before it gets bad. I need a cigarette. I've never known a winter so wet.' Struggling with the umbrella too huge indoors, leaving weaving lines of drops for a waitress to mop. 'Oh, yes, I can – that winter was wet, when you were ... when I ... you were a tiny little thing, you know, so easy to pass off as a bit before the right dates and all that.' Was the smile a device to forget, to remember?

A passing glance at the glossy case. 'Should have had the lemon cheesecake. And that's what's on your birth certificate, as you very well know.' A pointed look, half hidden by a hand patting brown waves, cheaply dyed at their stained bathroom sink. 'So you were Winmarley and that was that.'

'So really, then, I must be ... what?'

'No idea. No idea of the *name*.' Exhaling smoke. A laugh at a memory of risky irrational behaviour, of holding breath, of feeling a hot stab of something in the darkness of a parked car. Nothing happened. Nothing that mattered to her. Nothing that could not be tried again.

The house, cold, grey, smelling of everything and nothing.

'Why are we so slack, Mum? So lazy?' A cardigan, accusingly lifted off the sofa from a pile of washing, did not release creases.

'Tired, love. Exhausted.' The wry mouth of a bitter mother.

'We rest *before* we're tired.' Sharp accusation, soft voice.

'What I've been through, Missie? I'll be tired for a while.' Damp raincoat and umbrella flung into a corner. Another click of the lighter. A flame, an inhalation.

Something to clean the bathroom mirror with, quickly, before the feeling went, before steam from the hot tap could fog it. What could possibly appear? What could show differences and similarities – and to what, to whom?

Green eyes. Sandy hair, now loose from elastic bands, which trapped and tugged and ripped out three long hairs the colour of what? Marmalade. Dirty custard. Her mother's well-used credit card. Mud. Gold. The inside of a Crunchy bar. The inside of a Violet Crumble.

A nose unlike any other. A twin to that of someone never seen. A man when a boy who impregnated a woman when a girl; and now this? Not Winmarley. Then who, what?

Brilliant hair, he must have had, imagined swept back with a plastic comb kept in jeans back pocket;

ginger hair, and green eyes blinking with mischief, adventure. Straight, smart, rich teeth, braced by slick expenditure, stainless steel twinkling in the night in the depth of – what did she say? – *Galveston Avenue.*

Never heard of it. Heard only stuff of this town, of Winmarley stuff: fights, departures, money, neglect, false laughter, money, saucer-less cups on the draining board. Money. Laziness, cheating, the loneliness of no one to care if the sofa stayed full of washing taken from a line bristling with generations of clothes pegs. And a daughter not really his.

Her real father a mystery now. Curious. How could she have no idea of his name?

The mirror glinted it. Her eyes created it. Green. Yes, Green. Smart, savvy, a little on the naughty side. Easy to create, really. Make him up. Make up a name. Devil-may-care Josh Green. No – smart. Jonty Green. In expensive shoes. Glasses? Yes – glasses *and* braces. And clean. Brilliant clean. And this ginger hair.

A fortnight later, in a bedroom no longer grey, with curtains pulled back and panes made bright with hot soapy water. A grey face at the door opened without a knock. 'Birthday, dear. See? I remembered.'

'Thank you.'

'Doing anything?'

A definite nod from a head no longer seventeen. A head determined to right wrongs. Not to rest unless really tired. Really. Really tired.

In the city, grey dust and promises of change. She was on the way, watching her step, changing things, starting with her name. Much easier than she thought. Much more expensive, too, but worth every thought that went into the change. Perhaps, for sure, of course the bored counter clerk who took her money handed her a new identity.

'A hundred and sixty-five dollars. And oh, happy birthday, Miss.'

Yes, happy birthday. Happy, happy day.

'Name's Selby Green. *Selby Angela Maya Green*.' So the new sheet of paper read. Said out loud, by kind permission of deed poll, under her breath on the bus, a litany all the way back. 'Selby Green.'

The mother needed reminding about things. Prodding.

'Can I have a green top, and ... some green eye shadow?'

'Made of money, you think I am.'

'*His* money, Mum.'

'Yes, love – we'll be all right. More than enough. Just desserts for what I put up with.'

No point in arguing. She thought what she thought. 'We could hire help. You know – to ... um, clean and cook and ... fold laundry or something.' And before the exhausted mother could exclaim, complain, retort, think, 'Goodness knows. Mum, you deserve a ... um, a *rest*.' A hand sweeping, indicating a living room filled with dancing dust motes on lances of light through dead curtains. Damp washing on a dead couch.

'I do. I do need a rest from all this. Brilliant, Bec.' A smile like the idea was hers.

'Selby.'

'What?'

'I want to be called Selby.'

A slack mouth hanging open. 'What ... what's this now?'

No rants, no monologues, no explanations for effect. A shrug, eloquent or not, had to suffice.

'Not the name of one of those artists you read about, is it?'

It was possible to keep silent until her mother was

distracted by something else. In a clean house, everything was possible. And it was possible to make it clean.

'Could never make you out, could I?'

But now she knew why. All in her name. All in her eyes, in his eyes, in a newly-adapted sense of order. Winmarley money bought bed linen and shiny spoons. A new Green identity brought energy and cleanliness. Smelly living room rug expelled out the door; dead curtains afforded a decent burial.

'You can be so ruthless.'

'I can be what I want.' Which was the point. Her voice, though, lacking confidence. Her mother raising an eyebrow, not convinced, not convinced.

It came heavily that week; drops tumbling onto a mown front lawn, weeds shaven close, so close, they could have been anything. Anything in that downpour. Buffalo, dandelion, purslane, ragweed, onion grass, kikuyu. Their smell reminding sharply of a man in a grave, visited in the rain. A man not her father, but missed. This shorn lawn evidence of a new realization.

And someone fixed the gate. And the gutters, and painted the front door. That someone took away every single bit of rubbish, identifiable or not, from the garden. Drove away with a trailer of trash. A paid someone; like the paid maid who even organised the cutlery drawer and sprayed the bathroom ceiling back to something like the yellow she never knew it was.

'What's this? What have you done now?' A startled mother looking, looking, looking at a new style.

Selby – Selby Green – tilted a lighter head. 'Just a haircut, Mum. New look. And look, new cups. We do have the money.'

'You don't stop, do you?'

'Not unless I'm tired.' A pause. 'It's not only ... not

really *tiredness*, you know.'

There was no answer, but good tea was sipped. Hot, from a green teapot, almost exactly like in the café with the yeasty oven. But she did speak. 'It's not laziness either, young lady.'

Drinking tea; a more potent response than a denial.

A mother's insistence. 'Mmm?'

'It's knots, see? Knots of boredom. Of blackness.'

'Don't get all mystical on me.'

'Mysterious, you mean. Like why we went to the cemetery.'

An understanding nod. 'You still miss him.' A sweep of a hand like it was obvious.

It was undeniable. Clint Winmarley might not have been her father, or any sort of a father, but he left money. Told jokes. Left a trail of whisky bottles, but was a sodden drunk. Harmless, jokey, full of dopey affection that stayed unreturned. Full of a latent kind of energy he poured into work, work, work.

'You do.' Another sip of hot tea, and spoiling for an argument.

'Hm?'

'You do miss him.'

'I do.' Identical tea in identical cups. Brilliant clean. 'I can do my missing anywhere.' Nodded a shorn head. 'Here is good. Here's the same. Here, there, anywhere.' Different gaze. 'Why did we go to the cemetery, Mum? Exactly why? I cried and you didn't.'

She never cried. Not about the dead dog. Not about lost earrings. Not about Ian leaving. Not about dead Clint Winmarley. 'What did you say before?'

Sun could now channel through clean windowpanes onto an old clean tablecloth, found by chance in a drawer not opened for countless years. Small vine leaves, beautiful, embroidered by goodness knew which grandmother in goodness knew which country town. Sun touched the back of carefully-dyed brown hair.

'What, about missing ...?' Selby rotated a perfect plate of sandwiches.

'No. You said something about knots.'

'Knots of boredom. Monotony.'

'You and your bookish words. I'd never noticed before I was monot ... *bored*.'

'I'm curious.' Selby knew it would work.

It worked. 'About what?' Straight lipsticked mouth struggling with a sandwich to rival the café's.

'I told you. About the cemetery. About visiting Dad.' Not Dad, he wasn't her father. '*Clint*, I mean ... on a wet day, without real need.'

'Yes with *need*.' Said forcefully, said with a defiant gesture; finger pushing shiny teaspoon an inch, turning saucer an inch. Raising chin.

Silence let in street noises. The Smith woman from across, wheeling her bin down the steep driveway, over joins in the concrete. Roll, roll, thump, roll, roll, thump. The postman stopping everywhere but there. A plane going goodness knew where.

'What need? I don't need to ...'

'I need to!' An old, old plea. More tea. Prematurely old cheeks reddened with something more than Maybelline. Old eyes crinkled, blinking through cigarette smoke. Skin older than her years. Teeth slightly yellow. Gums inflamed. What was she now – forty? Forty-four?

If she waited, her mother would spit it out. When she waited, two days ago, the tablecloth, steeped in strong detergent, had released old stains. Rubbed with young inexpert hands.

'I needed to make sure, see?' A mother explaining.

Sorting out what it all was. Right there. At table, eyeing, eyeing, eyeing another sandwich.

If she waited, stains were released.

'I need to make sure from time to time. It's like pinching myself. Like telling myself it's true. It's true there's a grave.'

'*Mum.*'

'It's true. He's gone-gone-gone.' She rose. New rug fibres underfoot relenting to weight, to pressure, to pacing up, turning, pacing back. Spread arms, throat swallowing ham and cheese. 'Ha ha! It's true.'

Her mother was free. Goodness knew from what, really.

And here, right here, was Selby Green.

Two

Cleanliness

A bit unsure now, what drew Selby to him. *What attracts a woman to a man will eventually disgust her.* That's what her mother, so long ago now, years ago now, had said. Philosophical, under an umbrella, in a downpour. A mother gone, resting in peace, after – what was it? – seven years of irritation, twelve months of pain. Inhaling an agony. Exhaling a struggle. Resting before she was truly tired.

She'd been right about one thing. Whatever it was that attracted ultimately repelled. What pulled would eventually push. *Pull-pull-pull*, she had said, *push-push-push*; and Selby had no idea what she meant. Then.

Now she did. Now she looked at him, this husband of so many years. Pinched eyes, pinched mouth, nose an arc in profile, over greying moustache, long upper lip, popeye chin curved upward. She had liked the humour – once – the wit she thought of as sharp. Liked his clean habits. Immaculate kitchen, bathroom close to sterile, carpets free of dust or pet hair. Pet hair! She was the only pet. On a tight leash. That's what it was; the cleanliness. Now she was its slave.

Remembered the day the first stifling feelings of being trapped stared out from her own eyes in a sparkling hall mirror; art nouveau frame. Matching umbrella stand. Gleaming polished surface. Sickly smell of jonquils fresh from the kiosk outside his office building. Stared out from the bathroom mirror, too, under lamps regularly cleaned. Hot soapy water.

All planned, all orchestrated, her eyes said. Your fault, Selby Green. You walked up that aisle. You walked across that bridge. No one pushed you. You strode away from knots, bonds of boredom. Monotony. Bouts of blackness.

'No – it's not boredom.' Turning into her mother. No – not quite. Green eyes. Eyes of a half-invented father. Jonty Green. Hah! *Save me now, Jonty Green.*

Save me now. Goodness knew where he was. He might never have existed. He might have been a figment of her mother's invention, created from pure boredom. She never found a Galveston Avenue on any map, near or far. But where did the ginger hair come from, the green eyes? So unlike Clint Winmarley. Nothing of him in her.

'Nothing of him in me.'

'What? Who ... of whom?' Squinting, her odd words making him curious. She knew that look.

Looked up, arresting him, freezing him in a steadfast gaze. Interrupting his dinner. 'There's nothing of my father in me.'

'So?'

'Neither one, nor the other.'

'Other? You can't have two fathers.'

'I can have what I want.' Shook her hair, ginger, bright in the brilliant light. She saw it, immediately. Instant in his eyes. A look of deep annoyance. Close to contempt.

'None of us can have what we want.' His meanest tone. A husband's tone to put her in her place.

'Least of all me, right?' Too sharp. Too true. 'Yes – I know.' Her tone now intended to assuage. To stop just before he got angry. Never make him angry. That she knew. That she had learned. A soft wistful smile. It worked.

'We can always wish.' He rose from the perfect table, laid with care. Fresh cloth, posy in a cut glass vase, shiny cutlery now placed to one side after a perfect meal. 'That was nice, darling.'

It was always nice, darling. *A Book of Nice Recipes*. She could write it herself.

'And when you load the dishwasher ...'

Another smile, another wistful smile. Contrition, if it were liquid, would have stained the tablecloth. 'I know – put knives in point downward. I know. Sorry.'

'Replace the towel, too. Draw the curtains.'

How much apology in one evening? 'Yes, sorry.' Her eyes downcast.

How clean was too clean? How obsessive?

Floors on Thursdays, laundry on Mondays. Ironing all Wednesday afternoon. Longing to leave piles of damp shirts, heaps of creased trousers, clumps of unpaired socks on the sofa. Longing to leave smeared butter on the handle of a silver knife. Leave a teabag on the draining board. Leave a row of mugs stained brown inside. Longing to sabotage her own calm and quiet.

A coffee with Thelma might work. But what did Thel – four kids and unreliable car – know about an empty house that could stifle? Empty rooms, empty chairs, an empty breast, eyes empty of anything other than ... whatever was it that kept her captive, here, in this grey perfection?

Emptiness. It was not what kept Thel tied to her life. Far from empty. Buried in children's things, pets, mess, noise. A disorganized woman loved by her family man with a thousand hobbies, was Thel. And she?

And he? Kept on talking. 'And when you load the

dishwasher...'

'Yes, I'll put out a fresh towel, too.' And leave a couple of knives point upward, hoping one might neatly slit ... wistful smile. What *was* she thinking?

Three

Low pressure

Black-black-black her mother would have said. Despondent, moody. No, not moody: that would have been up-and-down, back-and-forth. She was unhappy *all* the time. Since Christmas. Which Christmas? No, since dinner with the Balcon-Wests. No, since her own wedding.

How long ago? Too long ago. Now that was a day. Memories of white-white-white, of cut flowers that reeked of a joy she did not feel. Of an altar that danced before her unbelieving eyes. A fear-filled imitation, a burlesque tableau out of Arthur Boyd's complex artist's mind. A ghost bride: herself. Goodness – a church, and she in it, mouthing vows that came out of her lip-sticky mouth, up a tickly nose that threatened to sneeze, sneeze, sneeze her into some sense.

'You'll never lack for anything,' her mother had said, through glaucous eyes. Perhaps she was right. Perhaps she would wake to something close to ... to what? Something less like imprisonment. No one to save her from this. Mother dead seven years, Clint Winmarley dead, Ian good as dead, Jonty Green a figment ... a figment. And now turned legally, matrimonially, definitely, with just a few words, from Green to Brixham.

It all came back. White, white, white. *Black-black-*

black. All these memories she never wanted to collect, from scowling at porcelain figurines, none of which she liked, but all of which needed dusting. Washing, better. Pulling out the yellow basin. Filling it too fast with water too hot, too soapy, too slippery for this job. Expensive porcelain. A tall pale overly-thin maudlin pastel female figure in pieces at the bottom. Sharp pieces. More evocative now than whole.

At dinner, with fork halfway to mouth, she paused. 'Broken. At the bottom of a yellow well of bubbles.'

'What?' Mouth full of bourguignon. Head full of office stuff. Face full of annoyance. Bearded chin stiff with ... dislike, regret, derision?

'I broke your Aunt Raelene's wedding present today.' Expecting a burst of anger.

None came. 'Only those who work, break.'

The loss of a hated figurine, then, was attributed to industry, or at least, to the absence of idleness. The eradication of laziness, which he loathed. 'Which one was it?'

'The tall Lladro thing. Improbably tall, improbably beautiful. She ... she disappeared.'

'*Disappeared*?' A crumpled face. Pent-up violence. He could slap her, slap her. Crush her. 'Listen to you. You need to get out more. Buy a bicycle.'

Her blank stare a provocation.

'You heard. Don't just mooch around here *reading*. Get out in the open. *Exercise*.'

Purple, it was, and efficient, with gears like silk. She rode it north, to Westcombe, east to the sand bar, south to Summermead, west to the new estate, where smells of fresh concrete, quarried stone, diesel-powered land movers, upturned soil, cut tiles, new mortar, poured driveways assailed and dizzied her.

In nine months, the new place teemed with new

life. Families tumbling from removals vans. Furniture spilling into rooms stinking of paint. The stink of hope. In nine months, she lost twelve pounds.

'Like a skeleton you are.' Thel combed through a shag of wet hair on one daughter's head. 'That bicycle will be the death of you.'

Little did she know how right she was. How easy it would be to dissolve, finish, under the huge front wheels of some barrelling truck.

'Eat something. You exercise like that, you need carbohydrate. Lots of it.'

A grimace. How could she eat? Why should she eat? Nothing could fill the hollow. Nothing could wake her from this numbness.

Thel laughed. 'You'll disappear.'

Now that was an idea.

He startled her. Came into the hall just as she got back home, with a sweater over his head, arms half through sleeves, back early from the office. His bunch of flowers on the kitchen table. 'There will be six of us to dinner on Friday.'

'Six?'

'You heard. The new marketing manager and his wife, and the Balcon-Wests. They're always good for conversation.'

'And ...'

'And Beef Wellington. That pommes thing you make. A couple of French beans. And a fancy dessert from Maison Whatever. *Don't* try and make it yourself.'

'Croquembouche.' A dig, a cynical hint.

'Sometimes you are ridiculous.' Sometimes his contempt was palpable.

Her high laugh was no response, it rattled the chandelier. Rattled him. Pretended it was a joke. 'Over the top, right?'

No answer from him, sliding on that grey sweater like a second snake skin.

Her skin no longer smooth. In the hall mirror it seemed pleated. Old skin, tanned from cycling, crinkling at the elbow, lining at the eyes. Misery pleating dry skin near her mouth. From living here. With an unhappy man. Thel told her.

'You're both miserable.'

'Both? Both?' Realization flooded, cool and warm in turn, all the way back on a bike too purple for comfort, too smooth for comfort. Well-oiled and fast. Over bridge, past warehouses, behind church, front of factory, past school, around the service station at Point Rigby. Up the smart driveway. *Same-same-same.*

'He's miserable,' she said to the mirror. 'Unhappy. Glum. Grey as a rainy day.' He hated her. Of course.

But she did it anyway. Carried a huge Croquembouche to the table on Friday. To five startled gazes, eyeing, eyeing, eyeing the tower of round puffs strung with pulled sugar. Gleaming under the chandelier. Gleaming.

'Selby!' His voice a rifle report.

Guest voices a blur.

Her voice. 'From Maison Whatever!'

Everyone eating fatty bombs of crème pâtissière. Smiles all round now. Embarrassment, anger, victory, contrition, regret dissolved in Chateau Lafite or whatever it was in those tall wedding present glasses. And coffee from that awful machine on the spotless kitchen counter. Gleaming in a gleaming kitchen.

'Are you miserable?' Later, her small voice in a big bedroom.

His miserable head shaken back and forth. 'They thought it was a joke. Worked in the end.'

It wasn't what she meant.

'At least you didn't waffle on about history, and *art* and ... whatever it is you read.'

I read. I read. I read. How crazy of her. 'I read biographies. How artists lived. What they did. Why they painted.'

'*Why* they painted?' Sullen face. Droopy eyes, wry mouth.

Glum-glum-glum, her mother would have said.

'I'm never miserable.' Corners of his mouth downward. Neck bent. The arc of discontent. Was it because they didn't talk? Was it because they had no children? Was it because there were so many questions that were never spoken, never answered?

'Course not.'

His head rose slowly. 'Do you mind if I sleep in the guest room?'

Did she mind? She had no idea. 'Sure.'

He disappeared.

She disappeared into muffling, rustling, crumpling mounds of bedding she mussed up more, heaping everything into the middle of the great big rigid platform they called a bed. Which she made up carefully every morning, tight as a drum. Pulled at sheet ends now, quilt ends, pillow corners no longer perfectly pointed. Creased the whole thing into an impossible fabric dune. Oh. Found bliss underneath it all.

And quiet. Perfect quiet.

Curled herself into something she saw in her night mind's eye. A Gustav Klimt figure wrapped in a hundred quilts, a thousand gold blankets. A million solitary, blissful, sleepy seconds.

Four

How to disappear

Photographs of his parents in frames. And he, graduation robe, tilted head, piercing eyes, dull glare. Her dead mother's live smile; so close to insolent, so close to devil-may-care, in a lonely silver frame, top of a chiffonier, near a figurine dusted every Thursday. A photo of her big form, so large, so deceptively maternal, under an umbrella.

No photo of Jonty Green. No photo of Clint Winmarley. And then her own bridal face, deceptively plump and deceptively jolly, full of life, in a frame blinding with the glint of fine silver. Surprised it was still there; surprised the passing years did not just melt it into dove grey wallpaper, lacy doily, shimmering oak sideboard. Looked closely at her Jonty Green green eyes. The mouth she could never decide was hers.

'Could I find him?'

'He'd be a hundred and four and demented.' Practical words from Thel, through lips clamping bobby pins kept out of reach of toddlers on the floor.

'No – surely in his sixties, or something.'

'Find yourself first.'

'What?'

A smile, benevolent, full of household wisdom. Kitchen sink sagacity. 'What have you ever done? *Do* stuff.'

'How can I just ...?'

'Nothing to leave behind but misery, I reckon.'

'Thank you.'

'My pleasure. Have a doughnut.'

She stared blankly at a plate piled high. Did nothing.

'Carbs – have a doughnut, I tell you.' Thel poured more tea. 'Get some flesh on those bones. See the world.'

'I can't just ...' through a nibble of cinnamon sugar.

'You can do anything you like.'

'But he...'

'He'd be relieved, after the shock.' Sharp laughter. 'After the surprise, he'd be happy you're gone.'

'True? You think so?'

Two children on her knee. 'Don't know. Don't know, really. Try it, Selby Brixham.'

Selby *Green*. She was Selby Green. She hated this Brixham business. 'Green.' Through cinnamon sugar. 'Selby Green.'

'There you go then. Whatever you want, I guess.' Three children on her knee now. Thel animated, voice a growl, a mock fierce rumble, over the sharp alto squeals of her children. 'Look in the mirror – what do you see?'

Selby stared and stared now, no mirror, just a friend across a cluttered table. Seeking meaning in this assured confident reliant reliable woman's eyes.

'You see yourself, if you look in a mirror.' A grimace typical of Thel. 'When I look in the mirror, all I see is four kids and a husband. I've disappeared, see. Can't even figure what I like, what I want, what I desire, what I need. I know everyone's needs but mine. I've *vanished*.'

'You mean ...'

'I mean this is the best way to disappear ... because you've wondered, haven't you?'

She had.

Thel reached long, stuck a finger in her chest, poked her gently. 'You've wondered how you can disappear. Go up like a puff of smoke away from this misery of yours. It's misery because you can hear it, see? I can never hear myself in all this.' Arms widespread, children sliding off lap. Squeals deafening. Doughnuts handed out. Wry sideways smile, sideways wink.

'Thel, I can't disappear.'

The woman laughed, poured tea. Gathered bobby pins in a neat pile on the table. Played with them a second. 'You're invisible already. What you need to do is appear in another place, honey. Poufff!'

It came heavily, that day – tumbling rain, spiralling, slapping onto her head. Dry-eyed, looking at the gravestone, now with a line to her mother's memory underneath Clint Winmarley's. Dead but not invisible. Gone but not really faded from life. Vanished but still present, sharp voice in her daughter's head. Gone-gone-gone. The smell of sodden weeds bringing it back. Her mother would say *buried-buried-buried*. Like some family ritual that never went away. Like tea at the café on Fridays. Like shopping at Dunfurlough's. Like umbrellas dripping in the hall. Like damp clothing piled on a sofa.

Thel was right. She didn't want children. Even though she had waited, waited, waited for years for something to change. Didn't want silver on the sideboard, or Lladro statuettes behind glass.

Couldn't stand another dinner where her left-handed resentment turned on her. Turned into success; pumpkin into carriage, croquembouche into social coup.

'Too quiet in my house.' Spoke to the mirror like it could solve all this. The misery was deafening. Didn't want a husband. Didn't want *We'll be eight for dinner on Saturday*.

Tried, attempted, struggled to write a list, like it said in one magazine. A list of wants. Needs. Wants. Had no idea what to want. What could she possibly have now? What could be left for her to want?

One thing. One thing. Two.

Five

Sibling similarities and differences

Found him. Incredible. Nothing like her, still the same Ian who disappeared at fourteen, leaving in a huff, leaving everything. Nothing of him in her either. Plenty of Clint Winmarley in those eyes; a lot of wry disappointment, a lot of sozzled humour.

'Didn't think I'd drink, would you, after all that childhood crap?'

'I didn't say anything.'

'Like you need to talk to say something. Everything's always written on your face, Bec.'

'Selby.'

'*Selby*. Have you changed *everything*?' Squinted through rank cigarette smoke, stale already from lips as straight as mother's. Reached for half-full glass, smiled the smile of the nearly-drunk. Winked the wink of the harmless sot.

'Wish I could.' Did not want to confide in him, really.

'Believe me, everything's changeable.'

'Except people?'

His laugh rolling through the pub, turning heads, creating weak smiles on desperate faces. 'Think you can change a name and change your whole .... what ... *personality*?'

Looked down into her glass, still slowly bursting

with impotent effervescence. 'Don't even have that.'

'You can have anything you want.'

That much of something in him she recognised. 'Ian Winmarley – have *you* got everything you want?'

'Except a dog, perhaps. More or less. No comparisons with anyone else but ... yeah.' A slow definite nod. 'Yeah. More content than I ever could be right now. Never thought I'd see you again, sis.'

Warm glow. Incredible flooding sensation of something indistinguishable.

'How can I call you Selby, Bec? It'll turn my mind back to front!'

'Try.'

'Hm.' Nodding, nodding, nodding.

'Ever wondered why I have ginger hair and green eyes, Ian?'

Ringing laugh. Sideways look. Pretending to be distracted by a dog passing outside the pub door. 'No – I have wondered, but, why I have freckles, black hair, and brown eyes!' Laughter reaching greasy lined-up fluorescent strips overhead, swinging slightly in cigarette smoke. The miasma of indolence, early afternoon. The sense of nothing going on. Of the world stopping, except for the sound of a distant police siren on the highway. 'What's this then? Why do you have green eyes?'

Told him. Said the words *Jonty Green* aloud. They felt real.

'Not surprised. Amazed. But not surprised. Tried to find him, then?'

'Nothing to go on. Where's Galveston Avenue?'

Scratched his head. Signalled for another round. Squinted eyes. 'Dunno. Not here in town, that's for sure. Not anywhere I've been.'

'That's where I'm going.'

Grunted. 'Yeah?'

'No – not really. I just want to find him.'

Gulped at fresh drink, patted pocket.

'I'll get it, Ian.' Paid for brother's drink with husband's money.

'Cheers.' Gulped some more. 'You don't want to find him. Not really. Pandora's box of family mess. Mess and bother. Murk and muck. Guarantee of muck, family stuff. No one wants to know their parents' unknown misery – we know that. The *known* misery is quite enough, thank you.'

Believed him. Agreeing, agreeing, but persisting anyway with her thought. 'It might make me ...'

'Happy? How happy are you? I mean – all this married in the suburbs lark. How happy is that? You want to lose yourself, not find him.'

More sharp wisdom. 'You and Thelma should meet.'

'Thelma who? Who's Thelma?' Piercing eyes through smoke. Through a decade and a half or more, or however long it was. Still could see through her. 'If someone else says the same – someone who knows you well, right? – it must mean something.'

'I don't know how to disappear.'

'Hah! If you could find me, if you could send me money, enough to get back here to see the old town ... to see you, I mean, and all that. Jeez.' Nodded and threw head back, eyes wide open. 'You can do anything ... what did you say you ... ah! Selby, you said. Selby it is now. Selby, you can do anything.' Thought again. 'Anything since ... anything but ... what did you say?' Glazed eyes, slurred esses. 'Disappear?'

'Hm.'

'Nothing to it. You got legs.'

Looking, looking, looking straight at him, like she

might at Thel.

'So what are we doing now, d'ya think?' The wink of the very drunk. 'Y'know? You were always a looker, you were always a quiet thinker – still read a lot? – but now … now you need something, um … something. What is it you need?'

She watched him without a word. Not knowing what to think, what to feel, what to want.

Ian, looking tired. Scratching head. Kindness, futility, contentment, benevolence, affection beaming out like it did from Clint Winmarley. 'You need to eat more, I reckon. What we do now is fish and chips. How much money you got?' Head thrown back like it was funny.

Six

Jumping to perceptions

Weeks after that auction, standing in a doorway. *Wet-wet-wet*. Waiting for it to stop. Waiting for drubbing, yawning, grating thunder to roll away. A break in the weather. Crossing to the other side. Find Ian. Lose yourself. She looked at the old house through pouring rain. Not hers any more. No smell of weeds here. Nothing but exhaust fumes doused by greasy rain. Nothing but the seed of an idea with nothing to grow it in.

Except for money, of course. There was the money.

Still in town? Need to talk, she said to her brother on the phone. Now walking towards another pub, far side of town.

He was not too far gone to talk, perhaps. Perhaps her idea would lift her from this.

The sound of brakes. Sudden. Sharp. Sharp breath. Quick step back. Quick exhalation. Unless something else got her first. Nearly mown down by a bus. Hand to chest. Exhale. Inhale. Close shave, that was. A close shave that could have ended it all.

It would have solved something. But no – a knot of determination, felt in her chest, under that raised hand. Life could give her more than this. No. She could *take* more than this for herself. Perhaps. Shaky, but walking surely, firmly, resolutely to meet her brother.

'Hi.' Eyes a bit blurred.

'It's not even four, Ian.' Wishing she could take the words back. How dare she make any kind of observation? How dare she even try to tell him what to drink and when? This was her long-lost baby brother meeting her when she called. So what if he smelled of beer and cigarettes? 'Sorry – you're here. I'm here.'

'Yup.' Sweet smile, taking in and putting out his entire world. Held out an arm. Embraced her. 'Smile – it might never happen.'

Old line. Old joke. Left her silent.

'Nearly got collected by a bus.'

'But you're okay, right?'

'I think I am.' Hand to chest, hand to forehead.

'Need to take things more lightly, sis.'

'Me?'

'You. I take things so lightly,' he said, eyes serious and opaque, 'that they're hardly there at all.' Blew through his fingers.

'But how can ...'

'Piece-a-cake, my love. Stuff happens. There I was, wondering what on earth could happen to get me out of a jam, and you call, out of a clear blue sky, and send a ticket. And here I am, out of the jam. Drinking with you at ... at ...'

'At Tony's Bar.'

'There you go.'

'All the stuff, Ian. All the old stuff from home – it's gone.'

'That's what I figured, long ago.'

'No. I mean, I sold it all. And the house. Now. Recently. And I have an idea.'

Instead of lighting up, his eyes now slitting, drooping, squinting like he didn't understand.

'Ian – I planned this. Are you listening?'

A raucous laugh. 'Always listening, love. It's what I do best. Suck at talking.'

Thought of all his slurred sentences, rushing out at her last time. Smiled. 'You see, the old house was Mum's. Furniture, stuff – mostly rubbish and junk. Sold the lot. Auctioned it off. '

'Had no idea there was anything left.'

'Oh yes. Clint Winmarley left ... some.'

'Worked like a Trojan, did old Dad. That I remember. But drank. Boy – could that bastard drink.'

'He was kind.'

'Kinda desperate, you mean.'

Never occurred to her. 'Desperate?'

'Unhappy. Cruel miserable, he was.'

What could he mean? All she remembered were smiles, yarns, slurred jokes. She shrugged, ordered a lemon-lime-and-bitters, grimaced, all at once. Turning to avoid his smile, his look, his searching for an expression that would tell him what she felt.

'That all you ever drink?' Pointing an expressive finger, a shaky finger on a trembling hand. He was too young for this.

Looking now, into black opaque eyes inside reddish lizard rims. No eyelashes to speak of, and nearly three years younger than her. 'No.'

'Won't make you disappear, you know, drinking.'

'I don't drink.'

'Way you live – the way I sense you live... I'd have been driven to the bottle years ago. You are a plucky one, you. Bec ... I mean, Selby love – it takes pluck to stay. Me? I shipped out. How old was I, fifteen?'

'Fourteen. And it wasn't from a marriage. Everyone leaves home at some point. I've been married fourteen years. Almost.'

'Family is marriage, see? Marriage to mum-n-dad is

the kind of marriage you never sign for, see? No wedding, no vows, just born into misery. Takes pluck to stay – the kinda pluck I don't have, Selby.'

'It takes pluck to *leave*, Ian. To leave a husband, a house, a crystal chandelier, silver in a sideboard. A good dinner set. Brocade curtains.'

'What would you rather, then?'

'What do you mean?'

'Think.'

'Mum said I'd never want for a thing.'

'Hah! She would. Money. Money was all she ever thought about.'

'And now, I can't think. I feel numb.' Was he listening?

'What kind of life do you have all sketched out in your head? What do you *want*?'

'For now... I don't know, Ian. Leaving is as hard as staying.'

Glugging down the last of a schooner of beer. 'Nah. You got legs, ain'tcha?' Looking at froth left at the bottom of the glass. Looking at the palm of his hand. 'How old you now, Selby?'

'I came here with an idea.'

'How old you now?' Squinted at the barman pulling another beer. 'Got kids? Am I an uncle now then?' His arm lightly around her shoulder. Strangely comforting, strangely familiar.

'Oh Ian.'

'Guess that's a no. Even easier. Jeez, girl. You even got a bus fare, is my educated guess.'

'So what's keeping me.' Not a question to him. Bitterness choking her statement, filling a throat, a breast, already full of regret. 'Thirty-five. Thirty-six soon.'

'You thirty-five!' Eyes suddenly sober sizing her up.

'Skinny old thing. Look more like seventeen.'

He was right. He was wizened and tough-looking enough to be her older brother. Possibly with advice to match.

She dropped her head. Raised it quickly. 'Huh.' Looked at the ceiling to run tears down back where they came from. Somewhere behind her chin, behind her nose, where hot pain welled. Didn't know exactly where it hurt, or why.

'So, Selby girl. Up to you.'

'I came here with an idea.' Safety in repetition.

'Do you still paint on that old easel? Long brushes, squares of card? What did you paint? Butterflies? Kites? Birds?'

'Gave it up.'

'Oh. I quite liked some ...'

'I came here with an idea.'

'So you say. Out with it.' Opaque eyes, wide smile. Beer stink all of a sudden acceptable, accepted.

'Money – money from mum's old place.'

'Ah-huh?'

'Half yours, half mine, right?'

'Depends.'

Ignored that. What could he mean? 'We could get a flat somewhere ...'

' ... far away from here.' He was getting it.

'And you could live there, and I ...'

'But I live in Inverell.' Eyes solid. Breath steady. His neutral stance annoyingly blank.

She paused. Trying, trying, trying to think. Tears sniffed back. Eyes suddenly clear. 'Alone? Do you have a ... a place?'

'Perceptions, see? They take us up the wrong river, see? You sent a ticket without asking ...' A breath. 'Yes – I have a place. No, I'm not alone.'

She was wrong. He was right. She had all the wrong ideas. Didn't even start to ask. Just assumed. Now he would tell her.

'Like who would put up with a drinker? Someone like me? Who in the world would take Ian Winmarley on?' Squinting. Laughing. Patting a back pocket. Again. Again.

Looking, looking, looking now. Good quality jeans. Crumpled but expensive shirt.

She had to start again. 'Let's find a table, Ian. Tell me about your life.'

Seven

Where are we bound

So it was not wise laughter she heard, all her youth and childhood. Not wise tired experienced laughter from a jolly mother. Tired mother, untidy mother, wheezing exhausted mother, in a grubby house. Years, years, years went by and now she saw it for what it was. Or was starting to see a glimmer.

'What are you saying, Ian?' Grilled her brother. Distant brother. Regained brother. Younger brother who knew more than her. Sensed more. Saw more. Remembered everything.

'What?'

'What do you mean he was desperate?'

Ian sat back. Gazing cross-eyed at ceiling. Gazing cross-eyed at her. 'Dad was the most miserable man we knew, see? The unhappiest bloke on God's little acre.'

'He drank.'

'Wise up, Selby love. You'd have drunk too. Drove *me* to the bottle. Why do you think I up and left at ... how old was I?'

'Fourteen. *Fourteen*. Surely you remember how old you were.'

'Why d'you think he died?'

'There's no reason why people die. He had a heart attack! You don't know anything. You weren't here. Soon after you left. A few months later, it happened.'

Leaned forward. Stared cross-eyed into her face. 'You were here. You saw, din'tcha? You heard. They were misery incorporated.'

'Sure, they fought, but...'

'You lived right in the middle of it, Bec. I mean Selby. Neglect. Grime. Fridge empty but for a dish of ... of rancid butter or something. A bottle with an inch of juice at the bottom. A pie crust. Sofa full of washing brought in too late – or too soon, or whatever. A carton of cigarettes all there was, sometimes, in that cupboard. Cockroaches. And lip. He was the most harassed, hen-pecked, word-bashed, long-suffering bastard this side of the tide mark.'

'What? What tide mark? What are you talking about?' But words took hold, hold, hold of her head. Long-suffering. Hen-pecked. Clint Winmarley – hen-pecked. Harassed. By a big blousy woman whose washing lay in big damp heaps on a grey couch. Whose grave was the neatest cleanest thing in her life. *After* her life.

'Tide-mark between purgatory and pure hell.' Hoarse laughter pulled his head back. Distorted row of bottom teeth like gravestones.

'Three reasons I left, sis. Two big fat reasons, one not so big. Surprise is, you stayed. And never noticed half of it, by the sound of it. Jeez.' Shook his head like a wet dog. Dipped hand in breast pocket, waved a fifty-dollar note between index and middle finger. Cocked his head. 'Another of those ... whatever it is you drink ... what is that stuff?' Stood and walked dead straight to the bar. The arrow-straight trajectory of the nearly-drunk.

Cup of tea. Pot of tea. Tea and sandwiches what she wanted more than anything. 'Wait.'

Ian turned.

'Nothing for me. Get yours and drink it. We're going to ... just drink it. Let's go.'

Shades of Clint Winmarley, he was, downing a half-pint so rapidly he could not have swallowed more than twice. 'So where are we bound?' Ain'tcha, din'tcha, jeez, and *where are we bound.*

'You're a mass of contradictions.' Not a scolding. She meant it literally. She smiled at him. Harmless sot, he was, like his father. Willing to be dragged, half-drunk, to a warm clean tea shop where the same old chandeliers were clean as the day they were hung, high above talking heads. Just like on the day of a mother's confession. *Not your father.*

'Brought me here for tea the day she told me.' Looking at him across a table laden with green pot, green cups and a plate of sandwiches, she told him how it rained that day. Watched his eyes. 'And it's still here, this place.'

Ian ate soft bread. She saw his enjoyment of it, watched his crinkled eyes, so unlike her eyes.

'How long ago, then?'

'Oh, years before she died.'

'And when did you ...'

'Tell me about Inverell, Ian. Is it warm there? Do you get storms? Tell me about your ... wife? Girlfriend?'

Dark eyes looked at her, no longer opaque; clear, clear, clear. Cleared by tea and good bread from a yeasty oven. Excellent butter and real ham.

'My house has green trim. Traditional, Federation Green. Love it.' Paused, looked for something in her face. 'Kept real neat and lovely. Can just see the courthouse clock from the back yard. And inside, smells of sandalwood and vanilla – from discs he buys in boxes. Air freshener. Had never given it a thought until ... you know, it smells clean. Always wanted clean. And lovely, stocked, clean fridge.'

Did he say he? Could not pull her eyes from that clear gaze. She had clean too.

'Brilliant clean, as you would say, Selby girl.'

How would he know what she'd say? 'Ian ...'

'Brilliant clean. '

Did he say *he*? 'So you ...' She did not want to probe.

'Look – I got onto the stage for a while. Plays, love plays. Did a couple of short movies.'

'Really?'

'Hmmm. What was I? Seventeen? Nineteen? Twenty-three? Don't know. Then went straight into radio, see? Love it.'

'You work on the radio?'

'It's where all the ugly guys in the business end up, you know.' Laughed so hard he made her smile. A hoarse repetitious bark and chortle that was so refreshing, so different. So happy.

'No one hears this voice though. Ha ha.' Bit the corner off another sandwich, and sipped, sipped delicately from his green cup. 'I sit behind the glass, so to speak.'

'Really.' Nothing else to say. Robbed of words. Quick, think. 'In Inverell?'

'Since Derry retired, yeah.'

'So she worked in radio too.'

'He. Derry Stubbs. I live with Derry Stubbs.'

For a minute the name meant nothing. 'Oh!' Goodness – Derry Stubbs. 'He used to do a quiz show on the television.' Her voice intentionally neutral. Disbelief and awe crowded in. 'Really.'

'Yeah – before his stroke.'

Raising a hand to her mouth. Oh. 'Oh – how sad.'

'Murder, Selby. Awful. It's pure ... hard to get on with things, sometimes. Sorry.' Looking away. Looking back. 'I'm frustrated out of my mind sometimes. When you got in touch? Relief. I get time out to think, see?'

A brief silence. Noises from the café crowding in.

'So...'

'So?'

'So how ...?'

'So I met him in Sydney after I didn't get the part of Banquo in some contemporary production ... do you want to listen to all this?' More tea, lowered brow, a question in eyes black again with something she could not understand.

'An audition?'

'My life used to be chain auditions. Back-to-back auditions. Addicted to rejection, some of us are.' But no real bitterness there. Acceptance, humour, cynicism and held-back laughter. 'Back-to-back auditions, queuing up with the same old faces. Same young faces, getting old.' Laughter ringing through chandeliers. 'And I answered an ad, because you know, even actors need regular money.'

'For a radio job?'

'Yes – irony was that I got it. Five minutes, it took. And then moved around for years. Years. Station to station. Met all the talk-back celebrities and cruised the pubs after I learned to push levers and knobs and balance sounds. All about the bass, baby. I was a jock in less time than it took to learn the Banquo monologue. *Beaten black and numb.*'

'Beaten?'

Signalled to a waitress for more tea, nodded. Grunted. 'Matter of speaking.' Laughing softly, laughing until the hot green pot arrived. 'That's right, pour me another cup and I'll tell you how Derry walked into the studio one afternoon, to do some voice-over ... some promo ... I don't know. I was awe-struck. *I mean*, Derry

Stubbs.' Hands held palm upwards, to stress, I mean. 'And we were drunk as skunks in Jason's Jibe on Little Collins until about three in the morning.'

She had no words to say.

'And he like what ... ten years older than me?' Bit into the last ham sandwich. Smiled. 'Twelve? I don't know.'

'Do you want a cake?'

'Why not. What's good?'

'Eccles cake?' To the waitress. 'And a piece of chocolate tart.'

'And it's been more or less so since. He is ... I mean – he thinks *I'm* wonderful. Go figure. Never in my life thought that would happen. My background and all. I don't even have a degree or anything. And he thinks I'm great. Wonder of wonders. And since his stroke it's been sometimes better and sometimes worse, see? Sometimes blissful and sometimes hell, see?' Dull, sharp, dull lights in the dark eyes. 'Nothing like your marriage, is my best guess.'

'I never even dreamed or imagined you were ...'

'... gay?'

Nodded. She could only nod and swallow.

'No one told you the reason I took off one morning, after the dog died, after a night of unbearable ... unbearable *conversation* with Mother Dear?'

'Mum?'

'Okay – you don't remember that side of her.' Shifted in his chair. Looked across to the café window. 'Do you remember then, how she made it a point to call you for something the minute you sat down with a book, or took up your brushes? Because I do.'

Now she remembered. Now she did. She did. Said nothing, pursed her lips. Taking up a brush, loading it with paint; loving, loving the feeling, the anticipation of making something worthwhile, something good. A bird that looked like it would take flight. Right there, right then, in her small room.

And the voice filtering through, from the living room, where the TV was always on, droning with some program or other. *Put the kettle on, will you, Bec? Bec? Hop to the shop, will you? Get us some cigarettes. There's a good girl.* A good girl.

'It's raining. Love this weather you have here.'

'She was ...'

'Impossible. Impossible is what she was.'

Eight

Cow print fabric

'Black and white ball, Selby. A week from Friday. In aid of … I don't know what it's in aid of now. Sent them a cheque this morning and already it's clean out of my mind. Too stressed, this week. In any case. Black and white, at the Hyatt. On the seventeenth, at eight.'

'But you know how I feel at things like that.'

'No, I don't. And please don't wear beige or grey or fawn and look like, like three times your age. Buy something. Something white. Something. Something good. Don't look frumpish, for goodness' sake. Don't look like Olive Oyl. Don't *stoop* like that.' Turned towards the mirror. Big bedroom. Booming voice. 'It's humiliating. It's embarrassing! I turn up with some frump in tow. I turn up with Aunt Mildred, in beige!' He foamed at the mouth. Angry at her. At himself.

'I don't …'

'I'm thirty-six. You're thirty-six, not *fifty*-six, for goodness' sakes! Most women your age – I don't know. They're alive, sexy … *alive*, Selby!'

Listened to his bathroom sounds, searching, searching, searching in the mirror for something, for a corrected stoop, for a saving element, for something to like; anything for a sliver of hope. A slice of something. Chocolate tart she ate with Ian. Gone now, back to Inverell, promising to return soon, with a plan.

Plan? How could she plan? Feeling crushed. A frump.

Black and white ball, now. Week from Friday. Stomach sank. Could tell, could think what it would be like. A sea of faces she could not put names to. Glamour and glitz, fuss and fakery. Money and discomfort. Black and white.

His voice from the bathroom. 'Top table – ten others. Please look good. Look decent. Not like you walked out of some charity shop. It's a charity function, but not the way *you* think, goodness' sake. Go to boutique whatever.'

Thel came with her to three boutiques. Child in pushchair, shopping bag slung from the handles. 'Face it, girl – black makes you look like, fifty. And skeletal.'

'White makes me dreary. Yellow skin.'

Thel, laughing. 'Reluctant bride, all over again.'

Stopped, turned. A ghost picture of Boyd's drowning, flying, dying bride in her head. Paintings. Paintings. Dreams. 'Is that how you ...'

'That's how you sound. I wasn't there, remember? We've only known each other since we moved from Bentleigh. I don't exactly get the picture, but, of a glowing picture of anticipation.' Laughing, talking above the whine of the bored pushchair-bound child.

'Come on, Thelma!'

Handing half-unwrapped muesli bar down to child, laughing still. 'Sweetie, Sweetie, it's got to be either black or white, or ...'

'Cow pattern print.'

'You crack me up sometimes.'

Selby grave, straight-faced. Hatching a plan. Slip, slip, slipping in her new jeans to the door. 'I'm dead serious.' Headed back to the hot streets, past slow traffic under the sun, in the dust, in the noise. A distant siren, a nearby squeal of brakes.

Made it herself. Sewed, capably and well, three afternoons, wielding scissors, biting pins between clenched lips, pressing sewing machine throttle, gingerly, like it drove a powerful racing car. Whizzed through, hemming, hemming, hemming. *Zig-zig-zag*, her mother would have said. Attached shoulder pads and zips, sewed on sixteen bright black sequined buttons.

His face, Friday night, stayed blank. Bearded chin sank a little. 'Are you sure?' His uncertainty almost enough reward for the hours of work. 'I like the bag and shoes ... but *that*?'

'Boutique Whatever. Up-to-the-minute. Just hope it's the only one there tonight.' Lied through beige lipstick. Heart in clenched throat. In her chest, thumping, audible. Cheeks fiery red. Not daring to look in the mirror, knowing cheeks and lips clashed.

Walking into the ballroom, regretting now her mad crazy spite-her-own-face scheme. What was she thinking? Everyone, but everyone looked at her big, swinging cow-pattern calf-length evening coat with shiny buttons, worn on top of long white pants and camisole. Why those over-large shoulder pads, which made her sway and sweep, like an animated clothes hanger?

'Latest trend?'

'The cocoon coat look – everyone's doing it. Not.'

'Your wife's a ... um, genius. Where does she shop?'

'Good God – where did she get that?'

'Is that Mrs Brixham ... what on earth?'

'If she weren't so thin it might suit her.'

'Honestly?'

Danced woodenly with manager of this, and manager of that. Said seven words all evening to anonymous faces. Chatted with the band drummer on the way to the 'Rest Rooms'. Listened to him say disconnected phrases. About the sea. About boats. About something. Came back to a roar of voices. Ate small pieces of bright food off enormous black plates. Food lacking smell, taste, or substance. Enormous glasses clinking and swilling with sediment-laden purple liquid she barely touched to her lips. Dessert a tiny chocolate sculpture in the middle of a drizzled plate. A forkful. Longed for a cup of tea and flat shoes. Thought of socks. Thought of lying in bed with a book. Thought of a ham sandwich. Thought of Inverell.

His voice booming in the big bedroom. Off with bowtie, off with his stiff new shirt. Off with his head, lopped from this angle in the mirror, looking from where she sat on the end of the bed. Headless, skinless, a snake without a slither.

'No one was wearing a pants suit except you.'

'Mmm.'

'Cow pattern, someone said.'

She made a small laugh. A small snort.

'And you talked to the band.'

'To the drummer. Not the whole band. The only interesting face in the room.'

'What did you talk about?' Slitted eyes. Jutting beard.

'The weather. The world. The South Pole. The Doldrums.'

'Sometimes, Selby, I just don't get you.'

'Sometimes?'

'Sometimes I think you need a hobby. Are you ... what? Bored? Tired? Upset at something?'

Thought of her hobby, her row of tiny cactus plants on a windowsill downstairs, which she watered and watched.

'Do you need a hobby, Selby?'

'I'm going to Inverell.' Her own words so surprising her eyebrows shot up.

A long-angled glance through the mirror. A short silence. 'What's in Inverell?'

'My brother.'

'You told me he disappeared in his teens or something.'

'I found him. I found Ian.' Her voice dull and low.

'Destitute, is he?'

Kicked off her shoes, shrugged off the evening coat. Pulled at shiny buttons. Peered at painted toenails, sickly beige against green carpet. Immaculate carpet. No pet hairs. Nothing. 'Not compared to me, he isn't.'

'What does that mean?' Swishing mouthwash in the bathroom. Swishing, swilling, spitting.

'I'm going to visit him. And his partner. For ...' Thinking. For how long? Thinking, reaching for something to say. 'A fortnight.'

He slid into pyjamas like it was the first time he ever did it. Shot the cuffs. Shot the cuffs of pyjamas. Looked down, ran a hand over the buttons, like to check they were still there. 'Shall I stay at the club?'

'Yes. Yes.'

'Will you fly?'

Fly! 'No – I'll ... Perhaps.' She hadn't thought. 'I'll take the coach.'

'God – you'll be ages getting there.'

'Yes. Yes.' Ages in a coach. Oh. With a suitcase in the compartment below. She had seen it done. Oh. Wanted to do it now. Thought of the honeymoon suitcases in the roof space. Wheelie things with retractable handles. Only hauled out once or twice. Holidays in some exotic resort whose sun blinded her. Sent her scurrying for shelter. Wheeled cases. Black, shiny black.

'Coming to bed?'

Distant, mind far off, detached. Thinking, wishing, wanting to sit in a coach for ages, right through it all with him. Right through his reaching for transient pleasure like it was necessary, after such a puny dessert. His breathing and murmuring, his clammy hands, his final grunt. Her fumbling to put her nightdress on again, retreating to the cold side of the bed, wondering how long it really took to get there.

'How far is it?'

'Hmm? From what? To where?' Already half asleep, his breathing slowing.

'Nowhere. Nothing.'

Nine

Chance encounter

Surprised, shocked, startled out of a brief reverie close to the butcher's window on the high street.

'You can't be Bec Winmarley.'

She wasn't. She was not Bec Winmarley. Hadn't been for years. Since she turned eighteen. Who was this?

He peered at her, tried to engage her eyes, and held her with one hand, above the elbow.

'Listen ...'

'You are. You *are* Bec – don't you remember me?'

Prim, prim as she could be. Brushed his hand from her arm. How dare he?

'Where did you go to school, tell me that.'

'None of your business. I'm in a hurry. Goodbye.' But she remembered him. Goodness – Morgan. 'Morgue' Pearson, whose father ran the funeral directors, down the highway, halfway to the lake. Over the long hill across town.

'I can see you remember me, Bec.' Nothing if not insistent.

'Hello Morgue.'

'People call me Gordon these days. I use my middle name.'

She had to smile. Turned her face away. Looked at their reflections in the butcher's window, among refrigerated chops decorated with plastic parsley and silicon lemons. Pulled her mouth straight. Pulling herself into courtesy, out of annoyance, out of exasperation. Lowered eyes, then raised chin, defiant. 'I'm Selby Brixham these days. I use my married name.' Voice sharp, her mother's inflections.

'Selby-Brixham. Double-barrelled surname? Fancy.' Looked her up and down. Looked at her ring finger.

'Selby's my first name. I'm in a hurry. Bye-bye, Gordon. Nice to see you again.' Side-stepped, stepped, stepped quickly away from him, towards the newsagent's. Towards the chemist's, wondering which door to enter. There was the cake shop, and the baby shop. The closest. Stepped in, suddenly blind. Felt the bar of a pram graze her side, felt the change in temperature. People were turning on air conditioners. Already. In October.

'Come and have a coffee.'

What – he followed her. Anger threatened to bubble up, show on her face. It would cause a scene. A shop assistant hovered.

She smiled. 'Morgan ... I mean, Gordon. You followed me.' Irritation in her low, low voice.

'Yeah. Come and have a coffee. So many years since school. I used to watch you.'

'Charming.' All the disingenuousness of a seventeen year-old. What was he thinking? What could she say? Hurried out for a bag of fertilizer wearing gardening jeans and her striped green jumper. There was a dot of potting mix on her shoe. 'I'm not dressed for coffee, Gordon.'

'Rubbish.' Took her elbow, steered her out, walked her adroitly across the street. To Crossingham's. Oh no, no, not Crossingham's.

'Not here. Down the street's better.'

'You know best.'

Did she? Mind blank. Mind cleared of everything but not wanting to drink coffee in her gardening shoes with this insistent male from a murky past. Who remembered high school?

Morgue Pearson did. The past rolled off his tongue, insistent sentence after insistent sentence. Classes, names, locations, school events.

'No, please – not the school ball.' Protested, but knew he'd go on. Had to grimace. Had to admire his nerve, insistence, intensity, brilliance, brightness, lightness.

He threw details at her of who wore what, and what the band played. 'You had on this brilliant dark green ... frock or whatever you call it.'

'Gown.' Remembered a mother's complaints about price, fabric, size, length, style. *Cheap-cheap-cheap*, buzzed in her head. Other mothers might sigh with relief, but hers grumbled when she did not pick the most expensive gown in the shop. 'My shoes didn't match, I remember.'

'Who remembers shoes?' Gordon Pearson ordered coffees, peered at her face.

'If they hurt you do.'

He laughed, out of proportion to her line; a laugh that engaged all others at other small tables. Everyone looked up. 'Do you remember dancing with me? Do you remember the fabulous ...'

Memories did not match. She was out of synch with his energy.

Mortified in shoes that hurt, a gown whose zip ripped, a sequined waist-ornament to make up for the fact she had no corsage, no date. It all came back. She was Bec Winmarley then. She was.

'So do you remember dancing with ... you know,

that guy who was the football and swimming ace?'

Now she remembered. Tanned face, steel braces. Smell of pool chlorine underneath school ball cologne. The smell of a hired tuxedo. The smell of dinner on his breath. And beer. 'Nick Byfleet.'

'Yeah! Nick Byfleet. What a guy.'

'Was he? I didn't know anyone much.'

'But we watched you. We all watched you going in and out of school. For years. Across the oval. Under the bridge.'

Could not believe him. Why watch Bec Winmarley, in blue pleated school skirt and too-large jumper, creased from being thrown damp on the sofa? Stared at him in silence over a cappuccino going cold.

'What do you do now, then?'

What did she do? Thought of her row of white standard roses in the front garden, behind her classic iron fence. Thought of weeds she pulled. Cow grass, milkweed, dandelions, wandering jew, onion grass. 'I garden.' She ironed shirts, talked to Thel, washed porcelain ornaments, polished silver, re-hung brocade curtains back from the cleaners. Planted bulbs. Jonquils, gladioli, daffodils, crocus. *Jonquils-jonquils-jonquils.* And now, her row of perfect cacti behind the sunroom glass. Identical pots, all lined up. 'I garden,' she said again. Remembered an abandoned easel. Abandoned paints, all those hard tubes. Bent brushes. A mother's disapproving face. Blank. Mouth bowed downward. She once had wanted to paint, quite desperately. So long, long, long ago. So distant and remote. All those pelicans, cormorants, pigeons, doves, seagulls, on card. Streaked and smeared. Frustrating. Forgotten. Never painted. Never painted *well*.

'That what you always wanted to do, garden? Remember how they asked us to write about our plans in high school. And how we had to have a Plan B?'

Had forgotten. Remembered now. Kept her eyes down, her lips thin, together. Had written *artist*. Ah – all those abandoned birds, all those bent, hard, useless exasperating tubes of paint.

'I wrote down meteorologist, even though everyone knew I'd go on with Dad's funeral business. I hardly knew what it meant. And *mountaineer*.'

She looked up. 'But you didn't.' Remembered not seeing him for years. Must have left town. 'You didn't carry on the business.'

'Didn't climb mountains either.'

'Who did you marry?'

'No one from school. And it ended before it started ... no kids or anything. No real cause for regret. She was Dutch, matter-of-fact, too cool and detached for even a decent memory.' Sad voice. Thick regret.

'Oh.'

'Yes. Yes – Oh is the only thing I've got left.' Looked at her. Sad, keen, jocular sad smile. 'What do you want to do, Selby Brixham?'

'Green.'

'What?'

Shaking her head. Stupid, stupid, stupid. 'Nothing.'

'What do you really want to do?'

'I want to go to Inverell. I'm going on the coach.'

'Really? Is that all you want to do?'

'I am doing it. I want to go to Inverell. Soon.'

'Tell you what.' Turning his head, looking around. Making up his mind about something. Nodding deeply, looking at her again, sideways, under sparse bristly eyelashes. 'Tell you what. I'll drive you there.'

'You must be joking. It's ... something like ... what? ... a day away?'

'More. It's only a few hundred kilometres out of my

way, anyway. Couple of hours. Maybe four.'

'No.'

'Yes.' Nodding, nodding. 'We'll drive there together.'

'Oh, Morgue.'

He laughed. Stopped abruptly. Looked around again, slowly. '*Oh Morgue, oh Morgue.*' Repeating what she said. Sad tone, flattened and defeated. 'Look – the weather will be atrocious, but we'll manage.'

Selby too confounded to ask what he should be doing, where he should be. Didn't he have a job to go to? Looked at her shoes, at the floor between her gardening shoes. She should go home. 'Okay.'

Turned his eyes toward her without moving his head. 'We must be crazy, right?'

'I know what we are, now.' She felt his understanding of her own cryptic words. Knew he would say yes.

'Yeah – two lost people, finding each other. Still lost.' Laughing, laughing, laughing softly under his breath. 'Still lost, but. So what the heck? Get your stuff together, Selby Brixham. Meet me right here.' He pointed at the floor. 'Right here at six. Yes, at six tomorrow.'

'Seven thirty. Outside.'

'Whatever you say.'

'Really? Are we really doing this?'

He took a pen from his pocket and bit off the cap. Crooked front tooth. Determined eyes. Took her hand, gently, from where it gripped the table edge, and wrote a long number on her skin, starting where her thumb ended, digging the point in near a raised blue vein. 'My mobile. Unless I hear otherwise, I'll be outside, right there, at seven thirty, tomorrow. Just after dark, it'll be. Now write yours here.'

'Just after dark.'

'We'll drive and talk. And I'll take you to ... what's in Inverell?'

'My brother.'

'Little brother? Black hair?'

'Ian Winmarley.'

'Stubborn little bugger with a straight mouth!' He remembered everything.

'Not little any more.'

'Nothing's little any more.'

Thinking. Shaking her head. Biting her lip. 'This is crazy. Mor... Gordon. Listen. This is crazy. Why are you in town anyway? What brought you back?'

'All my business here is tied up now.'

She tilted her head. Tilting, tilting, frowning.

'You remember where Dad had his business, right?'

She hadn't been up that way for years. *Pearson's – Funeral Directors Since 1964. Your plans, our organisation, your peace of mind.* Had passed it daily on the way to school. Every day for more than ten years.

'Well – it was boarded up long enough. I sold it off – it was auctioned by Les Corngold. He of the golden gavel, apparently. Came to sign off the last papers. So. So. All done.' Hands together, palm down on the table.

'No more links to this place then.'

'None. It'll be bowled over and townhouses will mushroom up, won't they? Like everywhere else. Bit of a shame. Glad I met you, though. Oh, and glad I did that, too, I guess.' Brilliant smile. One crooked tooth. 'Needed the money. Can you get your things together by tomorrow?'

She looked at her shoes. Looked at the ceiling. Looked at the side of his face, so strange. So odd. Thirty minutes ago hating the thought of drinking coffee with him, now promising to ride together, all the way to

Inverell. Not quite a perfect stranger. Perfect insanity. But with more smiles on a male face in thirty minutes than she had seen for years. 'I must be nuts.'

'*Be* nuts. What's holding you back? Be crazy. Go insane. What's holding you? The rain?'

She could make him a list. Brocade curtains, Lladro figurines, a line of potted cacti, beige bedspread, perfectly folded towels and sheets, an empty ironing basket, a brand-new sandwich maker still in its plastic bag, a tablecloth to hem, a fridge to clean out, socks to pair. Roses to fertilize. Big rooms, small rooms. The perfect bathroom. Nothing. Nothing. Nothing.

'Nothing.'

'I thought you said you were married.'

'I am.' Married to grey beard, creased forehead, tired sad eyes. Cruel eyes. Discontented mouth. Perfect shirts. Silk ties. Six to dinner on Friday. Shrugged. The muscles down her back stung, burned, burned through to her chest, lancing from the back to the front. Her breathing stopped. Started again. What was that she felt? 'It'll all still be here, won't it – nothing will move.' Her hand gripped the table.

He placed a tentative finger on her knuckle. 'I guess it won't.'

Ten

Recklessness

Thelma's voice tinny on the landline. 'What? He could be an axe murderer. He could rape you on the way. Bury you three miles from Inverell.'

Smiling. Hushing Thelma. Her turn now to seem in charge, knowing what she was doing. Great pretence. 'I know what I'm doing. He's nice.'

'Nice!'

'Hm. He remembers everything about school. What I wore to the ball.'

'Everyone's nice. Psychopaths have great memories.'

'You're envious, that's what.' Words to say. Words to say with a smile. Words only a true friend would take in the right way.

'Yes, I am. I am, Selby. Bright green with it. Look after yourself. So you leave tomorrow? What about ...?'

'Oh – it'll be okay.'

'Not a disappearing trick then. Not going off into the blue without a word.'

That was an idea. Oh. Looked at the mirror, where her strange flushed face, her hunched shoulders, her mustard hair all mussed up on the left, looked peculiar. Watched herself talking on the phone. Gardening jeans. Checked shirt. A smear of something on the elbow she hadn't noticed before popping out to the shops. Stroked her hair. 'I'll tell him tonight at dinner. He's known I've wanted to go off to visit Ian for a while.'

'Take your green jacket – it'll be cold there. It'll be rainy.'

'Cold! In Inverell. Thel, you're acting like a mother.'

'But not yours.'

No, not hers. Hers never told her what to wear for the cold. Never said anything about looking after herself. Never said she was envious with a voice full of smiles.

Packed a glossy black suitcase. Looked at flattened clothes all pressed into the corners, squared off, neat. Shoes heel-to-toe, cosmetic bag bulging with all that stuff from her side of the bathroom. Big fluffy near-new beige towel folded in thirds perfectly fitted on top of everything.

Pressing down the lid, pressing, pushing, zipping. A feeling both of finality and of starting a new something.

Explained over dessert, but said she was catching the coach. Did not mention Gordon Pearson. 'Will you be okay?' She wondered whether he would even touch the freezer. All that prepared food she put up all the time: Bolognese sauce, Beef Bourguignon, Chili con Carne, Butter Chicken, Lasagne, Thai Green Curry, Chicken Tettrazini, Osso Buco, Irish Stew. All dated, all labelled, all in uniform rectangular containers. Stacked, stacked, stacked.

'You know I'll be fine, Selby. I'll eat ...'

'There's heaps of food in the freezer. All our usual stuff.'

'... I'll eat that.'

'I mean, it'll go by like a flash.'

He looked down, straightened a knife. 'Will it?' Poured a long dribbly stream of white wine into his glass. Brilliant clean. Shiny. 'How long do you plan being away?' Looked up, looked at the window. Looked like he couldn't wait for her to leave.

This was the last night before she left, far, distant, removed from him on the other side of the bed. Listening to his breathing, sliding a hand to where his thigh flattened the mattress, sensing the warmth but holding back from touching, interrupting his sleep, waking him for more. Did not want more, but needing to check he was there, really there, before she left him behind.

Light slid from the window, over to the mirror on the other side of the room, touched it with gold, then dulled. A slither, a hiss of rain on the roof, a mass of grey darkening the room again. Had she slept? Must have. Did she hear thunder? Turning, turning, turning slowly, raising a hand to hair mussed on a hot pillow. Looked at the upright suitcase. It held some sort of promise. What would she talk about all the way to Inverell with Morgue Pearson?

Would she ever want to come back to this? Heard the rain lessen and stop. Heard a single thunder clap in the distance, heard a siren. Listened for the first bird call – there. Some honeyeater up above her daisies and roses and marigolds and spikes that would become gladioli in two months. Smiled in the lightening space that was her bedroom. Frowned in the space. Feeling skin stretch on her face. Touching lines up and down the side of her mouth. Heard his early morning snore. She should get up and what ... finish the ironing? Clean out the end cupboard over the fridge? Put in a last wash and watch it spin? Mix a can of liquid fertilizer and pour it over the beds where slaters and ants were turning and rising in the new light?

Lying there, thinking of Inverell, where she had never been. Where she might need her green jacket.

Where Ian was. Where Morgue Pearson was taking her, with some thought in mind. What did he want with her? Was it the same as what she wanted with him? Something new? Someone to laugh with instead of all this grey perfection? Someone to forget things with?

There was nothing to forget, perhaps.

Nothing.

Nothing.

Eleven

The Riverina

With Morgue Pearson at a roadhouse in the middle of nowhere. Had to ask, had to find out where all this flat country ... where ... it had to have a name. She stood facing the service station; flat darkly glimmering solar panels on the roof. Saw its emptiness. Its unpeopledness. Its lonely petrol pumps glimmering in the sun, under a slanting roof bordered with stars and stripes and dots and rectangles in all the primary colours. Dazzled. Dizzy. Still unbelieving she had left town. He had texted, wanting to leave earlier, earlier, much earlier, mid-morning. There was nothing for her to do. She was packed. Before long they were shooting along an unfamiliar highway.

Morgue now a metre behind her, facing the building. 'So that was an easy three hours, wasn't it?'

It felt like three days. Three minutes. 'Where are we? Where's this?' Blazing sun on a brown plain.

Looked sideways and laughed. 'Now I know I like being with you.'

'What. Why?'

'You don't count kilometres, or read every green sign like it was a tenet from the big bible in some geographer's mind.' They could not have been his words.

'Tenet?'

'Never mind my sarcasm. Or my sense of irony. I'm enjoying this. Are you?' Looked into her eyes. Tried to look into her eyes. 'We left all that rain behind us. We've come miles and miles. Already.'

She looked towards the horizon. Said nothing.

'Okay – I'll tell you. This is the Riverina. Welcome to the Murrumbidgee Irrigation Area. They grow ... okay, guess. What do you think they grow here?'

'Fruit?'

'Lots of it, and rice.'

An instant mental picture, a mirage, of paddy fields and conical hats, dispelled just as suddenly by his insistence that they get something to eat. Just when a rush, a sudden cool brisk rush of freedom wrapped itself around her heart. She was in rice-land all alone. Well, with Morgue Pearson, whose smiles made her feel at once alone and something else.

'I'll decide later.' Aloud, to a petrol pump, yellow, so yellow in the sun it was white.

'What will you decide later?'

Both of them walking to the sliding door.

'How I feel.'

'You feel wonderful. And hungry. Powerful hungry!'

And her phone vibrated in her pocket. Yes – the green jacket. Thel was right. If for nothing else, it was good for somewhere to put her phone. Looked at who was calling, now. Right now.

'Ian.'

'I found him for you.'

'Hello. Hi. Who?'

'I found ... the guy you call Green. Your father.' Breathless, like he ran a long way to tell her this. 'Listen, you really should come out to see me. You... you said you would.'

'I am coming.'

Morgue looking, from the distance of the sliding glass door. 'Come on. Coming?'

Nodded to him. Held up a hand. Held up a hand like this was important. 'I *am* coming, Ian. I'm on the way.' Into the phone, breathing through surprise and intrigue. Thinking. Now? Right now? Why this minute?

Ian Winmarley laughing in the phone distance behind her head. 'Sure.'

'Yes, I'm in ...' Raised her head. 'Where are we again?'

'Close to the Murrumbidgee River.' He was by her side.

'I heard that – who was that? Are you both coming?' Ian curious. Breathing hard.

She wondered whether this was a good idea. 'I'm with a friend. I don't know how far away we are but ...'

'You're near Wagga? Somewhere near Wagga?'

'Wagga?' she said to Morgan Pearson.

Nodding, smiling. 'About an hour away. I guess it's where we'll spend the night, okay?'

The night. It was blazing; a hot afternoon that promised no such thing as night.

'See you tomorrow, I guess then. Or the day after?' Ian deciding perhaps, to tell her more in person.

'Yes. This is amazing. How did you find him ... look, tell me when we meet.'

'For sure. Looking forward to seeing you again. And for you to meet Derry.'

'Yes. Say hello.'

Biting into something he ordered. Surprisingly good. And a pot of tea. Without even asking. Thinking about the night ahead.

'I've got something to show you.' He pulled out his phone, scrolled a few times. 'No. No, look – we'll go there. Just before dark. Just before ... this will blow your mind.'

'What is it?' Curious now, wanting something to distract her from thoughts of meeting her father. Her real father. Not Clint Winmarley. Not Jonty Green.

'Have another cup of tea. Have another one of these. We'll drive down to the Five Mile, just outside Narrandera. Just at sunset.'

She watched him eat two hamburgers, grasping them like they were alive, like they would escape if he loosened those spatulate fingers. Flattened fingernails. Tinged a kind of mauve underneath the broad ridged nails. Rolled up sleeves on his blue, blue shirt revealing sinewy muscles and hairs bleached and bristly. Working jaw, chewing, square, what Thel might have labelled strong and scary. He could be an axe murderer, she said.

'I told ... I said I was taking the coach. Except to Thelma. I told Thelma I'd met you again.'

Raised his eyes. Oh. Dark, dark brown in here out of the sun. 'Again?'

'Since school and all that.'

Laughed. 'All that you hardly remember.'

'Hm.'

Wiped his mouth in long drags, side to side, with a paper napkin folded into a strip, a horizontal thing, left to right, right to left. Taking a deep breath, smiling hugely. 'That hit the spot.' Drinking tea like it was necessary. 'Do you want more tea?'

She nodded.

'And something from ... a cake, or something?'

Oh. Wanting, needing, wanting to enjoy this properly. 'Ice cream. Let's have ice cream.'

'Now, Selby-Brixham-Bec-Winmarley, now go ahead and enjoy this properly then.'

How did he know? Walked over to the counter.

Watched the girl pile three differently-coloured scoops into a fluted ice-cream dish. 'Do you want nuts or sprinkles with that?'

Morgue calling from the table. 'Both! Both!'

It was a holiday. She didn't know, three days ago, that she wanted a holiday. Had not even wished for one. And here she was, dipping, dipping a spoon, taking turns with two spoons. Laughing. Scooping up green, cream, pink ice cream tasting of real cream, country cream. Avoiding the nuts in the dish. Sharing ice cream. With two spoons. Never done before.

'You don't like nuts.' Not a question, but a mental note taken. He would remember, like he remembered her ball gown.

'Are we on holiday?' Shaking, lowering her head and smiling. 'I must be crazy.'

'You are. You left town with this guy you hardly remember at school. Just like that.' Broad smile.

What was that in his eyes? 'Morgue ...' No words to say how she felt.

Driving hard again, on an undulating road with trees whizzing past on both sides, then vast expanses of brown paddocks, then trees again. Water in the distance, shimmering a mirage, then crags, and trees again. The landscapes of Boyd and Drysdale.

Talking, talking, just like he said they would.

'They can't have the same oven at that café, not after all these years. Yeah – I remember that place. Good cakes.'

'They make this amazing bread. The best bread in the world. I just keep going back. Used to go there with Mum.'

'Great um ... relationship you had with your mother, then.'

'I don't know. She had a way of not listening. Ian

says she ear-bashed Dad ... I mean, Clint – he wasn't my real father.'

'But you don't think so, do you? She was different with you?'

'I don't know what to think. I think differently these ... since ... I don't know.'

'You feel you're suddenly doing all this thinking.'

Turned to look at him. His profile. Driving. Eyes on the road. Did not blink. How did he know?

Talked more. Talked.

'Jonty Green? No one's called Jonty Green.'

'But that's what I called him. And I changed my name to Selby Green.'

Now he turned to look at her. 'Wow.' Eyes back on the road. 'There it is.'

There it was. The river, rushing. All the world's water caught between two steep grassed banks. Cattle on the far side. Trees leaning towards the water.

'See that outcrop there?' He pointed. 'That's not the far bank. That's an island. And wait for it ... When it's almost sunset.'

'It is almost sunset. Wait for what?' She turned to look at the sun, orange, red, yellow, behind the trees.

'Yes. Look. Wait. Look.'

Looking, looking, and seeing. Catching sight of what seemed like bits of black paper fluttering in the sky. First a few, and then dozens. Hundreds. Thousands of fluttering things approaching, darkening the darkening sky, towards them, on the orange horizon.

'Bats!'

'Flying foxes.'

'Millions of them!'

Amazed. Gasping, gasping mouth wide open at millions of flying creatures overhead, wings like brown parchment. Stretched. Waving, batting. Flapping.

Transparent. Brown. Gold. Too many. A never-ending stream of them. Silent and not. A burring, furring sound. An occasional call, or squeal, or screech, or howl. Fascinating. Fascinating – could not take her eyes off them.

'Are they dangerous? Do they bite?'

'Dangerous? No, not here.'

'How many? Will they stop?'

'There are always stragglers. Wait until they've all gone over.'

The last two, no three, no six ... nine, eleven. The last one flapped overhead. She turned, eyes following until the flight was out of sight over treetops, over roofs in the distance, under clouds, the sky now a deep indigo, nearly black on this side. Still tinged with orange behind her. Morgue a silhouette.

'Sometimes a straggler gets caught in the power lines. A little nipper.'

'Oh.'

'Poor little sods, you think?'

'Where are they going?'

'To the orchards in Leeton. They love plum blossom. Peach blossom. They eat all night, and return to the river islands at dawn. Gorged. Drunk on nectar. Sleepy.' He put both arms around her. 'You liked that.'

'Morgue...'

'You liked that.'

Nodding. Nodding against his chest. Blue, blue shirt smelling of liquorice. Of sweat. Of laundry detergent. She pulled away. Walked towards the water. Now it was dark, was afraid of coming too close to the edge of the bank. Stopped near a tree, placed a hand on the bark. Peered at it in the dark. Could hardly see her hand now.

'That's a scribbly gum. A scribbly gum tree.'

'Mm.'

Feeling the chill the night would bring. Feeling the dampness of the valley, of the river basin.

'Let's find a place for the night, shall we?'

'If we ...'

'Don't worry. It'll all fall into place. No pressure.'

'I don't know ... anything.' Arms dangling by her sides. Hands loose and nervous at once.

His laugh travelled over water, over crags, over grass, through trees, near the rushing river. 'Neither do I.'

Twelve

All a horrible mistake

Lying back on a motel bed, listening to trucks and road trains rumbling past on the highway. Somewhere to here, rumble, rumble, here to somewhere. To somewhere, like she was heading somewhere distant and unknown. And she didn't think Inverell. Lying back and feeling the motel rumble and roar. The ceiling pitched one way and then the other. Came from driving all that way. Her mind still sped on, closed eyes still seeing ghosts of trees whizzing past in the dark, great grey pools of fog embracing the car when they descended into a valley.

'Where are we? Where are we?' she had asked, many times.

'At the One Mile.'

'Is that the sea I hear?'

'Ha ha – no. The sea is miles and miles away. That's the swish of gum trees in the wind.'

'Where ...'

'See? That'll be the sign to the One Mile.'

'You know your way around here.'

'I hope so.' He smiled without turning to look at her. 'I don't need a map. See? It *is* the sign to the One Mile.' Without looking at her. Like they had been driving together like that forever. This was forever.

'I keep thinking ...'

'You keep thinking you're quite happy now.' He nodded. Dead serious.

This was forever and an hour. And a week. Where was she bound? No ironing on Wednesday.

'You keep thinking there's nothing to do.'

How did he know? 'I've never felt this ...'

'... free? This independent?' He knew. He knew everything and nothing about her. Nothing and everything, like he had watched her all her life.

Did he see her in that church, wondering how she had landed there, like some flake from outer space, all in white? Did he see her stare at her groom, wondering why it was this man, of all people, standing up in church with her? Did he watch her lay a perfect table for six on Friday? Cooking Beef Wellington? Arranging his Friday bunch of flowers in a cut glass vase? Ordering croquembouche from that special place? Washing ornaments in hot soapy water? Listening to Thel tell her that her husband was miserable, that it was a terrible mismatch? That neither of them was happy?

Did he see her pack a bag with perfectly folded clothes for a drive with someone out of a past, a youth, she barely remembered? Did he see her cloaked, covered, steeped in doubt, in panic, doused in her foggy unbearable existence? Did he see her leave home without a backward glance?

'I feel I've made a terrible mistake.'

He did not say a word or turn.

'Not coming here. Not leaving with you, I mean. It's like I've come out of a fog, a coma.' Shaking her head. Shaking. Holding head in hands and shaking. 'All those years. My whole life was a ... I hardly know why or how.'

'Numb? Like life happened to you, and you just let it happen. I saw that. Plain as day, all over your face.

Your face hasn't changed at all, you know that? Just like I remember in year twelve. I saw it, I tell you – clear as a bell. In a flash. Outside that butcher shop. There you were. And there was your whole life on your face. Another minute, and I might have missed you.'

'In my gardening clothes.' Shaking. 'What did you see?'

Lights. Street lights. Suddenly in a town, parked cars, a pub on every corner. Shops all lit up. Pulling into a motel forecourt.

'Here we are. Now listen.' Turned in his seat. Face inscrutable, serious, eyes invisible in the dark of the car. 'I'll get us two rooms, okay? We'll have dinner, and sleep as long as we can. Long drive tomorrow.'

'Oh.'

'You don't know whether to feel relieved or disappointed.' Squeezed his eyes shut and laughed.

She smiled. Sank back in the seat, took a deep breath. Had to take it in that he knew everything, all the time. Had to capture serenity, the pleasure of being significant. 'Do you know everything, Morgue Pearson?'

Laughed again. 'Come on, let's get something to eat.'

Now in bed, tracing ghosts of trees under eyelids, tracing the window's outline around badly-fitted blinds, with eyes wide open. The rectangle still there when she closed them shut. Open shut.

Lonely. Confused, out of kilter with the rhythm in her head of speeding car and fog-pooled valleys. Of long milky puddles glimpsed at the roadside. Of paddocks distant and near. Of darkness and light. Of bats streaming endlessly over her head.

Was it just a dream? Was he out there somewhere? There was really a man there, Morgan Gordon Pearson, who thought she was worth remembering. Who did not think she was beige or fawn. He had driven her further than she had ever been in her life.

Where was his room? Across the passage? Somewhere on this side of the motel. So, outside, across the car park? Struggling into jeans, tucking nightie deep in, slipping on unlaced shoes. Not allowing the possibility this was a bigger mistake than any other she had ever made.

There? Here?

'Morgue?' Rapping, knocking, tapping a fingernail against what she thought was his door. It was. Sudden bright light. He opened, pulled her in by a sleeve.

'Two in the morning. This how you treat a tired driver?' Warm and fuzzy from the bed. Naked.

'I don't ...'

'Shh. You're here now.' Grumbled, cleared his throat, turned out the light to plunge them in the dark. Dark, dark.

Guided to the bed. 'Morgue ...'

'Shh. Get in, get some sleep, okay?' Pulled her close, one arm, one leg folded over her, quilt pulled up. 'Sleep.'

Deep, deep, deeper sleep than she ever slept in her life. Drowning in it, and woken by his thick bristly hand stroking her hair, neck, back, under nightie. Dawn, yellow dawn, white with light, coming through the window whose blinds he never lowered. Noises from the highway rumbling in between deep breathing and noises recognized as her own sighs, oh, and rapid rapid rapid breath.

'Oh. Oh.'

Buried his head in her, his hair smelling of liquorice, hotel soap, liquorice, sand. Heavy over her, under her; she was weightless, transparent, invisible. Disappeared into a haze of something. Of nothing. Of something brilliant and light, and piercing and captivating and magical. Something sharp. Sharp and blurred and sharper than ever before. So sharp she half screamed. Weightless, caught between the ceiling and the morning sun. Pinned, a moth on a board of blue velvet, of white silk, of hot corrugated iron, of matted felt: a violet iris in the wind.

She exploded like the sun, burned, blacked out. He breathed with her, then stopped. Then turned her see-through and weightless again, floating against a sheet of glass, burning, hot, untouchable. And she was back, conscious, conscious of coming to from somewhere remote and white with exquisite intensity.

'Been meaning to do that since year eleven.' Mumbled into her neck, exhausted, brown eyes suddenly in hers. 'Bec Winmarley.'

'I'm ...'

'In my mind, you are Bec Winmarley, since I was sixteen and promised myself one day I'd do this with you and it would be heaven on earth. And you know what?'

'What?'

Laughed on his way to the bathroom, splashing water, laughing, laughing. 'You *know* what.' Emerged with a big white towel waving between those blunt hands with mauve nails. Big, broad, muscular, daunting, miraculous. Real. There. Clear. 'You know exactly what, because I felt it.'

Did not say a word. He wanted her all those years ago. A kid in high school whose wish came true after a dozen years or more. Here, grinning. What had she wished for then? Perhaps she should have shared that wish. Who knew what to wish for at sixteen? She did not.

'I did not.'

'Didn't what?' Stopped using the towel. 'Yes, you did. Your heart stopped. I felt your heart stop. I made it stop.'

It did. The bed slid out from beneath her, backward. Slid against the universe. Lurched her free. Free of everything. 'I didn't ... I lost ... I fainted.' Perhaps she should grin too. Smiled to show it was something good. Something she did not know existed for her. Until then.

'See? Look at your face. Heaven on earth. Pinch yourself, Gordon Pearson,' he said to himself. Laughed. Looked at her. Sat on the side of the bed and pulled her to him. A kiss so deep she touched the bottom of that rushing river, drenched in it. Sank. Drowned. Disappeared.

'Now – I'm going out to get coffee, coffee, and more coffee. What would you like for the first breakfast of your real life? Coffee?' Grinned. Sat on the end of the bed. Pulled on last night's clothes. Turned and kissed her again. 'What? Tell me.'

'Iced doughnuts.'

'We must work on your taste, Bec Winmarley.'

'I've had taste and perfection too long.' Thought of back there. She could never go back there now. She could not go back to Wingate Street, Portnoy Street, Galaxy Avenue, Bay Parade, Charles Roxon Street, Mayberry Avenue, Carlson Lane. Wingate Street. Wingate Street, Wingate Street. She could never go back now.

'Ah! I see. A vacation from taste and perfection, is this what we are doing?' Laughing, laughing to the door. 'And here I was, thinking we had turned the world on its ear. Felt like it, somehow.' Straight face. Brown eyes shot through with yellow light from the window. 'Don't move. Don't move a muscle. We have stuff to discuss when I get back.'

Sank back.

Sinking, sinking into a feeling so clear, so far from perfection, she blacked out, short of breath. Slept. Rolled, turned over. Rumbling from the highway never let up. Never. Rumble, rumble. A car horn, once, sharp. A siren in the distance. Then another kind of siren. Listen, listen. The hum in the distance. The rush of traffic. Never-ending. Eternal. Deep, deep sleep again.

Thirteen

Ian can fly

Waking slowly. Opening eyes. Trying to stretch. Content. Cold. Uncomfortable. Hurting. Cold. Caught under stiff white sheets. Achy and dizzy, disoriented.

'Hello. Hello, Mrs Brixham. Can you hear me?' Peering, someone peering too close into her face. A short-sighted stare through shiny glasses. Too much mascara. A light blue uniform, like the curtains.

Who was this woman? 'Who are you?'

'Do you know what day it is?' Face serious behind that smile. Forced smile, forced, with a pinch above the bridge of the glasses.

'I'm cold.'

'Do you know what day it is?'

'Cold.' She knew. She knew it was the last day. The very last day. The Wednesday of the very last week of it all. Of the last year. Of the last second. Flooding in, tears, muffled by something behind her mind. Sobs hurting where other sobs had been.

'What's today, love?'

'It's over. There is no-no-no-no day.'

'You're in hospital. Do you remember what happened?'

Noise. Noise like lightening. 'Tell them to stop that noise. Please. Please.'

Taking her hand. Taking her hand above the covers,

stretched tight like a drum.

'Take them off me. The blankets. Tucked in too tight. Where's ...' There was no one left. 'There's no one to tell, is there? No one to call. Cold, cold.'

Another face by the bed. 'She's not making sense. We might call Sister.'

'It's Wednesday, all right? Ironing to do. Please loosen these blankets.' Clouds descending over half the room. Sobbing catching at her throat. 'That noise.'

'It's only the dinner trolley, pet.'

'Crockery and cutlery, brilliant clean.'

'She's not making any sense. We might call the doctor.'

Choking. Suffocating on tears, and sighs coming from the other side of the white room. Blue room. Curtains hanging everywhere.

'Doctor came to your motel, do you remember?'

Sat up. Selby Brixham took a deep breath. Her head hurt. Right hand? Left hand to head. 'All I'd like, please, is coffee. Coffee. Coffee. And iced doughnuts.' Raised both hands to her face, and drenched them with hot tears. 'I hurt all over. Nurse, nurse ... it hurts.'

'Oh, oh. Don't cry like that. Don't cry, pet.'

Held by a nurse. In some anonymous hospital, out where she might not be. Where she never was. Where she could not possibly stay.

'We are treating you for shock. You've had a terrible shock.'

Sobbing like a child. Breathless and inconsolable. Hearing a male voice somewhere distant, somewhere insignificant. Feeling a sharp jab, a quick and capable rubbing dusting scrubbing with a ball of cottonwool. Sensing a chemical seeping through arm, neck, tongue, eyes, head. Sensing nothing.

Nothing for hours, and then asking for coffee again,

and asked what day it might be. And her chest devoid of a heartbeat. Empty.

'Empty.'

'Sorry?'

'It's Empty today.' Looking straight into her glasses. 'That's what day it is.'

'Oh.'

'May I please have coffee and an iced doughnut?' Looked at a tube and a needle under a pink plaster on the top of her left hand. 'Am I on a drip?'

'You have been quite out of it for ... for several ... um, hours.'

Her turn to ask. 'What day is it?'

'Friday, love.'

Morgan Gordon Pearson already dead two days. Three. *'Friday?'*

'Your next of kin is listed as your husband. Is that right? We've tried to contact him, but no one can find him. Mr Brixham seems to be un-reachable. Is there anyone else we can call? Can we get someone to come out to you?'

'Where ... where is this? Where am I?'

'Wagga Wagga hospital.'

Wagga Wagga Wagga Wagga. Numb. Numb. Pinching her own forearm. Feeling nothing. 'My brother is Ian Winmarley. Ian Winmarley. Ian. I need my mobile.'

'We'll call him. Do you know where ...'

'Inverell.'

'Oh, Inverell. Oh. God. Just over ten hours by road on a good run.'

'Ian can fly.'

'Can't we all, love? Now lie back and rest.'

And then she opened her eyes and he was there. Ian Winmarley. Straight mouth and hair not so black any more. Floods of tears. Heaving chest.

'Oh Bec.' Held her. Soft and tough and smelling of cigarettes and alcohol.

'Did you fly?'

'No – drove. Came as fast as I could.'

'I can smell again.' Through deep sobs, punching at her lungs, stopping, piercing, stabbing at her throat. 'No tears left.'

'They told me what happened. Something of what happened.'

'Take me away. Get me out, Ian. Drive me somewhere. Not home. Not home.'

'They can't find your husband. He's disappeared.'

'Not *home*.'

'He's disappeared, love.'

'He doesn't know how to disappear.'

'What?'

'It doesn't matter. Nothing matters. Take me out.'

'We'll go home to Derry, okay?'

Nodding, nodding helplessly. A child in a hospital gown. A different woman. A hand with a tiny bruise under a bandaid. 'My drip is gone.'

'You'll be all right now.'

Suddenly in her jeans and checked shirt. In her brown shoes and green jacket. In a wheelchair, under a deep deep porch where sunlight slanted to the spot a black shiny suitcase stood, its handle extended, its side bright with light.

'Goodbye, Mrs Brixham.'

'You've had a kind of mental breakdown. Nervous collapse. That's what they said,' he said in the car.

Not a real car. A truck, a ute, a high four-wheel drive. A detail she needed, to steady her. A nervous breakdown. Collapse. Deflated. Everything knocked out of her. All gone. Squashed. Pushed, spread, smeared onto the bitumen of a highway. Dead. Finished. 'What's this car?'

'I had to borrow one. Ours is in the shop right now. We have a Commodore.'

'But what's this one?'

'A Landcruiser.'

'Really.' Talked about cars. Had to talk about cars until they were out of there and driving along a highway. A highway. Road, road, robbing her of all that. All of what? Looked through the windscreen and saw nothing. Nothing. Held back tears until the salt boiled and sang through her arteries, stabbing like knives.

'We'll go along the Mid-Western Highway until we get to Temora, see? And then follow the signs to Parkes. It's the shortest way. The only way I know.' He turned on the radio. 'What kind you want? Talk-back? I think we can get ... music?'

'Anything you like.'

'Tell me if you want to ...'

'Talk? Talk?'

He accelerated. 'Anything you like, okay?' And hours, hours, hours later, 'Okay – toilet stop. Hungry?'

Waking, waking from a whizzed dream, with a crick in her neck and a wave of nausea. 'I slept all that way?'

'Come on, Bec love.'

'What's the time? I slept all that way?'

'You're sleeping off all the dope.'

Miles and miles of road. Too fast to think. Too close to the edge. Signs passed too rapidly to read. But she never read signs. Everything behind her. 'Were there police? I remember police now. Two women. Cops. And traffic cops.' Whirling, tumbling through her mind. Questions, questions, questions.

'They said you'd remember bits and pieces.

Disjointed, not in order, like. And yes – the police were at it, apparently, for hours. And someone came to say you could go. So I signed the discharge, okay? Said you must see a doctor soon. It was fairly obvious, they said, no enquiry, they said, and the other guy didn't have a scratch on him.'

'Other guy?'

'Huge accident, Selby – Bec. Huge. Road train and … and … '

'And Morgue.'

'That's his name. Yeah. Morgue? Anyhow, never knew what hit him. He drove right out into its path, see, and that was it. They said you must have heard it from the motel. Sirens, and all that.'

'Sirens all the time, everywhere.'

'I guess.'

'And nowhere Morgue. Coffee. Under the wax. Papering. Dis… when you *think*.' Sobs. Suffocating in her cupped hands.

He shoved her a handful of tissues from the squashed box on the dashboard. Started to pull over onto the shoulder. Tyres crunching, squashing, flattening gravel.

'No, no, keep going.'

'Sure?'

'Keep going, Ian.'

Tyres on bitumen again. Hot. Fast. Fast.

'We should sleep in Dubbo.'

She would never sleep again. Could not.

Morgan Gordon Pearson drove out into the path of a road train. It mowed him down, car and all, in an instant. A second. A moment all it took to cancel all her thoughts and hopes and what she had discovered that night.

'Or Gilgandra. Okay. Right.'

Ian did not know how to console her, she saw. She saw. Nodding, nodding without looking at him. He probably needed a rest. Could not share the driving. 'Can't drive.'

'No – they said not to let you. All those drugs.'

And then, out of a fog of landscape and road, road, road, they stopped outside a house with green trim. Pretty. Brilliant pretty. Neat. Timber painted green. White roses tumbling all over a dark green fence. Someone on the veranda waving.

'That's Derry. Say hello.'

Fourteen

And books everywhere

He was nothing like she remembered from television. Not slick. Not perfectly turned out in a grey suit with shot cuffs and permanent smile. Kind of sideways, lop-sided, skewed, asymmetrical, cosy, welcoming, grey, grizzled, warm.

He hugged Ian. Hugged her. Smelled of coal tar soap, peppermint, dust, compost. A gardener. Something she recognized.

'You have a lovely garden.'

'Surprised you'd notice. Pretty bad run of things, you've had, hm? I'm sorry. This house ... it's your house, until you find your feet.'

'Oh. Oh.' Overcome by such generosity. Moved to tears of a different kind. Flooded.

'Bring her in, Ian. I've made up the back room for your sister. But first, the kettle. I'll do that.'

Ian with more tissues. Through a stained-glass door, up a passage with an arch, through a tidy lounge, past a tiny shiny kitchen, to a brown door.

'The sunniest room in the house, Bec ... Selby. For as long as you like, love.' Wheeled her case to the foot of a large, feathery, fleecy, downy bed covered in a floral eiderdown. Slanted with sunshine from a wall of windows. Same fabric for curtains, pulled, bloused, billowed on either side, bunched on the floor, on the cream carpet.

'Oh!'

'Come and have a cup of tea, just to make Derry happy. He tries very hard. Takes him ages. Then you can do what you like.'

'Sleep?'

'Whatever.'

Such a tiny perfect dolls house. A table, haphazard with odd floral cups, chintz tablecloth. Lopsided like his face.

Derry, questions in eyes, stirring in sugar, one arm useless, puncturing an overblown cake with a blunt knife. Ian taking over, pushing the sharp point of a serrated knife in, exclaiming at cream bursting out and up. All laughing, all sunshine. Tiny slices, large slices, all uneven. Rose petals floating in a plain glass bowl. A loud loud loud clock ticking somewhere. And somewhere else, the lonely sound of a saxophone.

And cats.

Spoken to, like people. Barnaby Rudge and Penelope Keith. What? And Noam Chomsky. In a row, heads up, waiting for cake?

'Ian, I...'

'It's okay. It'll take you a while. We're a bit all over the place.'

'No. I never imagined you in this kind of a house. I never thought of you this way.'

He laughed. Looked at Derry. And laughing, laughing, both of them the same. 'It takes people a while to get used to us, darling. We're a bit fussy, fancy. Floral! And feline.'

'And books everywhere, Derry's, so feel free.'

Feeling disoriented, inebriated on tea and cream and strawberry jam in a Victoria Sandwich, they called the cake, eaten off plates with fluted edges. 'All from a charity shop, would you believe?'

She believed, believed, and tottered to the sunny room, drew curtains, and slept in the downy bed. For four days, on and off, staring at a wall of books, finding a life of Eric Gill, the works of Gwen John, Norman Lindsay's *Cats*; peeking into the back garden, wandering out, between showers, finding ceramic cats, porcelain cats, clay cats, wooden and metal cats among the foliage and flowers. Talking little, eating toast fingers off a white-painted tray, and chicken soup, and shepherd's pie, and Irish stew that tasted nothing like hers.

No one had phoned Thel.

Found her mobile, slept while it charged. Slept another eon, and woke to sunshine, a white tray with a mountain of toast and beautiful golden marmalade on a tiny crystal dish. Real butter in a cat-shaped bowl.

'But you want a dog.' Looking at Ian, sitting on the end of her soft bed.

'Thought about that. Thought about that a lot. Saw a few lovely dogs in your town. When I ... that time I came. Big binge, that was. Drank a river of beer, vodka, whatever. Took a break then, see? Not sure I could cope with his stroke. But look at him now. The OT does that, I think. Like miracles.' Smiled a grimace. 'Still drink, but.'

'And?'

'I thought, see? I have Derry and seven hundred cats. Does the job, most of the time. I might want a dog ...'

'But all ...'

'Yeah. You got it. All I want is Derry, really.'

Not what she meant, but amazed at this candid revelation. Had no idea, now, what she wanted. She didn't want anything. Everything she wanted was dead. Crushed underneath the sound of sirens. Crushed.

Listened for the ticking clock, listened for muted striking of the hour, the half-hour. 'That clock.'

'Love it or hate it?'

'It saves the night.'

He nodded, not understanding that she listened to the ticking, loud, loud, in the night house. So different from anywhere else she had ever slept. Wingate Street, no. Her mother's house, no. The motel where ... no.

'I must find a clock like that.' She nodded. 'Exactly like that.'

'You like it.'

'I like everything about you and Derry and this house. And the cats. Imagine. Derry Stubbs.'

Then spoke to Thel for an hour, her phone still plugged in the charger, her knees a mound under the eiderdown, the sun disappearing behind sunflowers against the back fence she could see through the huge window, and then a clock tower visible for a moment, and then darkness but for the white daisies hard up against the glass, and one of the cats peeping in. And the clock ticking in the house, and someone in the kitchen clattering knives in the sink, and then a saxophone somewhere.

And Thel exclaiming on her end, dropping everything. Sending the children out with the patient, patient husband. Crying with her. Saying she would phone the house to see where he was, Mr Brixham, she called him.

'No.'

'I shouldn't call him?'

'No. They said at the hospital they couldn't trace him. They couldn't raise him. He must be away somewhere.'

'At the club.'

'Ah. The club. Forgot.' That part of her life,

finished? The club. The big bedroom. The sterile kitchen. Echoing bathroom. Art nouveau mirror and stand in the hallway. Finished? No pet hairs. No noise, no mess. No ticking clock. No saxophone. No pain. No regret. No Morgan Gordon Pearson. Tears sniffed back. Pain in throat swallowed, swallowed.

Thel heard. 'Oh, Sel. So heartbreaking.'

'I'll get better. Ian and Derry are so ...'

'Get better, Sel. Stay there – your brother and his ... they sound wonderfully caring.'

'They have cats.'

'And love, by the sound of it. They have love. They care for you.'

'And mismatched crockery. All with flowers. Flowers everywhere. You should see the garden.'

Fifteen

A choice to be made

It fell heavily, that day – tumbling rain, spiralling, slanting, slapping onto heads. They paced rapidly, together, almost in time, rhythm broken only because her legs were shorter.

'We love this lake, see?'

'Yes.' She could see. Swans, ducks, all still sailing in the sudden downpour. The dam in the distance blue green and masked by rain. Trees already dripping.

'We love the rain, too. But Derry doesn't take the damp well any more.' Lengthened his gaze. 'Ah, good, he's already in the car.'

'You look after him well, Ian.'

'Rubbish, Bec – he looks after me, really. I'd be a wreck, a dero, if it weren't for him. His mind – his mind is so clear. He figures people stuff out so well. He keeps me straight. Ha ha – you know what I mean. True.'

Striding, splashing, squelching on towards the car, overtaken by running children, families abandoning picnics. Puddles formed before her eyes. Puddles splashed into, in haste and speed towards the car park. Grass squished underfoot. A landscape turned from green to grey in five wet minutes.

'We haven't spoken about him, yet.'

'About whom?' About whom?' She had said a bit about Morgue. Oh, Morgan Pearson. Oh Morgue. Her wrists ached, her throat tightened. Saw in her eyes squeezed shut for an instant the light rectangle of a badly-fitting blind in a dark room.

'Oh. Later – at dinner perhaps.'

Damp in the car, steamy and clammy. Windscreen and windows grey, all grey. Suddenly turned very cold. Back to the warm house. Shower so hot, so soothing, even though brief. Emerged in dressing gown, bare feet, towel-dry hair. Derry lighting the fire with one hand. Other held tight into body, hand clenched, not normal, not awkward any longer, though. She had been there long enough to understand he didn't want special attention. Knew not to do it for him.

'Was thinking of making my way back, Derry.'

Looked round, jerkily, mouth lopsided but the expression obviously full of something like disappointment. 'Oh no.'

'I can't stay here forever.'

Laughed. Laughed and finally lit the fire. Turned it up high, gestured her closer. 'You know you can. We'd love you to.'

'Because of my chicken casserole.'

Laughed again. 'No, not for that.' Moved slowly to the drinks tray. Glasses jingled, jingled. Slowly brought her a glass. 'Drink this. You'll love it.'

'Oh.' She did. 'What is it?'

'Moscato wine. Sweet. I've always loved it.' Looked up at Ian, fresh from his shower.

'That was some downpour. And we'll get more tonight. It's gone very cold, all of a sudden.' Cocked his head for the sound of rain on the roof. Only the clock. Only ticking from the arched passage. Only the clock, and in the distance, a slight hum of some truck up the highway.

'You drinking wine now?'

'I gave her moscato.'

Ian smiling. 'You'll learn to drink properly, with that. Socially, elegantly, without it turning into a problem, see?' Said like a warning. An ironic joke. A personal pang.

She looked down. Looked up to his erasing, cancelling laugh. And Derry's. No accusations, no contrition. His drinking not an issue, then.

'Must take the coach back. I'm so puzzled about ... you know, Thel thinks he's still at the club, but no one there's seen him. He hasn't been there at all. I called twice and spoke to two different managers. So since I left, on the fourteenth of last month, he's been gone. Goodness knows where. So I'd better go back. Goodness knows what he thinks must have happened to me.'

'He's disappeared. People do that. Especially if they're not ...'

'... not happy? Thel says he was miserable. That we were a mismatch.'

'There you go.'

'So why did you say, Ian, that we must talk about him?'

Lifted a beer can to his mouth. Looked at Derry. Looked at her. 'Not *him*.' Looking, looking at his shoes. 'I found your father, Bec love.' Looked up. 'Or rather, he found me.'

'I'll start dinner.' Derry limped down the passage, turning lights on and off as he went. Click-click, click-click.

It came back. Ian's phone call, as she walked behind Morgue towards a glass sliding door at a petrol station in the absolute middle of nowhere. It came back, her surprise, her annoyance that it should come right then, right there, when she had least expected an intrusion. Remembered the ice cream. *You don't like nuts.*

Wept into the sleeve of her dressing gown.

'I'm sorry.'

'Oh Ian – it's not you. It's not finding my father. It's ... It might always be like this, remembering tiny minuscule things out of an interval so ... *brief*.'

He said nothing. Looked at her from the distance of the sofa. Tilted his head a little.

'You'd think it wouldn't matter. So brief. Too short. Too inconsequential or whatever the word is.' Sniffed. Sniffed and raised her chin.

Derry, from the doorway. 'It was important. Nothing, no law, no one says something important has to be *long*.'

Oh. Right. Right. He was so right. A revelation. 'I felt I'd come alive, see? I felt there was someone who thought I was wonderful ... since he was sixteen.'

'Since ...'

'He was at school with us. He was at *school*.' Sobbed into her sleeve, buried her face in her elbow, crouched by the fire, feeling it hot on one side of her face. Her shoulder, her flank, one foot.

'So that's how. Ah. You met again. He came to town?'

'Pearson's. Remember Pearson's?'

'The funeral director – that guy everyone called Mort ... no, Morgue, at school? Ah! Yup – thought so.' Ian shook his head slowly. He remembered him vaguely. Vaguely. Stood and poured himself a shot. 'Didn't know I knew him. Well – didn't. I was years behind you guys. But you know...'

Sudden noise. All eyes to the ceiling.

'Hail. Noisy, noisy hail. It's loud on an iron roof. Listen to it!'

Drumming, ticking, drumming again. Loud and insistent. 'Nearly mid-autumn, too. So maybe timely.'

Derry came to help her up. Fumbled and missed her arm.

She rose, swaying, swaying. Moved to a chair.

'I'll get you another moscato, hm?'

Nodding, wiping her eyes on her sleeve, grateful for the distraction the hail brought, warmed by the fire, comfortable in her seat, sensing armchair springs cushioned by upholstery beneath her, supporting, holding her up. Leaned back, eyes closed.

The noise started again, abrupt, drumming sharply. Stopped just as suddenly.

'Love it, really.' She looked up.

Both men smiling, grinning, looking at each other. Relief in the room like a presence.

'Tell me about my father. Do you know his name?'

'Edmund Eben.' Ian leaned forward, an elbow on each knee. 'Some name, I thought, see? Only spoke on the phone. Let me tell you, it was a surprise. Gave me his number. Gave me an address. Said I should take you.' Searching her face for a reaction. Wanting to see how she felt.

'Some name.'

'I think he had a slight accent. Slight, but. Not too foreign, you know?'

'Foreign? Where is he?' She could not imagine a place for him, a location. Nowhere. Who could he be? What kind of a man? *Where-where-where*.

'I know where he is because I have an address, don't I? But I could also look him up. You know ...'

'What – Google?'

Ian nodded. Raised his face to hovering Derry. 'Derry kind of thought it was a familiar name. He'd heard it before. Have you?'

Stalling, stalling. Ian was stalling. Should she know that name? *Edmund Eben*. Shook her head. Looked him straight in the eye. Waited. One of the cats, then another, circled her, then sat on the carpet in front of her chair, close to the towelling of her dressing gown. The third cat, Noam, perched high, on top of a glass cabinet full of floral china. Everyone looked at her. A frozen moment, with the power to make her look at herself. Looking, thinking, wondering whether she wanted to know who Edmund Eben might be. Clear. Clear as day. No obstacles to this. Then murky, muddy. What other complication would this open up?

'I don't know, even, whether I should look. For my husband. For my father. Are they lost, really?' Thinking aloud.

'If someone's gone, of their own choice, they might be lost to you ... but not to themselves. Choice is the thing, here.' Derry lowered himself, lower, lower, onto the overstuffed sofa, wriggling, wriggling to find a comfortable position, pulled the useless arm into his lap, leaned forward. 'If someone wants to be found, they will.'

'Uh-huh.' Ian understood.

'They make themselves findable, see. Or if they don't care, they don't care. Or they go looking, to see who might be seeking *them*.'

Ian squished open another beer. Effervescent noises, a hiss, before he drank. Stood with his back to the fire. Straddled legs, looked straight at her. 'It's easy to disappear.'

'No, it isn't.' She looked at Derry for confirmation.

Derry nodding, then shaking, his head. 'It is, if you know no one cares, and if you care for no one.' Shifting, shifting, on the sofa. 'No one cares enough to look. So you're all alone.' Head turned toward Ian. 'Isn't that right, Ian? That's when it becomes real freedom. One of the real genuine freedoms.'

Ian would know. A mother's words returning. *As good as dead, is Ian.* Wanting, wanting to ask Derry if anyone had ever looked for him. Wondering about his answer if she did. Knew nothing about him. Thoughts returned to Edmund Eben. Derry was right. He wanted to be found. Did she? 'So it's whether I want to be found.'

'Yes.' Rubbed the side of his lop-sided face with the good hand, reached out to take his drink from Ian.

A choice to be made, he said.

And, 'Dinner's nearly ready,' he said.

Sixteen

The end of Jonty Green

His bank accounts not touched for more than four weeks. The house cold and bleak. Selby going room to room to room to room, starting at the big bedroom again, again, again. Surprised the lounge, the statuettes, the photo frames looked dust-free. Everything still spotless. Smelling of plug-in room scent. Patchouli. Lavender.

The policewoman at the station said it was up to her, her choice, her duty even, to make a report. Report him as a missing person. Was he missing or just gone?

'Name?'

His name missing from her mind, had never lived in her heart. Her chest void, echoing only with the name of Morgue Pearson.

'Mr ... Brixham ... Mr Brixham. Francis Xavier.'

Fourteen years in that house meaning something? Nothing. Only her garden, her garden – jonquils, crocuses, daffodils now runs of fallen stems and lanceolate leaves, all leading one way, and then the other, dominoed lines of leaves, pointing, pointing at unpruned roses, fallen petals on the mulch, slaters rolling, feasting, scurrying in and around them. And everlastings springing, starting up between the gladioli, whose last trumpets withered, wilted, waned in front of her eyes. Yellow, white, yellow, crimson.

Her colours diluted. Her sun white. Temperatures rising and falling without her. This place, except for the garden, was pristine, clean, perfect. Uninhabitable. She could not stay. How could she stay?

Automatic watering, Tuesday, Friday, Tuesday, Friday, Tuesday, had seen nothing perished; but what devastation, what a return to wilderness in the green borders. How victoriously dandelions swung prickly yellow heads. Winning, winning, over her absence.

'I was gone just over a month.'

The policewoman hummed. 'Mm. And now you're back. Did you speak to the bank? To insurance? Superannuation, the banks – now the banks usually have a good idea where the accounts are sourced from. If and when.'

Tried to find words.

Policewoman found hers first. 'Date of birth?'

Easy to remember.

'Do you have a photo of him handy?'

'On my phone.'

Policewoman finding more words. 'But listen, people are crafty, you know. Did you know how much he made – do you know how much you spent? Statements from the bank? Take one from the other, my dear ...' Looked to her left and right to see if anyone listened. 'Minus. Minus one from the other, okay? That'll tell you if he hoarded money away, to run away on. Runaway money. See if you can minus your way to that.'

'So...'

'So look at old statements.'

'So ...'

'So your sums will tell you if he wanted to get away, see? Intentional disappearance. Voluntarily missing, the inspector might say.' Breathing more regularly now, back in authority, duty-bound to ask questions. 'There's a form to fill. Okay – I'll ask you the questions. Do you have reason to hold fears for his welfare and safety, Mrs Brixham?'

Reason? Reason? 'I don't know.'

'Is this disappearance out of character? Has he taken off before, or said something, or threatened to leave, they mean.'

'No.'

'No, no family to go to. His father died before we got married.'

'No'.

'No.'

'No.'

'Was he diagnosed with a mental illness. Depression? Ever show suicidal tendencies?'

'No.'

The last of the noes. The last of the policewoman's looks. Observed Selby's hand gripping the counter. 'Okay if we come home and have a look?'

'Of course.' Thought nothing of it.

'Called everyone he knows? Work?'

'Yes.'

'Everyone just as puzzled, you think?'

'More puzzled.'

'This inquiry private – or can we make the details public?'

Couldn't think.

Thought and thought. All boxes ticked, all lines filled at last.

Had no idea they would be so thorough. Went through all his things, and hers, and the house, and the garden. Went through all her answers about the last time she saw him, spoke to him. Showed them her phone. Took his number again, again, again. Took a photo from an album.

'Now we wait,' someone said.

'Breakdown in communication,' someone said.

'No history of mental illness or substance addiction,' someone else said.

'No history or evidence of financial or gambling problems,' someone said.

'Last signs of cleaning and gardening at the house pre-date his last appearance at work,' someone said.

'Wife in Wagga hospital for some of the time. Got that.'

As if she was not there to listen to them.

'One of those voluntary ones, looks like,' someone said.

'One of those mysteries of life,' Thel said.

Sitting, sitting across Thel's cluttered table like the intervening weeks never happened. Children growing, noise growing, clutter worse than ever. Smiles better than ever.

'Oh, Thel.'

'Don't cry. Yes – cry, let it out.'

Tea and doughnuts. Oh doughnuts. Oh, Morgue. Could not talk about him.

Then the reek of good cheddar. Thel slicing cheese for sandwiches. 'A nice cheese and ham sandwich, I think. You never were one for doughnuts.'

'No. Yes. No.'

And the smell of cheese. *Not your father.* 'Ian found my father.'

Thel silent, buttering bread. 'Is that good?'

'He wants to see me. Looked for me.'

'Wow.'

'Yes.'

Thel expertly cutting sandwiches into nice tri-angles. Arranging them on a plate. Piling, piling a hundred sandwiches. Two plates.

'Can't just let the kids look on, can we?'

Teabags in mugs, spoons of sugar. Glasses of cordial for the kids. Fresh carton of milk. Sunlight streaking clutter on the table white, yellow, white.

'So he wants to see you. Do you? Want to see him, I mean?'

Didn't know, didn't know. Yes, she knew. Curiosity sharp, sharp in her mind. But the end of Jonty Green was difficult to bear. Who was she really?

'I don't know who I am, Thel.'

'Oh! *Oh.*' Turned, whirled, swung quickly from pouring hot water into mugs. Embraced her clumsily. Awkward hug. 'My best darlingest friend, is who. Loveliest person ever. I know who you are.'

Reassurance exactly the same as Derry's, filling her. Filling her with warmth and wet-strong sensations in stomach-pit. Like Ian's drunken smile that first time in the pub. *Never thought I'd see you again, sis.*

'And Ian doesn't drink as much as I thought, either. Am I wrong about *everything*?'

'About that huge grey handbag, you were. Wrong size.' Laughed, hysterical, nodding. 'Wrong colour. Ha ha! Wrong shape. About that cow pattern jacket thing you probably were wrong, yeah. About that job you once ditched, remember? Yeah, *that* was the right thing to do, I reckon. But you're a bit stubborn.'

'Am I? I sometimes think people walk all over me.'

'Some folks are just people-walker-overs. They squash others, whether they're stubborn or not. Or they try. They give it a good try.'

More kitchen-sink wisdom. Thel just described her old dead mother. Her missing husband. So alike, come to think of it. People-walker-overs. So unlike ... 'You should meet Ian and Derry. Derry and Ian. They're such a pair.'

'No doubt it'll happen.' Bit into a sandwich. 'Come on, eat something, you broomstick. Let's get something into you.'

Best thing to eat since the Riverina. Best thing to eat since Inverell. Something inside was getting better. Something inside just died.

The end of Jonty Green came when she flew to Melbourne, to find Ian waiting, just as he said. "Arrivals" lit up behind his head. Waving a bit until she saw him. Her shiny black bag rumbling on industrial carpeting, his familiar smile muffled by a light embrace.

'Shall we have a drink or do you want to settle your bag at some hotel first? I haven't booked. I've just got in myself.' Looked at her familiar bag. Her new shoes. Looked at his own unstructured bag; overnight canvas grip with three swinging padlocks.

'I reserved two rooms at St Kilda – all right?'

'Oh – clever. Not too far, then.'

'Looked it all up. The places mean nothing yet. How's Derry?'

'Missing you. And the cats. They sit on that chair you liked. His arm is better. Gripped a mug yesterday. Starts speech therapy soon. All good. Radio getting busier – that's the funniest part. Something to do with going digital.'

'Oh. Good?'

'Yup – bulletins every half-hour now. Funny that. Changing demographic, or something. Everyone growing old, they mean! Hubby back?'

'No.'

'Might not be such a bad thing ... I mean ... not that...'

Had to agree. Could not tell him she was empty inside. Empty. Not missing her husband at all.

Profoundly, deeply missing a man she knew for a day and a night, so much her wrists hurt, and the space behind her eyes ached when she swallowed. Throat congested with grief. Still. Still.

'Doing anything new, anything good, Bec?'

'Talking to Thelma, that's all. She thinks I should get a job.'

'Perhaps?'

Shook, shook her head. Wanted only to do things she had never done before. Wanted only to keep moving. Or stopping. She didn't know.

And then there was the meeting. A shock, a surprise. A chiming doorbell. A high threshold, a wide-open door. His eyes exactly like hers, perhaps, but behind glasses. Half-frames. Intelligent stare. High square forehead, fringed with white, white straight hair, and creases on both sides of his wide mouth a permanent smile. A small scar on the cheek. But those piercing eyes, dark green, steady.

His house in Elwood easily found. Ian showing the way from the map on his phone. 'He told me to bring you to him,' he had said on the way to the hotel.

And here he was. Deep, deep voice, but soft. 'There you are, then.' Held out a hand.

She took it. Selby took his hand and he embraced her with the other, quickly, so she hardly knew it happened.

'Please come in.' Stepped off his threshold, his threshold in Elwood. A house at once stylish and threadbare. And smelling of paints. Of paints. Of turpentine and linseed oil. 'Please come in, both of you.'

Stepped with Ian into that smell, down a long wide hallway hung like a gallery with pictures, framed and unframed, some with copper bar lights over them, glowing. Glowing in the night. Was that why he arranged to see them at sunset? Impressing them with this vision of dark and light paintings under yellow light, butter yellow walls. Through to a large, large space that filled her eyes with a thousand impressions at once.

Turning, edging round to look at his soft black shirt, buttoned to the top, underneath a soft grey flannel jacket. And jeans, a well-loved pair, it seemed to her, paler at the knees.

'The table is laid, so we might as well ...'

'Yes.'

Turned to her, suddenly. Held her gently by the upper arms, at his arms' length, smiling, smiling. 'Let me look at you. Ah – you could not be more like me if you tried. Look at your hair. Green eyes, too! Thin and resilient. No matter what we eat, eh, we'll be thin, thin. Could not be more like me. But pretty. Eh? Pretty.' Nodded, appreciating her. 'Now sit. Tell me... tell me.'

'Yes?'

'You must have a million questions.' Soft esses, a slight, slight accent.

'You were born somewhere else?' She did not know where to look, how to start. His eyes so piercing, so knowing, so bright.

'Prague. A very very long time ago.' Laughed. 'But I've been back a few times. I visit regularly. City of a hundred spires, and all that.'

'And you paint.'

'That's all I do.' Beamed, raised his eyebrows above the spectacles.

'Did you know, Ian?'

'Yes – it's on the internet.'

She had not dared look. Did not want to know, until ... until this.

The older man, beaming, clasping hands. 'I've been

painting a lifetime, so some people know my name. Some people buy my paintings, yes.'

'It's funny – I used to paint, but I ...'

'You used to paint! Fancy that, eh? Not any longer? Why not?'

Selby hung her head. She didn't know. Felt she knew nothing, nothing, now that the idea of Jonty Green was erased. Eradicated. This man so real, so calm, yet so eager. Looking at her, up and down, appearing so happy to see her.

Ian so silent, watching.

'I still can't believe – or come to terms – I don't know. This is surreal.' She regretted the words. A hand to her mouth.

'I can't either. This is very strange. But true.' He turned to Ian. 'Tell us this is true, young man.'

And that was it. Consciously or otherwise he banded them together, she and he, related, linked, for Ian to observe from across some divide they all suddenly saw was there. She was connected to this man. He was her father. *Tell us this is true.*

'You used to paint. That seems wonderful. Later, I will show you something. I must show you something I did years ago. The whole reason this is happening now, you see. Eh? The whole reason.' His fingers, thin and expressive, spread like sun rays.

'Oh?'

'But first, let's have something. I have here a little plum cake from round the corner. And the kettle needs a button pressed – there!'

And she looked at pretty porcelain plates and cups, etched glasses tinted blue, gold rims on everything. Delicate cutlery. A tablecloth deeply scalloped with white-on-white embroidery. And suddenly knew why she was like she was. Why she sometimes gripped the edge of a table just like that. Just like he did now. Why she liked what she liked. And failed, utterly failed, to see what he might have seen in her mother, all those years ago. Her mother, who would not have known the meaning of the word elegance. Or style. Or understood why this was so subtle and sophisticated. And very nearly threadbare with daily use; some not-so-obvious economies of scale. Refined scale, but neat, ordered, and cared for, and elegant, and brilliant clean.

'I have known about you a long, long time.'

Another jolt. Selby's eyes showing it, wide, clear, green. 'Oh! Oh – I had no idea. Until I was eighteen I had no idea. There was no way for me to ...'

'I tried. Until she was alive, your mother, I was not allowed to do anything. She returned, gifts, money, letters, cards. All sent back. *Return to sender*. She absolutely forbade it. She said that you had to turn twenty-one. Then I heard she died, and I tried, but you had vanished, disappeared.' Thin fingers spread out again.

'Disappeared?' And she knew why. Of course she was unfindable.

'There was no one of your name anywhere I looked.' Tilting his head, turning, and looking with those intelligent eyes. 'No Rebecca Winmarley. Which I knew was the name she gave you. And I could not possibly make the journey, see, and come and knock on your door.'

'She. I could never understand ...' Stopped. 'I'll tell you why. I changed my name, by deed poll, the day I turned eighteen. The very day.'

He poured some kind of fragrant tea into her cup. 'Now tell me why you did that.'

'My father... stepfather, died. My brother ...' looked at Ian, who nodded, accepted his cup. '... Ian left home.

I wanted to be different. Different from her, I think.'

'So you called yourself – ?'

'Selby Angela Maya Green.'

'Green!'

Blinking, blinking away the thoughts of some eighteen year-old. 'Because of my eyes.'

'Bravo!' He clapped. Clapped long hands with thin oval nails, a band on his ring finger. Creased hands. He had to be – what? In his early sixties at least. 'Vanna will like that.'

A silence. A look at Ian. A possibility never entertained, never thought of.

'My wife, Vanna – she returns from singing at almost exactly seven. And then we will eat. How does that sound?' Rose from his seat, a little restless, turned a light switch, whirled and clapped again. 'She will insist on calling you Maya. She will love you.'

Seventeen

Overwhelmed

A small quick woman, like a stouter Edith Piaf, she was. Entering, brushing the drops of a shower from her shoulders, fluffing up short hair. Looking around the room, back and forth, and back; a small bird, grinning, wrinkling that beak of a nose, grinning. 'So she is here. How good! How nice! Yes? Mundo?'

She called this tall thin man Mundo, and scurried about, taking off a large coloured cardigan, checking the table. Looking at Selby. Touching her, touching Selby on the shoulder. 'Come give me a kiss. How lovely you are. Just like ... So thin, like Mundo. Like your father. Hah ha! You had tea? Good?'

'This is Vanna. Yes, we had tea.'

She filled the large room. Tiny, but bigger, bigger than her tall husband. Noisy, talkative. Looking at the table, at the cups, chirping, chirping, exclaiming and straightening things. Pale nail polish, loosely curled hair.

'Her name is Selby Angela Maya!'

'Oh – ooh. I shall call you Maya!'

'See?' A grin. A wide grin.

'And this is her brother, Ian.'

'So nice! Brothers are good. Of course, of course.'

'And we had tea.'

'And did you tell her? Did you show her? Did you

see, Maya – did you see, how it all began?'

'No, Vanna. Not yet. We are still ... still finding things out.' The man, rising, beckoning. 'There is something you must see. I have waited decades for this.'

Vanna hovering. 'Exactly thirty ... I don't know exactly ... or nearly. Tell her!'

'Yes, yes.' Happily leading her and Ian to the long gallery of pictures, where he stopped, turned, looked into her face.

'We have all waited for you, see? This is the day we all waited for. We all knew. All the time. Vanna said, look before it's too late. So I did. I looked for the name Winmarley. I found Ian. And now you are here.'

There were no words to say.

'And Vanna, ah – Vanna, the most capable, talented woman ... not only in Melbourne, but on earth, eh? She does a thousand things, all successfully. And all I can do is paint a little. And she does everything else. To make sure I can paint. And she is lovely – was used to wealth and elegance. Ah, Vanna – do you know she is half Maltese and half Sicilian, descended from a hugely wealthy but very eccentric Sicilian count?'

They reached a doorway, and he stood back. On either side of the door were paintings, of all sizes, some framed differently, some framed the same.

'Now look – look. I ...'

Selby looking, looking. Astonished at a portrait, a picture of a young woman in a room slanted with sunlight, sunlight in the squared-off shape of a window, spilling onto floor, door frame, wall. A delicious palette of gold, brown, beige, tan, amber, ochre. But her hair, her hair, in shades of coffee, caramel, oatmeal, taupe. And then her thin frame, her lowered head. It was unmistakeable. How could he guess how she was without seeing her?

'How long ago did you paint this?'

A smile. A nod. A hand on her elbow. 'Decades. I tried to guess, only a guess. A long time ago. A very long time ago. I tried to think what you might look like as a young woman. I was not so far off, eh? Not so distant from the truth.'

She had no words. Turning, turning to him, trying to mouth something through the emotion. 'Why?'

'Ah. It's how I do my thinking. Brush in hand. Too long ago. First she told me about you, in a letter, your mother. Then she forbade anything to do with you. I have no idea why.'

Derry had given her an idea why. Could not speak. Could not form words. Captivated, charmed by the painting. 'You painted ... me.'

'The only way I knew how to ... and Vanna of course was right. It was her idea. She places a brush in my hand, and then I can think. She is always right.'

'What I can't understand is how different you are from ... I can't see how ... what ...'

He understood. 'Ah – I was young and ignorant!' Laughing, shaking his head. 'Sowed wild oats, tried to become Australian in one short and turbulent year. Knew nothing of life, of love, or of art ... or of anything. Got into a spot of trouble here and there. Did not understand women, especially young women. Until Vanna.' Placed a hand lightly on Selby's shoulder.

They were the same height, he starting to stoop, only slightly.

'Are all these – is this all your work?' Craning her neck, standing back to take in the entire hallway, wide and long.

'No. We collect, when we can, works of others. Friends, acquaintances, some good but small pieces by ... you know, the Heidelberg school. Conder, mostly. Ah

– Conder!' He pointed at a long seascape. A horizon, a beach, a boat, a dock in the distance.

And then paused, pointed to the other side of the doorway. 'And this. Can you guess ...?' It was painted in the same style, same palette of colours as the portrait, the imaginary portrait he had made of her. It hung in a similar frame. It was of the same size, same weight, same importance. Two young men, alike, one standing near a window, another sitting with a cello between his legs. The same light as the other painting, the same hair colour, one thin form, the other shorter and more robust, and the same sunlight from a square window falling on the floor, angling up a door frame.

A sharp sensation gripping her, punching her in the stomach. 'Oh.'

'Yes, oh. Yes, yes – oh. These are Julius and Igor, my dear. My very dear girl. Julius and Igor – twins. Julius no longer with us.'

And Vanna suddenly behind them, bustling, noisy, placing a hand on the frame that held the picture of the two youths. Smiling, smiling, tilting her head.

Selby looking down at this strange woman. 'I have ... goodness, I have *three* half-brothers.'

Vanna shrugging, eyes wide, blinking, comical. 'Half? Half? No such thing as half! They are your brothers. And Ian. Ian? Come, come. Come and see! These are Maya's other brothers. We have photos, too, of course.'

Ian at the end of the passage, approaching slowly. Silent.

'No such thing as a half-brother, am I right? You are either a brother or you are not! You either have blood or you don't!' Laughing, smiling. 'You love or you don't. You belong or you don't belong! No halves. Eh, Mundo?'

'No half-measures for you, my dear.'

'No – no. No such thing. We lost Julius.' Her face saddening, crumpling. 'He went, he went, very young. We think it might have been ... but that's neither here nor there now. This picture is how Mundo imagined he might be as a young man. Much easier to imagine, since he has a twin. Much easier to make than yours, of course. Your picture was hard to conceive.' Stopped. Looked up into her face. 'Ah, dear Maya. You are here at last.'

To be so welcome, awaited, for so many years. This was beyond all expectation.

'The stories, in the end, are not as vital as the people, I suppose.' Vanna led them back to the big room, and gave Ian the task of stoking a large cylindrical potbelly stove with split logs. 'We are extravagant with our fires. Autumn and Spring, too.' Looking now at Selby. 'When people meet and part, part and meet again, it's not the stories that count, is it?'

'And where ... May I ask where Igor is?'

They both laughed. 'You must know ... everyone always knows where Igor Eben is.'

Ian looking round, raising his chin. 'Oh! Now I know why the name's familiar. Igor Eben, musician, right? Cellist. Soloist. I think he is ...'

Both of them, clapping, beaming, nodding. 'We rarely see him. He goes from concert hall to theatre, from auditorium to amphitheatre, from hall to arena, all over the world, all the time. I think today ... today he might be at the Concertgebouw in Amsterdam. We save as much as we can, we're frugal, and manage to go and watch him play, twice ... three times a year. He lives with his family near Frankston, just thirty kilometres away from us! But he is rarely there. Somehow, they manage a togetherness, don't they?'

Ian standing, the fire roaring behind him. 'You have

a famous brother, Bec.'

'Did you say family?'

Vanna spread her hands, counted on her fingers. 'A wife – Jacqueline, they met in Paris – she plays the piano. Divine. Beautiful and talented too. And their children, Horace, August, and Pearl.'

Turning away, turning, and sitting lightly on the arm of a leather chair. Nephews ... and a niece! A ready-made family. Not knowing how to take this. Not wanting to see the look on Ian's face. How would he take this?

Both dumbstruck. Looking at each other. From a life so impoverished of emotion, excitement, sentiment, passion; to this.

The old couple moved to the far end of the room, clattering dishes, preparing things; discreet and prudent, but conspicuous in their empathy. An elegant empathy.

No more words said. Selby's throat tight. Eating, dining, on that glorious white-on-white embroidered tablecloth. Delicate stewed veal, French beans, creamed potatoes, a sauce in a boat edged in faded gold. The splendour of everyday use. Knowing they always ate this way, in faded style. Threadbare glory, sturdy established grace. Nothing like what she moved from in her mother's house. Nothing like what she attempted at Wingate Street, using garish wedding presents. Did she know what it was she strove for? Couldn't have.

'I didn't know.' Bowing her head over a simple dessert of crème caramel.

They understood. 'You couldn't have known.'

Wanting now to run, hide, disappear from this. Wanting it too much. Needing something like this house, these people, to anchor her.

'I can't ...'

'How long are you in Melbourne?'

Selby shaking, shaking her head.

'Maya – my dear Maya.'

'Oh!' How could she endure another name change? And yet it was one she chose, one she wanted. One selected so carefully by an eighteen year-old, an eighteen year-old she no longer recognized, a numb eighteen year-old she did not know would grow more numb, with no idea any of this was there for her. Maya, they called her. And such attention, and such expectation.

Shaking all over now, emotion grabbing, seizing her by the throat. Head lowered onto arms, arms crossed on the table. Sobbing, the sound of helpless sobbing, in that large space, accompanying the crackling of logs and the startled cries of anguish from the old couple.

Eighteen

The otter

A waterfall, a torrent, a rush of chlorinated water. Clear, clear, and brilliant clean. With stars dissolved in it, evenly, splintered and melting, parts of the sun staining, painting, etching, engraving the sides of gullets, eruptions, spurts of water with the same gold. Metallic water, disgorging from a spout both natural and contrived, between eroded rocks, huge rocks drenched in gold, stained with silver, copper, nickel, platinum, lead, chrome, zinc, tin. Mesmerized by it, this waterfall sending a continuous never-ending stream into a kidney-shaped swimming pool, also bounded by large rocks.

Big, beautiful, home to a girl who dived, and swam, and dived again, over, through, and under water; a mermaid, a seal, a selkie, a manatee, an otter. Yes, an otter, running and diving and drenched to the skin, inside a skin-tight costume. Blue, blue, streaks of blue, celeste, navy, royal, aquamarine, turquoise blue, she was, with skin and lips to match, hair plastered in a long thin streak down her back. Hair very nearly the same colour as Selby's. Bec's. Maya's. Skin the colour of her mother's. Agility the legacy of her wiry grandfather.

'One more dive, Auntie Maya? Now? Just one?'

'Just three, and we'll go in. They're all waiting. No need to call me auntie, you know. No need.'

Eyes wide open. Edged in pink. Hazel eyes darkly wide and staring, used to opening under water. Drenched eyelashes spiked, wet, clumped like rays of distant myopic stars. 'What, just Maya?'

'Just Maya.'

'It's not what Uncle Ian calls you. He calls you Selby-Bec. Can I call you Selby-Bec, too?'

'You can call him Ian.'

Blue lips, swollen, crinkled, starting to shiver. 'Oh.'

'He'd love it. And call me Selby, okay?'

'And will I always be just Pearl? Can't I have lots of names too?'

'Dive another three times, and we'll go in.'

No second bidding. In, like the otter she was, graceful under water, submerged and mobile, wet. Wet and gliding upward, pushing effortlessly through greenish water, emerging and diving once more, deeper, faster, and again, and rising on flexed arms at the other end, glossing the rock with runnels of wetness descending over the tight young body. Legs slightly knocking at knees, a tremble starting from the shoulders, shrugged quickly under a fluffy fall of blue towel, held, held, squeezed, rubbed, hugged by Selby.

All gathered inside, an audience of faces. Expectant, waiting, eager to know her better. And the smell of food, and the tinkle of glasses, the clink of good china. And somewhere, an orchestra, muted and vague. Digital background music to this gathering of similarities and differences.

Some paintings on the walls recognizable as Edmund's. That rich distinguished palette of golds, browns, creams. His portraits, full and half-length, contained squarely in painted rooms drenched with rays of light shaped by windows; square and rectangle light, thrown onto architraves, floors, ceilings, walls and faces. Architectural faces, squared off, angular, and yet so like the ones in that house. His son's house.

Igor, a bit awkward, a shoulder slightly higher than the other, a shirt billowing over his skinny frame, managing to talk about different things to three children at once. And his wife, Jacqueline, quiet and stunning in dark beauty, unassuming; leaving the talk, chatter, noise, passion, gesturing, laughter, to the Ebens, of which she was not one, visually speaking, but who she loved, loved. Her black eyes following each one in turn.

The children impossibly noisy, bright, asking questions, questions. Asking about time, place, events, sounds, objects, quality, time, time, time; abstracting like adults. Questing minds in little bodies. Green eyes, hazel eyes, dark psychedelic eyes brimming with confidence. Such confidence. Such buoyancy and comfort in this house, where cooking smells were remarkable but unremarked, where an enormous cheeseboard – an entire wheel sawn from a tree, polished and perfect – presented a metaphor for completeness. That delicious reek of good cheese.

Selby observing, noting that she grew up without confidence, now she knew, seeing these three young things. She grew without searching conversation, without boisterous affection; without cultural curiosity; without art, save that she found in books; without a philosophy, without fun, knowing only the sozzled humour and half-love of Clint Winmarley. Where he now?

Even the noise and clutter of Thel's children was nothing like this. What was this? Exhausting, discomforting, pulling her out of, pushing her into a place she occupied only tenuously, she thought, but such a revelation.

'But,' she heard Ian saying. 'But ...'

A laugh. Edmund Eben clapping him lightly on the shoulder, nodding, tilting his head, attempting to straighten an encroaching stoop. Looking always for Vanna's eyes, and finding them. 'Is it not so, Vanna? I must paint Ian. And of course you are *family* – do not be preposterous. Maya is family. Things equal to the same thing are equal to one another. And when I paint you, eh? And when I do, it will be quite something for me. A challenge.'

She could not think why. Neither, from the look in Ian's eyes, could he. Months had passed, months in which her attempts to heal, to become whole again, to find a kind of life in the wreckage of a 'nervous breakdown' was at times difficult, at others intensely perplexing.

'So now that you have moved to Melbourne ...' Igor asking her. Asking her with the familiarity and ease of a truly poised artist to whom the world belonged. Did he not resent her intrusion into his hallowed sphere? He'd been until then an only child, a prodigy, a success, a curiosity. This new brother for whom she had no context, no parallel, no framework or perspective. A cellist. Whose brother was a cellist?

'Oh – sometimes I feel I've always been here. Melbourne is such a city. But on some days ...' She had no words.

'It can overwhelm some people. Ha ha – it can.'

Edmund nodding at his wife's words. 'I think Maya means what the move signifies in her life, not so much the city itself, eh?'

Selby thinking, thinking, how easy it had been to put a tenant in the house on Wingate Street. How easy it was to lease a flat in Elwood. How simple it was to extricate what money was calculated to be hers from the whole that was, in her mind, Brixham money.

'It takes seven years to calculate and distribute a missing person's estate,' some authority or other, some lawyer or other, some specialist or other, had stated in writing. 'But we have ways to ensure you are not rendered destitute in the meantime.' They installed a manager of the 'Brixham estate', such that it was. She had not felt it necessary. She could work. She had the money from her mother's house. She would move. She would rent out the house indefinitely. None of that was difficult. Not difficult, either, to pigeonhole him as gone.

Gone-gone-gone, she remembered her mother saying of a dead husband. Hers might or might not be dead. Would anyone ever be able to tell for sure? A mystery, a question, but not a quandary. A disappearance Thel labelled convenient. She had gasped, gulped, inhaled the meaning of it all. *Convenient.*

Lonely. Cold but for communication with Ian and Derry. Arctic and numb but for communication with the Eben family. Now turned, developed, grown into interaction to thaw her out. Here, in this Frankston house where Igor landed, as on some stepping-stone in a garden crowded with blooms, and would soon step away again, to play in Vancouver; his wife calm and tacitly charming, accepting, managing the life of their family as if by stealth, by sleight of hand.

'But this is delicious, Jacqueline!' Vanna exclaiming, beaming, doling out more little servings to the young ones, who breathlessly called her *Nannavanna*. Serving food to her Mundo, and cocking an eyebrow at Selby. 'You must have some more, Maya. This is truly very good.'

It was. Nothing like the frozen rectangles from her

own freezer. Nothing like what she once thought were bourguignon, or stroganoff, or chili con carne, made from easy recipes she found in the local paper and on the backs of packets and pouches. Nothing was anything any longer, compared to this.

'This is real.' Under her breath. Under her thoughts, under her contemplations and comparisons. What was. What could have been. What was. What was.

And to discover such a wondrous little person as Pearl, the water nymph, all of nine years old, who held them all in thrall, mesmerising her, especially. Such an illustration of who she could have been. Same mouth, almost, lips just a bit more plump. Hair very nearly the same shade, but nothing like her. Even the green of her eyes was profoundly and exquisitely different.

'I shall not play music.' A declaration, a table conversation stopper. 'I'm going to dive off the highest springboard into the deepest pool in the world!'

Clapping, a huge applause from proud grandparents. A benediction in the form of a half-smile from a mother, behind that curtain of dark, dark hair. Boos and hisses, laughter and pretend jeers from two brothers – August a young clarinettist, with strange arpeggios all of his own making, Horace a capable manipulator of drumsticks and mallets; both playfully bent on contradiction. And an accepting shake of a head from their father, a master cellist whose eyes held such love. 'Not even a bit of piano, Pearl, like Mama?'

'That is not a *bit* of piano! She plays everything, all the time. So much. And every day she says she must play Czerny. Nannavanna says she plays like an angel. And I am not an angel.' An otter, she was, with eyes still pink from gazing through chlorinated water. A naiad with a mind of her own, understanding very well how to capture an audience for her announcements. 'I don't want to play Czerny.'

And later, Selby standing on the wide expanse of lawn, handed something in a tall glass by Igor, watching the sky darken next to Ian, who was texting something on his phone to Derry, who had expected him back that night; taking in what to anyone else might have been a perfectly normal day spent with family. But which to her proved to be an exposé, a revelation, a discovery of how the world could have shown itself to her, but did not.

Not until now. And nothing, nothing, to use as a stepping stone of her own, a link back or forth or up or down to something she could call stable, dependable, her own.

But there it was, in the sky. In a sky darkening to a profound blue, tinged with streaks of red and pink from clouds settling over the distance, the distance she calculated to hover over the big, big westward bay, a startling surprise in the form of a sparse flight. Creatures she recognized. That pulled at her chest as if they had crawled, clawed there.

The children pointed. 'Look, Nanna! Flying foxes.'

Oh, the emotion, the memory of flying foxes in their thousands teeming over her head and that of Morgue. A century ago. A lifetime before all this. A vision to flood her with tears. No one could guess. No one knew. It was hers alone.

'It is an omen!' Vanna raising both arms, spilling a tiny drop of champagne. Exclaiming, laughing, declaring the bats to surely be a sign of good luck, blessed fortune.

'It is the Moreton Bay fig trees, Vanna. They come to the trees.'

'Yes, of course it is, Mundo! They adore the things, the little fruits – to us inedible, but such a lifesaver to these fuzzy creatures.'

A child laughing. "Ha ha – fuzzy. Fuzzy.' Pointing to the sky, to the disappearing bats, whose wings, at once stretched and golden, transparent, parchment-like, and opaque, glowed like the material of some ancient manuscript.

And there was Morgue, alive, in her head, lifting, lifting her above him, in the brilliant light of an uncurtained window, his face turned to hers, lost in hers. An eon ago. Yesterday.

A threatening tear, brushed away. A brilliant smile, to be transported in this way to pure joy, whether it was lost or not. Nothing was lost if she knew where it was. In her chest, in her throbbing wrists, that sang with the memory. In her aching throat, that longed to sob. In each breath. In each beat of a bat's wing.

Nineteen

Take up a brush

Occasionally, fleetingly, she received sensations of heady freedom, emanating from a source exterior to her mind or body. A sun bath from something she did not control. A warmth she welcomed. Almost two years, already, and no sign of him. An occasional letter from the police, to say no sightings, and the bank accounts still untouched. No attempts to get in touch with her. That part of her life over, perhaps. Perhaps. Possibly because he wanted it to be over. If so, his desire was fulfilled. Granted. Actuated. *True-true-true*. What did the policewoman say that day? Voluntarily missing. Selby breathed more freely these days. Vanna was right. Acceptance of things, hacking one's own path through the thicket of life, was liberating. *Free-free-free*.

Derry much improved, his asymmetry blurred into a kind of balance. Visiting with Ian, he embraced her, looked into her face. Hummed, mumbled, said sweet things. Came to Melbourne on a plane. Just to see her? Incredible. Walking along Elwood beach, and on the promenade, dog-breed spotting. Regaling her with décor ideas for the rented flat; Edwardian, but quite bland. Looking into her eyes, grief-spotting, progress-seeking. She smiled and smiled, wondering whether it ever reached her eyes, this half-imagined happiness. This new-found autonomy. This occasional contentment she could not hold on to. Looking regularly, morning in and morning out, in the bathroom mirror to check smiles, teeth, make-up, hair, smile.

'I'm going with them ... the whole entire family, to see Igor play in Antwerp. Next year. All planned, Ian – said I should ask you to come.'

'Who knows what we'll be doing next year.' Trying to get Derry's attention. Blank face. 'Hm, Derry?'

'They have this big concert hall there. Elizabeth something. Is that where?'

Neither of them accepting or refusing. Both wanting to wait, stall, procrastinate, dither, and she? Smiling again. So like them sometimes. Walking at a leisurely pace, to match Derry's, to a popular bar. And then later still, in her little flat, unable to let the thought go. 'I wonder, sometimes, what might have happened if ...'

Ian downing his drink, pouring another. 'You're full of what ifs. Have another moscato.'

'No, listen. What if something terrible happened to him, Ian?'

'In that case, it happened to him, see?' Arm around her. Then away, away across the room looking for something. 'Either way, there's not much you – or anybody – could have done.'

'You have a nice new life, here in Melbourne. Gee, it's nice here. All these bookshops, all these galleries. And you're painting ... show me.' Derry now quite stable on both legs.

Beaming, shy, 'I don't know ...'

'You don't know whether to show off or hide.' Walking pretty steadily to a stack of canvasses leaning again a wall. 'You must help with this.'

Stood them apart, perhaps a dozen paintings.

'All birds. All birds. Oh, sea birds. Nice. Ian – can

you see this one in our ... will we be your first buyers?'

'Buyers! Take it. You must have it.'

Derry took the canvas square. Lifting it, lifting it so Ian could see the pelican against a deep watery background. 'No, no. Of course not. Goodness knows, hm? Goodness knows how amazingly things might go if you say Derry Stubbs was one of your first clients. Hm?' Face full of humour, a cynical smile. Knowing, knowing his career was over with the stroke. Knowing the fickleness of his industry. 'Now look at that sea. Such a palette of blues.'

Ian smiling, nodding, mouthing *yes, yes* to her.

But the best, the most valuable talks for her were with Vanna, alone in her lovely little sitting room, just the two of them, set apart from the huge room where everything else happened. Edmund painting, kettle singing, radio playing, fire crackling, other artists visiting, glasses clinking, bass voices rumbling.

A small quiet room; plump chairs, book shelves, an exquisite inlaid table bearing a silver tray, etched glasses, a few foreign-labelled bottles.

'Now you must promise one thing. But first – Mundo said you are working now. How good! How clever you are.' Handing her a tiny glass brimming with some fragrant liqueur. 'Look, this is Rosolio. Smell it first. Such an aroma of Sicily. Made with rose petals and mandarin peel! There is nothing in the world like Sicilian citrus oil. We shall drink a *brindisi* to your new work. A toast. Tell me about it.'

'I only work three days a week.'

'Ha ha – not how long, but what. And where!'

'I started at a nursery – a plant nursery. In Caulfield. At first all I did was handle a hose, and trim dead flower heads off pots of plants on sale.'

'Happy? Happy? And now?'

'And now they have me in the greenhouse. I love it. Propagating. Striking plants. Growing from seed.'

'So very rewarding if it works. You must be such a good gardener. My talented girl!'

Hers. Her girl. Selby struck, surprised and pleased by the emotion. A full warm feeling rising inside, like a wave, like the warmth of alcohol she had not tasted yet.

'Smell it and taste it. What do you think? And are you looking after your hands? Let me see. I shall give you a tube of cream that is miraculous. Miraculous, I tell you!' Laughing, pouring herself a tiny glass of the pure gold liquid. '*Mannarinu* – say it, say it!' Such enjoyment for her to be sharing a quiet moment with Selby. 'It tastes of Sicily, too. Ah! Everything is so intimately tied to its history, is it not?'

Selby feeling her tense shoulder muscles go suddenly warm and lax. Breathing deeply and sensing the prickle, prickle, prickle of pleasure making the tiny hairs on the back of her neck rise. Listening to this older woman who made no demands, asked for nothing, and gave, gave, gave.

'Now listen. On the first Thursday night of every month Mundo and I host an open house. People come if they can, if they want to... ha ha! And many want to sometimes. Poets, artists, musicians. Sometimes even Clement Shenton comes along! All in the big room. All night, sometimes. Talking, talking. They bring wine. I make a very large dish of baked macaroni, and that's all! Someone once arrived with a tray of oysters. Someone once brought a basket of blackberries.'

'It sounds wonderful.' Not saying daunting. Not saying unnerving, perhaps.

Vanna searching, searching her eyes for the true reaction. 'Come just once or twice. You can disappear into the crowd. It will make your father very happy.'

Oh. *Her father.* How striking still to hear him described in that way. How so very astonishing, unusual, to have them linked like that. How could that clever, gifted, affectionate man be her father?

'You will meet other artists. Sometimes people read poetry. Their own, even. Melbourne is lovely for this, you know. How exquisite is this liqueur?' Sipping like a bird. That beak of a nose sometimes elegant, sometimes grotesque, sometimes impossibly striking and elegant. 'And sometimes someone will pick up a guitar and play. When Igor was younger, and he and his cello lived here ... ah! How quickly it goes. How short childhood and youth are. How brief and transient. It broke my heart when he went away. Young, he was, young, travelling with an orchestra.' Gesturing with short fingers. 'But look how happy he is ... they are. How can I not be happy to see his family? Jacqueline comes sometimes, on our open night.'

'It all sounds so wonderful. But ...'

'But you will be shy, a little. Talk if you like. Or not, if you prefer not to.'

'It does sound perfect.'

'So come.'

Talking, talking about novels and novelists, about music, about painting. And now that Vanna knew what she did, about plants and seeds and soils and fertilizers.

'And you are painting ... birds!'

'I walk along the beach at Elwood, down here. I watch the birds.' Wanting to say it was Vanna's idea. *Take up a brush*, she had said, some time ago.

'You must make one for our wall, for the gallery.'

Flattered, taken aback, but knowing them now, understanding their broadness, their wideness, their acceptance of things. 'You must have seagulls. The first one I did was of four seagulls. I felt like such a fraud at

Deans, buying paints.'

'Really! Ha ha. A fraud? Not you. Not you, my dear girl.'

Talking, talking about how good it felt, rather than lonely, in her small flat overlooking the golf course. How she felt no need to seek someone, to form a relationship.

'That, Maya, is the most important realization of all; that you have made. You came to this on your own. You are quite complete – there is absolutely no need to chase all over the place looking for someone to make you whole.' Vanna sat back, both short-fingered hands on knees, genial, bright, gracious.

'Do you think so?'

'I know so.' Nodding, emphatic, certain. 'When one is truly self-determining, truly integral, people see it. They feel it. They are struck by it. And one is liked for who one is. And then your friends are those who choose you for your amazing individuality. For your strength. Men or women ... I think sex is immaterial. They choose to be with you for your distinctive... what shall I call it? Alone-ness!' Pausing, eyes like opaque jewels in the room's light. Voice hoarse with emotion and age. 'Well – perhaps I mean singularity.'

'And yet people ask... at work they ask.'

'Of course. They always ask whether you are yearning to meet that special person. Because they want it – some people never feel whole until they find someone. Hah! Their *other half.* Ha ha! No halves. They do not really know who they are. Do you want another of these? Yes? Delicious?' Pouring another drink. 'Never mind the questions. It is not rocket science, you know. Be yourself. You do know who said that, don't you? A famous prime minister. I rarely talk politics, and if you come one Thursday night you will find three or four people who go off into the garden to talk politics, and smoke, while the rest of us wax philosophical, as the night wears on. Ha ha!' Making a joke of it. 'As if we are experts on Schopenhauer, Derrida, Popper, or Foucault!'

So there were the famous Thursday nights, when all Vanna's observations and promises came true. Babbling conversation, humming music in the background, which sometimes erupted into life and took the centre of the room, played by some guitarist, or some violinist visiting Melbourne. Poets, urged to read from hesitantly but gratefully unfolded sheets of paper, sat back and nodded to discreet applause. Ordinary wine poured, poured into unmatched glasses. And Selby noting the special Sicilian liqueur was absent, reserved for her special sitting room visits with Vanna.

And there was the trip to Antwerp, to the newly renovated Koningin Elisabethzaal, to watch Igor perform.

'Igor knows this is a special performance, because his sister will see him play for the first time.' Edmund Eben, grinning, spectacles glinting, taking her hand and tucking it in the crook of his elbow, leading, leading her onward; and that was how they took their seats, perched high above the stalls, floating above the orchestra. Wearing a new gown, an evening gown bought with the memory of another green gown, worn so long ago, at a graduation ball whose ghost of a memory she now courted; dancing with Morgan Gordon Pearson. Flying, her heart, flying to the sky over her head, where bats beat their wings in an orange sky.

And now, sitting between them, between Vanna and Edmund, both whispering, whispering, before the lights dipped and the conductor walked on to loud applause, which thundered when Igor took the stage. Small orchestra behind him, enraptured audience before him.

'Tonight the Elgar, I think, Vanna.'

'No – no, the Dvořák, and then the Shostakovich.'

They whispered across her, sweet, proud, knowledgeable.

And then nothing but music, music, and Igor the focus of all present. Thin, her brother, in a dinner jacket, animated, hands flying and expressive, hair waving in time to his playing; glinting with the colours of Edmund's palette in the stage lighting.

And returning to Melbourne, after an exhilarating ten days in Belgium, where buildings, people, night lights, theatres, museums, rivers, castles, trains, and family exhausted her. Tired, tired, but so full of the sense of being wanted. Belonging. Unpacking that small black suitcase, hanging the green velvet gown up, to the sound of someone knocking at her apartment door.

Standing there, just standing. A grey man, with grey eyes, and a grey sweater. Her heart gelid, seized by a sensation neither elating nor defeating. A numbness, numbing her. Disorienting. Where was this? This was not Wingate Street. It was all a ... 'What are you doing here? Where have you been?' Startled into speaking first. Thrown into disadvantage by his silence.

'May I come in?'

'Where have you *been*? Do you know how much ...?'

'May I come in?'

Walking backwards. Stepping, stepping backwards, blindly, holding the door open. Wordless now. Struck dumb. Could not, would not say his name.

He not voicing hers.

A pause, an empty pause. Three years rolling away and back. A wave of emptiness. A wave of nausea. A wave of something unhinging, threatening, foreboding. This was Melbourne. He belonged in Wingate Street.

'There is someone else in my house.'

'I ... I reported you missing. To the police.'

'Who's that living in the house?'

'How did you find me?'

Silence. Words hard to find. Hissing, humming, droning from traffic out there beyond the golf course. Melbourne coming alive at six in the morning. The scent of something annoying in her nostrils. Turning to the kettle for solace, for something to do with her hands. For sustenance. Feeling faint.

'She said you were overseas.'

Turning, turning towards those grey eyes. 'Who said?'

'The woman upstairs.'

'I was. I've just come back. I rented out the house in Wingate Street. Ages ago. It's leased until ...' Thinking, counting on mental fingers. 'Next month, I think. I can't think. I don't know.' Seeing he placed a small bunch of kiosk flowers on her table. Cellophane wrapped, creased and crushed where his fist pressed, pressed. Pouring hot water over teabags in a pot. Two mugs from an overhead cupboard. Two teaspoons.

'What are you doing, Selby?'

Recalling, remembering, bringing to mind Vanna's words. Squaring her shoulders, pouring milk into a tiny jug. She was someone altogether different now. 'Have a seat.' *It is not rocket science, you know. When one is truly self-determining, truly integral...* Turning, turning on her heel. Truly strong. 'Tell me why you looked me up.' In charge. Placing him squarely across from her. Putting him in a responding position.

'You vanished.'

'*I vanished!*'

'Look, Selby – there's one thing I want from you.'

Nothing she was willing to give. Nothing she was

willing to take. Not even explanations, now. Waiting, waiting for him to speak again. Waiting, waiting for a fresh wave of fear that this life might be taken from her. Must not. It could not. It could not; she ... this was how she wanted to be.

He silent. Waiting. Sitting.

'I hate shop flowers. I hate cut flowers. I like them growing in a garden. In a pot.' She wanted, wanted to propagate plants. Geraniums, lilies, euphorbias. She had just germinated a row of poppy seeds. At a nursery she loved. She had bagged hundreds of bulbs. Gladioli, crocus, daffodils, snowdrops. *Jonquils jonquils jonquils*. Thought of the cut glass vase that used to hold his Friday flowers, from the kiosk outside his office. Ugh. Thought of the garden in Wingate Street. She could never go back there.

She loved the first Thursday of every month. Thought of last month. Listening, quiet, holding a glass of sparkling wine, to poets reciting their words, to a woman in an orange dress playing the piano accordion. To a young man reading from *Ulysses*. Looked forward to the next evening with the Ebens' friends, could not wait for that night to come.

'I have been ...'

She cut in. 'I really don't want to know where you've been. Just tell me what you came here to say.' Staring icily at his blank face, noting the pallid skin, the sunken eyes. Even without her he was miserable.

'I want a divorce.' His dull words in a bright room.

Selby inhaled a quick breath. Rubbing the back of a hand against her mouth, trying to think, rubbing an itch on her shin, she paused. Paused. Exhaling, breathing again, in through the nose, and out in a small puff. An almost imperceptible shrug. Squared shoulders. 'Send me the papers. I'll sign what you like.' Her words powerful and in control.

So it was he. Vanna would say it was he who wanted freedom. Thel would say the same. He thought he was trapped in some way.

His head bowed. Apologetic, contrite, confused. 'I'll see you get what's due to you, Selby.'

Staring, gazing at the door long after it had closed behind him. That was a shock. Her hands trembling, her heart beating rapidly now. Her hand on the round side of the teapot. The tea still hot enough to drink. It had taken all of six minutes, and she was now out of that skein of complication. Unravelled, straightened, wound right.

The flowers. She stepped on the bin pedal. Jerking, jolting back, bumping the wall behind, its lid, and back, on top of the small bunch of daisies, stocks. Whatever they were. She pushed. The scent now trapped in plastic, metal, anything it took to contain that smell.

Vanna listening, a day later, cocking her head a little, clapping softly. 'Oh, well, that is so good. Hopefully we shall never have to talk of him again. That is the way. Draw a line under all that. You have a new life now. With family.'

'A new life.' Safety in repetition. Needing to appear judicious, clever, balanced with this wonderful woman.

'If we are going to discuss men, my dear Maya, then we discuss poets, musicians, philosophers, sculptors... ha ha! All the better if they are dead!' It was a humorous nudge, Selby saw. Elegant, sweet, clever in her nudging. Steering her to a plane from which she could see things clearly.

Talking, talking to Thel on the phone. Promising to visit. Hearing the noise in the background, feeling the distance.

Preparing a canvas, a small one, with gesso.

Standing it on her easel, not so brand-new any more. Streaked with shades from her palette. Her blues, her clear blues. The greens so subtle and challenging .

Preparing a range of sky colours, from indigo to orange. Orange for a sunset streaked with faint cloud. A range of difficult greys. Greys among the orange, and hesitating, waiting, pausing, stalling, before she could add her intentions.

Preparing but showing no one. Alone in her flat, in the front room cleared; a studio, and wide-open window lined with plants, a view of rooftops and the golf course. A view of sky over the grey water of the grey bay. Nothing like what she wanted to paint. Difficult. Difficult to capture what she remembered. Tried again. A sky that had never kissed the ocean. A sky that knew only the glistening slide of river, of river, of river that skimmed trunks of trees, banks of grass, pools of grey mist in hollows.

And overhead? A poised brush. A handful of prepared dabs of colour. A knife, perhaps. A hand shaking with the emotion of memory. Triangular shapes taking form. The gold of stretched parchment wings. The brown, the gold, of dusk light on an extended wing. Ochre and orange to signify flight. And orange and ochre again. No, no. Painting over a wing, adding a hint of blue. Stretching a power line across a corner of canvas. Silhouettes of triangles, and others over, above, below, beside them. Darkening an orange sky. Silhouettes of trees. The silhouette of a man.

A man immortalized, captured on a canvas. Taken from within her to where he could be viewed.

And telling Vanna what she had painted, how she disappeared into the making of him.

'Ah, painting, painting. You are like him, I can see. Like Mundo. You can place something in a painting, and it heals you. It sorts out your involvement, your connection, your preoccupation, your unease with something. That's clever. Clever, you are, my Maya.' When it was she who had suggested painting. All those months ago.

Pouring golden liqueur into tiny glasses. Holding one to the light. 'And tonight they come, all of them. Tonight Jacqueline comes too, and she brings little Pearl, who has written a poem.'

Seeing, seeing so clearly how that little girl, that otter, was nurtured, propagated; a seedling of her surroundings. A miracle.

'Tonight we also have the accordion, I think, if Marilyn comes. And the macaroni is already in the oven. Nothing to do but wait.'

Sitting and talking. Of the future, of how fashions changed, of the importance of music in Mundo's work. The importance of her presence in her father's life. And a propos of nothing else, out of the blue, she made it seem, 'And tonight we might see Clement Shenton. Such pure philosophical thought, from that man. And I think you like Clement Shenton, no? I know he likes you, my dear.'

Part Two

1947-2009

One

The artist as a young man

He did not speak, or often think, of how he came to be. It was the kind of thought that could erode the man he had created, almost out of nothing. Out of nothing he had sculpted an imaginary persona, such a long, long time ago; and squeezed his tall sparse form, his bright hair, his wide mouth, into it; often stooping to better portray the image he held – sometimes so tenuously – in his head.

It was indeed a long time ago. In another place, another time. *Well-educated. Jews perhaps*, he was told vaguely about his parents. That was all. And he a child, alone, solitary, a bit separate from the rest, in a Catholic orphanage. So he added, fabricated, invented a story he told himself as a lonely youngster.

Descendants from the ancient Celt glassmakers of Bohemia, they were, from a basin incredibly rich in wood and sand, wood and limestone, limestone and sand filling the life of his family like salt. Sand packed among the roots of his imagined family tree, leaving no room for air. No room for flightiness, for dreaming. Space and time only for practical endeavours. Occupations with real outcomes.

Sand and wood. Silica and burning logs. Molten glass and ashes. Ashes. Ashes; what filled his mind when he listened to the Sister at the orphanage describing how his father could have been among those burned, possibly alive. *If* he was one of the men at the glass factory. *If* he was one to perish in the incendiary blast that reduced half the building to powder. No one really knew.

To anyone who would listen, he would childishly boast of his father's mastery as a glassblower. A mythic occupation for a made-up man. He would describe a crystal menorah, one he had seen in a book, and invent stories of how he remembered it in a dining room, next to a window full of light, a window that sent slants of sun down architraves, up walls. It was of course impossible; the nuns said he was barely a week old when they found him.

The Sister also surmised and dreamed up, to soothe him during some tearful childhood mishap, or when they shaved his head to prevent lice, how his mother was a survivor, who could have been one of those who travelled, in the company of some merciful family of strangers, across the dense forests of Moravia. A fugitive from change. But what did that kind-hearted nun know? She knew nothing. All that the Sister remembered was the arrival of a baby boy, that day in 1947, when Soviet armies marched in from the North, from the East, and filled them all with a deep sense of confusion.

'You arrived like Moses, child,' someone said to him once. 'In an apple basket.' She whispered; 'Circumcised, unlike the other little boys.' Continuing in her normal voice, 'Wrapped in a length of hessian. Underneath, an old soft woollen shawl was your only garment. A woman's shawl. It was soiled, so they threw it away.'

They threw away the only clue that would have told him something about his mother. About the woman who placed him in an apple basket, and left him 'so bravely', to be raised by nuns, rather than risk his death in the freezing forests. So he grew up a believer of stories, in an alien world, seeking solidity. Seeking foundation. Seeking a woman with a soft woollen wrap around her head and shoulders, to adore, to adore.

They called him Moses. Moses Nalezenec, which meant *foundling*, and taught him arithmetic, ink drawing, and beautiful penmanship. He drew pictures of a mysterious woman with head and shoulders veiled by a soft fringed shawl, whose face was always turned away, or lowered, or shadowed, or indistinguishable in some way. As he matured, the pictures became more realistic, more detailed, more mysterious.

He almost found her when he was nearly seventeen, almost a year after he left. Nearly old enough to leave anyway, on his fourth – and finally successful – escape from the orphanage, now called a *college*, now stripped of all its Catholic paraphernalia, since the communist regime had taken hold; since all the children had reached college age and were leaving, either to be employed in Prague's factories, or to join the armed forces and the police.

'Never forget you are a child of the new freedom, Redhead,' some sarcastic college boy had mumbled through twisted lips before he vaulted the fence. But all he thought of was sand and wood. Wood and sand. Silica and ashes. And he found his first refuge in a dusty, sandy squat on the edge of the woods, sharing with seven other homeless runaways and delinquents from all over the country, drawn inexorably to that smoky awe-inspiring glass factory.

And that was where he was given his first job; in

that huge new oven of a place that somehow – through some modern magic – turned out lead crystal. Bohemian glass, the world called it, since the Renaissance. Glass that scintillated, glimmered, twinkled, sparkled on tables around the globe.

Beautifully etched crystal glasses and decanters for the world to pour its wines into were wrought from ashes, chalk, and sand; faceted crystal vases for the world to stand flowers in. Jewel-like candelabras illuminating halls, ballrooms and stairwells.

The factory belched smoke and steam into the Bohemia skies, sending fragile wares out, proclaiming mastery of the new press technologies, which out of sand, out of potash, out of an ugly square factory that stood, grim and stark, like a concentration camp in a clearing, produced such shiny, delicate, gorgeous artefacts.

There were epergnes, punch bowls, sconces, tazze, and there were chandeliers. Ah – the chandeliers! They hung in lines, shimmering in the bad factory light. Who could guess what they would look like, suspended through the centre of some grand spiral staircase; hung in a line along a broad ballroom; swinging slightly in the upsurge of incense and prayerful exhalations in some lofty cathedral?

He had a panicked terror-filled moment when he thought they might make him feed the furnace. They accepted him, in that labour shortage, even if he could give them no fixed address. Even if he so obviously had no work experience. They showed him around. They had two furnaces, someone said, one new and one old.

A furnace was a furnace, no matter how new they boasted it was. He would be consumed by heat belching from its mouth, and end like his unknown father. The father who emerged, a pure fiction, from his mind's eye;

a captive intellectual, feeding some kind of real or imagined furnace. A pile of grey powder. A heap of ashes.

'Can you read and write?'

A nod.

'Can you draw?'

An emphatic nod.

So they put him, almost immediately, in a large noisy cigarette-smoke filled room where women dressed in beige, faun, dun, taupe dresses wielded pencils and stunted pens, whose nibs were the only sharp shiny objects he would see for a long time. They showed him how to copy drafted drawings of facets, facets, facets. Prisms, prisms whose light he could only imagine. He drew vases. He drew glasses.

He wanted to draw landscapes, rivers, the difficult whorls and whirls of water. He wanted to understand colour and how to make it dance in the eye. All they wanted were elevations of crystals, angular pendants, bowls, bowls, stemmed glasses and tall vases. Punch bowls, when he had never tasted punch.

He drew bowls from a number of angles. Sometimes, to soothe his restlessness, he imagined he was drawing only the light these objects bent and projected.

He drew finials, spires, tents, and nozzles. The girl with the newest pen told him the names, showed him the differences, and what each piece was for and where on the chandelier it fitted.

'Listen,' someone said. 'Hear that buzz? It's the sound of the wheel.'

'Wheel?'

'The abrasive wheel, Nalezenec. What sort of a name is that, anyway? Do you know what it means?'

He nodded. Of course he did. 'Moses. Call me

Moses. What abrasive wheel?'

The girl rolled her eyes. 'The edges are fluted against it, by hand, do you know nothing? One by one. The blown nozzles are cut and decorated on the wheel. The edges are bevelled on it. Listen!'

He listened to the sound of the abrasive wheel cutting facets into glass laden with a weight of lead. Lead which, contrary to his intuitive thinking, made the glass clearer, sharper, lighter, more translucent. A weight of lead whose danger turned into light. Sand, ashes, and lead. Wood, silica, and lead. Lead, lead, lead.

He lifted his head after more than a dozen months, trying to harden his resolve to resume his search for that woman. The one who would wear a soft woollen shawl around her head and shoulders.

But the factory was too mesmerizing. It held him in thrall.

Two

Red pigment

The war might be over, but another kind of struggle had begun. It was talked about, hinted at, in secret, among friends. A struggle born of hope; imprisonment evolving out of the glimmer of salvation. Few dared breathe opposition to the infiltrating soviet forces. Few dared utter a single complaint about the new stringent bureaucracy. Freed from one thing, some said, and immediately imprisoned by another.

It hardly affected Moses. He spent a few bewildering weeks in the preparation room, sitting at a counter, marking long lines of glass vase and bowl blanks with a kind of red pigment, a kind of sticky ink made of red-lead and turpentine, which stank the whole room and filled and stung his lungs and the places in his head behind his nose and eyes.

Carefully following design plans, understanding the wordless code of vees and cees and circles and ovals and tiny arrows, he placed his red marks. Here and here and here a diamond facet. Here an annealed handle, here a v-shaped bevel, here a line of nodes. Here a garland of wedge cuts.

Sometimes, to battle boredom, and to give rise to something brewing in his chest, something undefinable, he would ignore the plan sketches, and order the marks on a glass blank according to some design in his head.

He would lie awake on the lumpy mattress in the squat, trying to summon warmth into his limbs, thinking of designs, and would devise symmetries and arrangements of marks; configurations and assemblies that, with the onset of restless sleep, would fly and weave and form into shiny glass shards. It was like making up stories, like painting transparent pictures without the aid of a brush.

It was nothing like what he really wanted to do, but it was satisfying enough. Painting, now that would be heaven. To hold a real brush, to plan and perfect landscapes. Brushes – huh! The expense was breathtaking. Paints? Just as out of reach. Even if he somehow found the money, where would he do his painting? Where?

The thought of a portrait was the height of fancy. Would he ever paint someone ... would a woman sit for him – present her most bewitching profile, her most captivating pose?

Off on off a glass bowl, his red painted marks magically transforming into deep printies, scavos and stipples. After a day or so, the pattern took shape in his head, oozing out of his red-dipped brush onto a glass blank, which then joined the line awaiting the abrasive wheel and the artists – they were nothing short of artists – who took up blanks and set down fantastic artefacts of dense light.

Whether his rebellion was noticed or not he never knew, and sometimes wondered where his pattern – so surreptitiously and insubordinately originated – would finish. On some grand sideboard? In the middle of a big round table? He had so little experience of the interiors of normal homes it was difficult to imagine anything other than the orphanage refectory table, the dormitory with its lines of metal beds, or the Mother Superior's dark brown office.

He drew steady red strokes codified to demand a fretwork of *latticino* lines, in the Venetian style, like he saw on some of the Western magazines someone had stacked outside the manager's office.

Nipped diamond waves, his hand described, so neatly, so cleverly. Intricate v-shaped hobnail patterns he could only imagine; he marked them all, about one in every hundred or so vases a creation totally his own. Ones he would never see; that he could only imagine. An intaglio forest scene, he even dared describe in red, which some cutter or etcher must have looked at with some surprise. And a waterfall. Was it erased and returned to the line of blanks waiting for red marks? Or did it make it to the wheel, and then the acid bath, where a brilliant lustrous finish was coaxed from the glass? He would never know.

Sometimes he watched the glassblowers, those magnificent artisans – how strong, how capable, how accurate. They handled the long blow tubes deftly, blew in measured breaths, stood close to furnaces so hot it was a hazard. They dropped blown blobs of white-hot glass into the moulds and blew again, blew; looking down the length of tube. Twirling, rotating. They turned out the rows of blanks he worked on. Vases, hundreds of vases blown, sheared, marvered, shaped, tweezed and blocked.

A young woman called Uršula was brought in and seated by the supervisor at the end of the long bench while he was there. A bit older than all of them, with evasive eyes. Her hair was always tied up in a knotted square; checked, like a man's large kerchief. She had no earlobes to speak of, but her dark brooding eyebrows were remarkable, expressive. They gathered over the bridge of her nose when she concentrated hard, following the design notes, making her red marks.

Moses tried to imagine her with a soft woollen scarf draped over her head and shoulders. Those bony shoulders. Any sharper, and they would have slit through the drab light brown dress she always wore to the factory.

Sometimes they took a break together, and stood silently outside the enormous sliding warehouse doors. He rolled her a cigarette, and she took it without a word. Once, her eyes caught his for a second, and he saw they were a kind of dirty blue, with a sliver of black in one of them; intriguing. Was this the kind of face one could call attractive? He had little to compare it with. All the wimpled nuns were more or less the same. All the other factory girls wore confusing red lipstick and black lines drawn around their eyes. This one was a soap-and-water beauty, if beauty she was. He knew nothing.

'They must have come and taken him away.'

Moses knew she spoke to him, even though her face was turned away. 'Who?' He watched smoke escape through her pursed lips. She blew it out, long and narrow. A funnel of grey.

'My husband. I woke up last Thursday, and he was gone. The front door stood wide open. The new enamel kettle was missing. Only the kettle. I have no idea where he is.'

He had no idea what to say.

'Because he wore a crucifix around his neck, I think.'

At last he found a word. 'Really?'

'Would I make up something like that?' She exhaled again.

'Could you not ... you can report him missing?'

The grey funnel of smoke dissipated in the cold air,

and she ground the butt into the gravelly ground. 'Let's go back. We have *decanters* to mark.' So she did not like her work. 'And no – it would be pointless to report a disappearance to the very people who probably took him away.'

'But aren't you ...?'

'Disappointed? Married just fifteen months? Of course I am. Devastated.' She laughed, dryly, acerbically. She wore sarcasm like that square of checked cotton on her head. It hid her hair, making the thick presence of it under the fabric more pronounced. Her sarcasm hid something Moses could not make out. But it was as dense as that hidden hair.

'How would it feel, I wonder, to be free of all this tightness?'

He knew what she meant. He wondered himself. He yearned for freedom from fear. Freedom from grinding poverty. He wondered what it would be like to live in that depraved, evil, democratic world out there. Immoral and corrupt, they were told it was. But the life he lived, even in this factory, was hardly free of corruption.

Another time, she squinted, between blowing out thin funnels of grey smoke from his cigarette, 'I see what you do, you know.' Her face was turned away. She gazed at the line of trees they could just glimpse past the factory gates. She tucked an errant strand of hair under the kerchief. 'You'll get caught one day, putting *your* own fancy patterns on those bowls, instead of theirs.'

Moses was silent.

'You never know. You never know – I might tell them.' She moistened a finger on her tongue and passed it along one eyebrow, then the other. Then she turned. 'How old are you, Nalezenec?'

'*Moses.*' He hated a surname that meant *foundling*. What about *Malíř?* What about *Umělec?* They would have made better names, if they were going to make one up.

But that was the precise moment he realized he had been there, in that factory, drawing subsistence wages, for nearly two years. And there was another base, intuitive nudge at his stomach, but he ignored it.

'How old are you, *Moses?*'

'Nearly nineteen.'

'God in heaven.'

She left him speechless. He wanted to say things, to stand tall, to behave like his imaginary father might have, after he had hand-blown a row of bowls, of vases, of rummers with a knop in the stem.

She dug each fist into a light brown pocket, which made her shoulder blades fan outward like sharp hidden wings. 'I have fresh *česnečka*. Veronika from down two storeys felt sorry for me, all alone in my place, and brought me some good bacon fat. So now I have vodka *and* soup.'

Moses said nothing.

'So come, after your shift. We finish together tonight.' She turned away, ground her cigarette end into the rubble at her feet and walked away. 'At six, don't we? At six. No kettle ... but you know ...'

It was surprisingly warm in her apartment.

'Living at the top means everyone's heat ends up here. It makes up for all those stairs. But it cools at night. It freezes. Sit there.' She kept telling him what to do.

He kept wondering whether he should do what he was told or show an ounce of initiative. What would a real man do? He looked around the small brown crammed space. A wide divan, a table, two deal chairs, an upright armchair that looked like it was stuffed with gravel. An ancient rag rug. Curtains held together in the middle with clothes pegs. And everything – everything – made of the same checked fabric as her head scarf. Everything was brown and checked. The pillow cases, the tablecloth.

He fingered the tablecloth edge. Now he knew what that folded fabric square around her head felt like.

'Cheap cotton. Someone sold me the whole bolt. I would have been silly not to take it. I see it everywhere, even with my eyes closed.' Her voice grated in the small space. 'Where do you live?'

He doubted he could call it living. He inhabited a tight corner in a squat where an irregular number of youths came and went. Half the house was gone, and the other half was slowly engulfed by wiry creepers and long weeds from the forgotten garden, whose mangled fence and drunken gates he could see even when wrapped up in his grubby blanket, lying on his lumpy mattress. The corners of the room furthest from the wrecked half were composed of crumbling plaster, most of it scrawled and gouged with names, numbers, initials, hearts, crescents, arrows and other symbols of despair and half-hearted hope. Some corners stank so fiercely of human excrement he never went near them.

He propped a line of broken shutters up, angled over his mattress and things, when he left for the factory, but often found things missing on his return, and the shutters thrown about over the muddled belongings of the other boys. It was a dormitory, at best, but so unlike the one he had left, where the nuns had deliberated such order, such sparse cleanliness.

'Where do you live?'

'Praha Eight.'

'What – Ďáblice? Dolní Chabry? Where? How do

you get there and back every day? You don't ride the bus?'

'Mm.'

'We are all so secretive. That's what I want – freedom from secrecy. Freedom from having to lie, lie, lie.' She raised her hands to her head, undoing the knotted square. 'Even to each other.' When the bit of cotton was loose, her hair cascaded.

Moses stared. It was amazing, that hair; black, like tar, thick, dense and full of a life of its own. It was massive, falling below her shoulders. How such a quantity of hair could be imprisoned in such a tight square of checked material he did not know. It was so unlike his, which seemed to emit light. Hers absorbed it. There were threads of almost imperceptible grey there, but the whole shimmered darkly, and smelled of something he could not place. Lavender? The ordinary fatty yellow soap they all used? No. Orange blossom?

'Your hair!'

'My hair. Uncontrollable. Twice ... three times Heddy Lamarr's waves.'

'Whose?'

'You know nothing.' Her blue eyes, her dirty blue eyes swung round to his in the small brown space. There was no escaping them now. 'That is what I figure. Nothing.'

The česnečka was good. Its floating pieces of stale bread were to his mouth like ambrosia. Not since the nuns' refectory had he tasted anything so hot, so fatty, so sustaining. 'Very ...'

'I know. Lots of garlic. Too much garlic. But I like it that way. I rarely get colds. And coughs? Hah – only from smoking.' She wielded that tin spoon like she held the brush laden with red pigment at work. She stooped over the enamel bowl without looking up, spooning until it was empty, still steaming slightly. She drove a finger along the bottom and licked it. 'Nice?' Her spoon steamed.

Moses nodded.

'Eat it all.' She kept telling him what to do. 'Later we can share a glass of vodka. Veronika gets it cheaper, somehow or other. I pay her for it right away. You know – being on my own now is hard. How can I stand in line for provisions, *and* work at the factory, hm? You tell me how.'

There was nothing he could say.

'So I pay Veronika to stand for me, in my place. When there is lard, there is nothing to fry in it. When there are beans, there is nothing to eat with them. When there is meat, everyone goes crazy. So because I have to pay her, everything I put down my throat costs more than anyone else's. See?'

Now he felt guilty for eating her soup. 'I'm sorry.'

'What for? Don't feel sorry. Chin up. At least I don't have to pay you to keep me company. Do you know what it feels like here, in the cold and dark?'

Dark, dark. He knew dark. There was no electric light at the squat. He too knew cold and dark. And it was twelve times as bad as hers.

'The power goes too often. Sometimes the heating stops. Sometimes I wonder...'

He nodded.

'Is it all worth the struggle, I wonder.'

He nodded again.

'Everything is such a damned struggle. At least when he was here I could stand in the lines while he worked. We had bacon sometimes. Sometimes the good sausage, you know? Not this stuff filled with mystery meat and sand.'

'Sand!'

'Dust. Sawdust. There is sand in everything. You feel it between your teeth. If I ever caught sight of sugar again in my life, I would bet it was cut with sand!'

'The glass we work with is made of sand.'

'Do not mention the word glass to me.'

'So what...'

'What happened? I'll tell you what *happened*. He went out seeking freedom, is what happened. He either walked off to run the gauntlet of the forest paths, trying to get to Germany, or they carted him away to Siberia for wearing his damned Catholic cross. Or they shunted him off to wash windows and sweep streets in Kladno, or feed the furnace at the Poldi steel factory ... because he had a degree in *literature*, you see. That's what.'

It was not what Moses asked, but he nodded.

'They still came and turned this place inside out. Impressed, they were. Impressed by my neatness. It's so easy to be neat when you are this poor, I almost said. I asked no questions. Because they would not answer them, you see? I was not worried. They would not find a thing that had *words* written on it, nothing, in any shape or form. I even destroy the labels from meat cans. No seditious literature here. None.'

'Do you miss him?' He missed the nuns, the women in the large noisy kitchen of the orphanage, even the scolding he got each time he tried to escape.

Her extraordinary eyebrows rose. 'I miss ... his usefulness. I do not miss the beatings, or ... or all the rest. You know, a woman wants something ... I don't know. Perhaps watching those films in the war was a mistake. It makes a woman want gentleness sometimes. Even the occasional *kiss*.'

Moses coloured. Her eyes did not lower. Her ambiguous anger was not something he could decipher.

'So you must learn to be gentle. You – yes I mean

you, nineteen year-old.'

'Me? I ...'

'One day, make some woman happy you met me.'

He started to grasp what she meant. Watching her take the empty bowls to the chipped porcelain sink, watching her rattle tin spoons, watching her wipe thin forearms on a brown checked piece of cotton, watching her grab a packet of cheap cigarettes without looking, pulled his heart back to a normal pace.

She lit two cigarettes at once, and handed him one, after twirling it expertly backward in her fingers and squinting at him through her first puff, one eye very nearly shut. Then she flicked her hair, her thick wavy hair, over one shoulder and walked over to the divan. Cushions were thrown to one side, and an enormous quilt with a checked cover was pulled down from its place on a deep shelf.

'Later, we'll come back, and you can stay here. No use returning to *Praha Eight* in the middle of the night. Mm?'

He wanted to ask where they were going, but words failed him. Asking too many questions would display his naïveté, his lack of social ability. All he could do was watch.

She wielded two brushes at once, and beat her hair into a kind of temporary submission, in between taking puffs from the cigarette, which she perched on the edge of the sink. Then she inserted – with a twist of the hand – two tortoiseshell combs, one over each ear. She patted her forelock, shook the long tarry mass down her back, and peered into the mirror.

'Freezing,' she muttered, as she wet a small flannel, wrung it out, and rubbed it all over her face, roughly, as if it belonged to some other person. As if she was a child at the orphanage, flannelled vigorously by some enthusiastic nun. 'When I had a kettle, see, it was a matter of using what was left of the hot water.'

She led him part of the way down the concrete stairwell, and knocked vigorously on a brown door. 'Veronika!'

He was not prepared for how different Veronika was from other women he had seen. One of her legs was in a black caliper, and her hair was cropped sharply just below her ears. And she was stout, round and stout. Together, the three of them descended silently down one more flight of stairs, at Veronika's speed. A door on that level stood open. Moses heard the incredible sound of music wafting, as if visible, into the landing.

'Havel *found* a radiogram. I don't know how he does it, but in the evening there is a music program. So we listen. As long as there is power, we can listen. We don't have to pay him. He accepts cigarettes, or vodka, or even half a loaf of good bread. Sometimes I bring him a piece of medovnik. Ha ha! Well – what passes for medovnik now.'

Three

Always gentle

It was amazing. A whole orchestra in one room. Moses had never heard anything more marvellous. There was a small harmonium at the orphanage, which a Sister would pound, producing hymns and accompaniment for the boys' singing. It had disappeared one day, together with the crucifixes, the bibles, the nuns' habits, and the pictures of the Good Shepherd from their walls. There was never a radio.

The voice of a man speaking some other language stopped, there were a few crackles, and then the music went on. It was heaven. This was heaven. Moses closed his eyes and let the rapture take hold of his entire body. It was nothing like when the players would come round to the streets outside the orphanage when he was tiny, and they would all crowd onto the balcony to listen. No. No, this was something else altogether.

'Nice?'

He nodded, opening his eyes. The room was lit by a single naked light bulb, which swung slightly to the combined breath and cigarette smoke of a dozen motley souls. It flickered occasionally, and they would all look up, hoping the power would hold for at least the length of the piece. Symphony or march, cantata or aria, musical or opera, popular song or anthem – he had no idea what anything was, but it was indescribably beautiful. 'Music...' he said. He had no other words.

'Hm. What would life be without it, mm?' Uršula said the words with a wink – less cynical or acerbic than anything else she ever said. She seemed soothed and comparatively happy.

They listened to a male choir, Russian voices, perhaps, which filled the room with resonances and echoes. They listened to what someone said was a saxophone, so Moses swore to himself his life would never again be empty of music. On their way out, she passed Moses an unopened packet of cigarettes to hand to Havel.

He ascended the stairs behind Uršula a changed person; one shifted from inertia to a kind of resolve. But he had no idea it was there, no idea it might have a name.

'Are you going to stand there and freeze, or are you going to join me?'

He stood and stared at her, stripped down to a mean cream-coloured cotton shift, after she folded the brown dress over the back of a chair and threw thick stockings over a rod that swung above the sink. She had climbed in under the thick quilt, and held it up now for him to slip in under the covers with her. 'Get out of those clothes first. And those socks.'

He had once shared a bed with another boy at the orphanage, a little scrawny child who had appeared with three others without notice, out of nowhere. The nuns got some of them to share beds. But this was different. This was new and disturbing, and soothing, and startling, and enlightening, and mystifying and revealing, all at once.

Changes in his body that had filled him with questions months ago were now answered. She kept telling him what to do. 'Always gentle,' she said. 'Always be nice.'

It did not occur to him that she was wresting for herself, out of the entire brown struggle that was her life, something she had come to hope for, and to almost despair of not finding. She taught him what she wanted, what she so desperately desired, for herself.

'Like this. Like this. Like *this* men are, in fantasy. In the films. But they are black and white ... no colour. No colour. Colour is real life. Colour is violent, see? You must be black and white, and gentle. Like Robert Mitchum.'

'Robert...?'

'Shh – nothing. No one. We can't see those films any more. Now we watch propaganda from the North. From the East. No Cary Grant. No Humphrey Bogart. No Yul Bryner.'

He had no words in response to this soft mumbled barrage of unintelligibility. He did what she said. Put his hands where she showed him. Alarm, disgust, awe, and revulsion ... surprise, curiosity, inquisitiveness, unease and arousal all melted with the night. They smoked another cigarette, sharing it this time. And then she rose, poured four fingers of spirit into a small jar, and brought it to the bed.

'Vodka. Don't hog it all.'

He sipped. It was not like the beer they drank at the squat. This liquid loosened his chest, his joints, and seeped upward into his neck and head, to the space behind his eyes. It rounded his tongue. It swelled his lips. After that, it was all easier, and more blurred, and less frantic and fumbled and confused.

He woke because he was so cold. His feet stuck out past the heavy quilt. He was naked, uncomfortable, and alone.

No. 'Don't lie there all morning. We have a factory

to reach. Work to get to. *Beautiful vases* to mark.' Uršula's hair was once more contained, hidden under that brown checked fabric. Her face was scrubbed and pink. She showed no signs of the night's drinking, smoking, and rolling under the quilt. No evidence either of the beautiful music they had listened to downstairs.

'Come on. Drink.'

'What is it?'

'This is boiled chicory. I have to make it in a saucepan now, but never mind.' She handed him the enamel mug she was drinking from. 'I left you half. Hurry up.' It was bitter. Bitter, black, and scalding. How did she drink it? He gulped, and gulped again while climbing into his canvas trousers and thick jacket.

'Let's go.'

The sky outside was bluer than before, wider, more distant. The clouds scudded and blew. It would rain later, but for now he found everything clearer, bluer, whiter. He emerged different, a changed person from the one that entered the night before.

For seven weeks, or perhaps nine weeks, or perhaps twelve – he was losing count – he rode back and forth with her, abandoning everything he had left at the squat. Leaving his mattress, his spare canvas pants, his other boots with the threadbare soles, his real leather belt, to anyone who might happen on them. He left his cardboard suitcase to chance.

She marked this milestone by telling him to shop. Showing him which lines to stand in, in her place. Keeping Uršula happy was a matter of doing what he was told, being scrupulously neat, filing down to the music with her and Veronika, and eating whatever they managed to scrounge between them. On his day off he stood in line at the shops, buying what he could.

'No cabbage?' Her voice was getting hoarse from smoking.

'Half. Half is all we could buy today.'

'Better than nothing. No carrots?'

'Yes – three.'

'And lard?'

'No lard. But if I had a bottle I could have bought oil.'

She brightened. The little black triangle in her eye sparkled. 'Oh! Wash out that one. Take it with you next time. Or I will.'

He moved to see if her face would register a reaction. 'There was a man called Petr, who said he knew you. I think he recognized the fabric of the shopping bag. Did you say I was your *nephew*?'

'Petr! He's a miner.'

'Yes – he said he works at the Klodno mine and he knows where to get English *chocolate*.'

'Sure.' She stared at him with those eyes, her eyebrows gathering over her nose. 'Sure. And champagne. And salmon. And blood pudding. And perhaps French *brandy*.' She placed a fist on each hip. 'Eh? Brandy!'

'Yes! He did say blood pudding.'

'You would believe anything, nineteen year-old.'

'Nearly twenty now.'

'Where on earth did I find you? *Nalezenec* – d'you know what it means? Foundling ... exactly. Exactly!'

'I know what it means.' Would he ever find freedom from that name?

At the crystal factory, he continued to mark blanks, setting them in their long line. He had less need now, to mark his own designs. Every so often, though, he devised a pattern of deep wedge cuts, Venetian lines, and wreaths and swags of pinch-notches.

One afternoon, just as the greyness outside those freezing panes turned darker, the supervisor from the acid room walked up to him, with a tall vase in his hands. 'This your work, youngster?'

Moses swallowed. He did not raise his eyes to face the man's anger.

'Answer when I speak to you. Is this your design, you little rebel? Stand up.'

Moses stood. He did not dare look over to where Uršula worked. She did not raise her eyes.

'You think you are clever, eh?'

What could he reply to that?

'You think you are something, in any case. Something other than what ... Tell me your name.'

'Nalezenec.'

He laughed. 'An orphan, hm? All right. Look – report to the design room and make a proper plan for this, and pass it to Domek, you know Domek? Good. Tell him I sent you. Do you know how to adapt it to a bowl, and a charger? Do that. Tell him I told you. You know who I am? Pavlicek – tell him Pavlicek sent you.'

Four

Fear and restlessness

In a young man's mind, six months was an eternity. Time stood still at work, it stagnated. After a month of envious ribbing, Uršula accepted that he was a designer now, a designer. He was free, she told him. Free of the smell of red pigment.

They moved him into the smaller room where three taciturn men in grey looked, peered, frowned at him. They smoked the entire time; they sat around and did little. He was in there now, and that was it. He was *free*. Not free from their smoke. Free from inhaling something more like blood vapours.

They held their lit cigarettes tucked into the cupped palms of their hands, thumb and forefinger pinched into a kind of mean claw. They hid the glowing end of the things as if they crouched in some dark forest. As if they hid from some marauding force, that would shoot at a glowing end in the dark. They were surreptitious and skulking, sidling and secretive, fear-filled and cagey, even inside a factory room. He watched them, hoping he would not grow into that kind of old man.

Moses drew designs onto stiff paper. When there was a shortage, they drew on coarse brown wrapping paper, which arrived in stacks tied with twine, instead of the flat boxes they were used to. He took to drawing with thin white tailor's chalk, and then white pencils someone thought to bring in, goodness knew from where, but they were good.

When the men went out on their brief breaks, he stayed in and drew on a stolen sheet of paper. Folded in eight, it made a nice little booklet. Sketches, sketches of trees and bushes, hills, birds, grasses, flowers, and clouds. Figures were difficult. He taught himself how to watch human movement and translate it into lines, crosshatching, angles and arcs. Occasionally, he copied his own hand, or quietly sketched the profile of one of the other men when he was not looking.

'What's this?'

'I doodle. Don't we all doodle?' He did not want to sound too defensive.

'All right, all right! What is it though?'

Moses turned the paper round.

'Oh! The warehouse, in the rain. How depressing.'

They laughed at him. His steel ruler was replaced by a set square. He didn't care. They hid his protractor. They took his cigarettes right out of his breast pocket.

His prisms lengthened, his ideas for chandeliers grew more fanciful. There was much, much less to do there than in the marking room. They had time to scrawl on his ideas, to ruin them, to criticize, to draw red circles around his numbers. When they gradually tired of their teasing, they left him alone. One tried to outdo his extravagant design for an epergne.

He countered their intrusion, their derision, with contrariness. He did not cower and apologize. He smiled and joked. He gained their approval when he asked for advice. He learned. Not about design, so much, but about people. About men. About how they needed to have a win every now and then.

He longed for something else he could not name.

And he yearned for music. He looked forward to the evenings he would sit in Havel's crowded room, listening to some programme relayed from some other, more exciting city. More exciting, distant, scary, daunting, pulling, drawing. Sometimes he drew closer to the radio, because the others would chat and ignore the programme.

'Your nephew likes wind instruments,' Havel said to Uršula. "Look how he sits up when there are saxophones.'

'Hm.'

'He is your nephew, isn't he? Do you have music in the family?'

'Believe me, we have everything in the family.'

'Tell me, tell me – what is that? What *is* this instrument?' Moses pointed at the radiogram, ignoring what they said. Chat was not what he came here for.

'Clarinet, I think. Yes, clarinet.'

'And what is the ... what's he *playing*? What is it?'

Havel exhaled cigarette smoke. 'Free music, young man. From the West. Now look at you – all of a sudden you want to go over to the depraved and so-called democratic side of the world, where corruption and laissez-faire will eat your soul.'

He did. He wanted to go to wherever that music came from. To hear it first-hand, without the crackling, without the threat of another power cut. He overlooked Havel's ironic tone. 'What is it, though?'

'Didn't you understand? The announcer said it's called *Stranger on the Shore*, and the genius playing is Acker Bilk. I think he wrote it. Try finding him, if you can. All the way in America! Ha ha! Go and shake his hand.'

'Acker Bilk. Acker Bilk.'

'Yes. Didn't you hear what the man said? It was the

most popular piece of music in the world, a couple of years ago. You are behind the times, ha ha!'

'I'll go to where that music comes from.'

'Ha ha! Listen to this one. Konstantin! Come and tell this man about your brother. How long has he been waiting for a permit to join your cousins in Canada?'

'America, I said!'

'Same thing – emigrating anywhere takes time. A long time.'

Konstantin did not mind talking over the music. 'Who, my brother Juraj? Yes, it's taking some time. But that's because he had to apply twice. There was a mistake the first time. It's taking a while. It's normal.'

'A while! Tell this man Moses how *long* it's taking Juraj. How long, Konstantin?'

'About nine years, or maybe longer – I'm not counting. It takes time to get the right papers. You have to get everything exactly right. And then you have to get the right stamps, from the right departments. And they might expire, so by the time you get the last stamp, you might have to get the first one again, and perhaps the interview that went with it, because it might not be exactly right any more.' Konstantin's tired face seemed proud he was able to give all this valuable information. 'Start early, is my advice.'

'See?' Havel strutted and glared.

'And get all the right papers.' Konstantin was willing to say more.

Moses shook his head. He was not about to wait nine years for the right stamps from the right departments. And how would he fare with an orphan's certificate? But he did not know how to get out of there, how to leave this place, how to free himself of sarcasm, how to head for the border, where he heard he could get through East Germany, and from there to the coast.

He could only imagine the terror, the excitement, the panic of doing it all on his own. Other boys travelled in gaggles of three or five or seven. They spoke about strange music, about getting to where everything was free and wonderful, about four boys called The Beatles, whose rhythms took years to reach them. They spoke of escape. Of democracy.

It was madness, he thought; it was the quickest route to Siberia, at gunpoint, with soldiers barking at you, toes frozen off, and nose blue and numb. It was deprivation some people lived long enough to speak about. Many were never heard from again.

The 'new program of socialism', promised for so long by various politicians, was taking an eternity to arrive. Edmund wondered whether any changes were possible.

He knew the apartments of some people were seeded with listening devices, despite promises to deregulate broadcasting. Even the rumours they would allow frequent and easy emigration to certain destinations was still a dream, and people were still disappearing for attempting to walk through the forests and over the mountains. He began to fear being caught at Havel's place, listening to western broadcasts, western music, people babbling in languages he could not understand.

'No one survives unless they can speak English,' someone said. Moses did not know a single word of German, let alone English. He was trapped for good. Liberty might be corrupt and evil, but it was out of reach.

It was a kind of gilded cage, after the dump that was the squat, to stay with Uršula in her apartment. Comparative luxury, with sporadic electric light, running water they could boil in a saucepan, and a door that locked. There were the evenings at Havel's, which made up for her fear of anything printed or written.

'No books. No books! No magazines, no *pamphlets*! They persecute you – they punish you, if you are found with printed pages.'

'Only if they are seditious, only if they are political pages.'

She blew out defiant smoke from pursed lips. 'Learn this – everything's political.'

He learned it when the unmistakeable thrum-thrum-thrum of soldiers' boots came up the concrete steps. The electricity was more erratic than usual, the cold was numbing. They listened in silence, holding their breath, wrapped around each other under the enormous quilt.

'Is the door locked?'

'Shh. Yes, yes.'

The boots thundered past the door to the apartment at the end of the passage. The sound of knocking. The sound of peremptory voices, the sound of low responses, like moans. Then the thrum-thrum-thrum again past their door. Had they taken someone away? Was anything wrong?

'Should we have a look?'

'Shh. Stop it. No.'

'Should ...'

'Are you joking? Shh – *no*.'

They heard the following day, on the bus to the glass factory, that the couple at the end of their passage was taken away for questioning, because someone had heard them mentioning the names of German entertainers, Italian singers, French actors. Was it possible?

'But Marika is a singer. Of course she ...'

'Shh? Marika? Do we know a Marika? You can't say

anything. *Don't* say anything.'

'So what about Havel...?'

She raised those eyebrows, frowned at him, bit her knuckle at him. 'Shh. Do we know a Havel? Who's Havel, anyway?'

'What?'

'No one knows anyone else. We don't know Marika either, do we, *Moses Nalezenec*?'

'We don't? Ah – I see. No. No.' Moses had seen her expression, her eyeballs moving left, left. The small movement of her eyes. The infinitesimal lift of her chin. The person in the bus seat behind them might very well tell on them, relay everything they said, spill all their confidences, betray all their movements to some bureaucratic ear.

It was stifling. Numbing. Claustrophobically limiting. He took on her paranoia. He had to get away from this. He needed to move. Moses needed to get away. But from what, to where? The thorn of restlessness poked his ribs, lay under his clothing, stung his breathing. But what about Uršula? What about his position at the factory? What about standing in line for her, to get oil and cabbage and beetroot? To get cans of jellied meat that sometimes had *fish bones* in it?

To where, to where? There was nowhere to go, except to where that music came from. He had to have a plan, but he had to hide it from Uršula.

She had said it plainly, more than just once. 'If you go, go.'

He was nonplussed. 'What?'

'If you decide to leave Prague, just disappear. Just go. Don't tell me your plans, or your destination. Nothing. No one should know your ideas. Don't share your plans. That is not how to disappear.'

He did not want to *disappear*, exactly.

'I don't want to know. Because they will come. They will ask. They will take the place apart again. Understand?' Her expressive eyebrows telegraphed fear.

It was clear he could not let that happen. He had to make a plan, yes. But his last departure had to be from some other place than her little brown apartment. He had to leave that checked environment, that nest of brown cotton. That huge quilt under which he had learned everything. Where to put his hands. How to be tender. How not to be selfish. Learned how to be always nice. *Always gentle.*

'But we love each other,' he had said once, muffled under that quilt.

'Oh yes?'

Her blunt question stung him into silence. He dared not even breathe.

'Oh yes? This is love now?' She was sharp. Brutal.

Stung. He turned away from her, feeling suddenly too young for her. Too hopeful, too naïve.

'You're looking for someone to adore. You told me. Someone wearing a soft woollen shawl. Have you seen anything woollen, or soft, around me? Hm? Someone to *adore*. Well, it's not me, Moses.'

He curled into a ball of disappointment.

'It's not me. I am not someone to *adore*. You have it all wrong. Your point of view is all skewed. Catholic nuns ... they can do that to you. *Listen* to me.'

He turned.

She had already lit two cigarettes, flipping one round in her fingers for him. 'Here.'

He sat up and inhaled cheap dull smoke. His chest and shoulders shrank in the cold air, so he pulled the quilt higher.

'It's the wrong way around, do you not see? Inverted thinking. *God* in heaven. Find someone who will adore *you*. Who finds *you* absolutely ...'

'I thought ...'

'You think too much, foundling.' She gave up. Her thin form shuddered slightly. Her thick black hair fell forward. When she stretched, holding the quilt to her chest, to tap ash into a chipped saucer nestled in the fabric channel between their shapes, he looked at her sharp shoulder blades, flared like wings.

'Fill the jar, will you? We need it, I think.'

They sipped vodka from the old jam jar, taking turns. It was from a new bottle Veronika sold her. It had a yellow label with a hare on it, and a crown cap, but it was better than any other they had so far. 'Hm. Things are looking up.' Her sarcasm rang in the small checked space.

Five

No comfort

Moses left as quietly as he had appeared in that line of young men and women looking for work, almost six full years before. With no letter of release from the factory, no warm farewell, no good wishes; nothing but a small fabric bag with two changes of clothing, his identity card, and a few klobasniky wrapped in greaseproof paper.

Perhaps he could have stayed longer. Perhaps he could have found some other kind of work closer to Kladno, where he would have felt less under scrutiny.

'Watching? Who do you think is watching you? So you think you're important?' A new girl, given the bluntest pen at the factory, had asked once, when he pushed some drawings across the counter for her to copy.

'Hush. You don't know ...' Moses attempted to silence some political comment she started to make.

'Rubbish.' Her riposte was arch and smug. 'We are all insignificant factory workers. No one cares about us.'

'On the contrary...' One of the other girls pointed the end of a pen at her.

Another cocked an eyebrow. 'You mean we are the salt of the earth.' Her voice boomed from across the room. '*Monuments* will be erected to us workers.'

'They are going to bring in price and wage

guidelines, yes!'

Moses did not know whether what they said was sarcastic or genuine. Fake, or constructs intended for listening devices.

'You know what I mean.' The new girl did not seem to know either.

But the feeling of unease stayed with him, especially because of the incursion by soldiers in their block; especially because Marika's man had disappeared. He could not put Uršula through all that again.

He would have to return to the squat, where none of the squatters' names was on a lease. Because there was no lease. Where he could – yes, he could make up a name, a fake name, a false identity. He would lay a false trail. But he had to find another squat. And it had to be closer to the border. And what would he use for papers?

It was far from easy. First, he needed to plan it all without writing anything down. And without asking too many questions. And without letting Uršula suspect.

It turned out to be another counter-intuitive move. He needed to journey further east to eventually move west. It took him a whole month to figure out, and a whole day to get to Zábřeh, even though he had learned it was a mere three hours by train or road. He had left without a word, which wrenched at his chest. But that was the way she wanted it. She wanted to know nothing, so any answers she might have to give to interrogation would be the truth. Nothing, she had told him several times, showed in the eyes more clearly than lies.

'Some men from the other glass factory are going to walk through the forest to Germany.' The new girl knew nothing about prudence, nothing about discretion, nothing about danger. She had probably never listened to the thrum of military boots on the landings of her building.

The information, however, was valuable. They would all think he had walked away with them. All he had to do was time his departure to coincide with their 'disappearance'. He listened carefully to the new girl, who displayed her knowledge with a smug look, with words everyone in the copy room seemed to ignore. It was stupid of her, but it was valuable to Moses.

On the first Tuesday of September, he did not clock in for his morning shift. He did not accompany Uršula that day, but stayed behind, telling her he was going to buy oil, and rode a bus that took him round the other way, almost to the rival factory at Kladno. Taking only what he could pack into her checked fabric shopping bag. Taking his time. Taking three klobasniky from the enamel dish on the stove. He could not dare to look like a traveller; no suitcase, no canvas backpack, but everyone carried shopping bags made of material scraps and remnants. Everyone rode buses looking for provisions. Getting to Zábřeh from there was not much harder than from Prague.

And then, finding a corner in a squat turned out to be fortuitously easy. He just followed one of Uršula's frequent behests. 'Enter a shop. Listen, don't talk. *Listen.*'

Listen. Listen.

He overheard some vital words. He followed a young man in a light brown jacket at a distance, stood in a queue of shoppers in a cold unseasonal wind for an hour, and heard what he had to hear. Drew near, drew nearer, approached an abandoned house, spoke casually to a man with a shorn head, and took up a corner. No mattress, no comfort, and a heart much heavier than when he had joined the first squat, as an innocent seventeen year-old.

He already missed her. He already regretted his stupid plan to get away. He rued coming all the way to Zábřeh. What was he doing there? His stupid claim to freedom. Freedom from what? And nothing to show for his time with her. All he had of hers was that brown checked fabric bag. And it tugged at his heart.

'I have to get to where they make that music,' he said to one of the boys at the squat.

'What music? Are you crazy? Everyone makes music. We have plenty of music here. Come on Friday night to the hall where ...'

'Stranger on the shore.'

'What?'

'Acker Bilk.'

The look he got was enough to silence him for as long as it took to find his way to the border. The look he got taught him a lot. The look he got prepared him, in a way, for other looks, in other places, from others who were just as annoyed or puzzled or *something.*

He paused, and after a safe interval of nine days, he got to the border, which was so much further from his present position than it was from Prague. He was closer to Poland now. How to reach East Germany was still a problem.

He lay in the dark, hands behind his head, gazing into nothing, doomed to gaze into nothing forever, listening to cheap lighters buzz briefly, before a flame and an inhalation, over and over, until they would all fall asleep, and thrash and snore and utter their desperate dreams that turned into scribblings and scrawls on the dirty walls around them.

A voice in the dark. 'Have you any more tobacco, Karel? What did you say before?'

'I said there is a van leaving Zábřeh for Dresden,

but you didn't hear it from me. And it's about time you got your own tobacco.'

'What?' Another voice in the dark, hoarse with sleep.

'You heard. Three of us. Only three. Myself, and Karel ... and you ... who was that who spoke just now?'

It was a voice in the dark and damp of a room thick with smoke from hand-rolled cigarettes. A room thick with the smell of unwashed boys, unwashed socks, damp jackets. He hated it. He should never have left. No.

Yes, he would get to Germany, but he would go alone. He would not go in a van with Karel and two other boys. The plan took form in his mind, and all he could think of was a thick pair of boots and canvas trousers, a fur-lined jacket, and a thick klobouk for his head, because he kept his hair cut very short now. And Uršula's checked fabric bag. He thought of practical details instead of philosophical concepts. Freedom – what was freedom? It was a construct. It was abstract. Perhaps it did not even exist. But music; that did exist. It changed things.

There were ways out of there and towards that music. Towards art that he had seen on magazines smuggled from who knew where. Western music and western art – art it was a crime to even look at. Art he yearned to create. Art it was a crime to even think of.

People who committed crimes, he heard someone say, were now being forced to emigrate. It was an idea, it was an irony – such an irony – but what kind of crime must it be? Would he risk the kind of punishment they had heard about during the purges?

How was he to make a life for himself if he kept thinking someone at Uršula's apartment block or at the factory would report his absence? If he kept looking over his shoulder? He remembered his escapes from the orphanage. They had taken him back so many times, sulky and defeated. Hands behind his back, head down, empty feeling in his chest. Would it be a return to that kind of setback, over and over again?

He would not let it happen again. He was an adult now, and it was more dangerous. They would deal him the kind of treatment he heard about, standing in shopping lines. They would interrogate him, detain his acquaintances. Arrest Uršula. No.No. He had to listen, like she said. And think, think, think. Think of a name. Call himself something else. Something different.

He thought of the doorstep where he had perched to eat one of her klobasniky; how he had swallowed, swallowed past a throat sore with held-back tears.

'Find someone who adores *you*,' she had said. Now it was clear; why had he never realized? It meant she did not love him. That he was there to keep her warm at night, stand in her shopping queues, accompany her downstairs to Havel's, tidy the porcelain sink, fold the checked quilt, bring her oil in an old rinsed-out vodka bottle. That was all. That was all. She did not love him.

Perhaps she still adored the man who beat her, who did not care if she was cold. Who staggered up the stairs drunk. Who took all her cigarettes. Who smelled of other women. Who left her.

Perhaps she only loved someone who had disappeared. Who was absent. Who was no longer there to aggravate her moods. Perhaps she would adore him *now*.

Six

The smell of brine

The smell of water. A glimpse of flights of what looked like water birds. Seagulls? Seagulls? Could they be? He had no idea, but it all took his mind off what happened on the train. Seagulls! They must be seagulls or some sort of tern. He had heard and read of terns. Yes. He was there. It had proved a nightmare, but he was there.

To produce his factory papers for a ticket to somewhere was not what he wanted to do, or could do, in Zábřeh, and he had no letter of release, no permission to travel or leave Prague, so he had waited, waited in the dark, got into the yards through a triangle of lifted fence wire, and waited some more. He had a clear idea of what he wanted to do, but he was exhausted and hungry. He had two cigarettes left, but he saved them for when he knew he was over the border.

The rail yards were full of rolling stock, a maze of stacks of timber, dilapidated carriages, huge brown rain puddles, and half-visible rails. He needed to find a train marked *Bremen* as a destination. It was easy to stay out of sight of the station windows, even though there was no light there. Even though he felt it was deserted. Bremen, Bremen, Bremen.

Was this a crazy thing to do? He could buy a ticket to Dresden first – but no. He had no idea of the layout of that city, no way to find out the best way to get onto a goods train to the coast. He could not speak German. This was his only way out of the country. Narrow, narrow. His choices were very narrow.

Military police patrolled the fence. He heard their boots and their baritone voices just as he crouched out of sight behind a mountain of planks, stacked at the edge of a milky puddle whose edges were starting to ice. Then he saw it.

Yes. A yellow card sign, wedged in the front of a long line of rolling stock. There it was. *Bremen*. And a boxcar in the middle of a train, just behind a flat-bed trailer of logs, just in front of a tender, partly hidden by a bin-trailer covered with a black tarpaulin, it was. *That* was what he sought. The sliding door was open. Just a crack, just a vertical strip that looked darker from that distance, but it was open. It was a goods boxcar, full of something destined for Bremen, just like he was. And there was bound to be room for him inside.

The police moved out of earshot. Other male voices in the distance hailed each other about going home, about soup and vodka, about women. A hoarse laugh rattled along the rails.

Moses – no, he was not *Moses* now. No, no. He had made up a name, a new name for himself, and he had to remember to *be* that name. He was Edmund Eben. He said the name. He urged Edmund Eben to move, *move*.

Crouched like a squirrel, and just as fast, he hoped, he hurried out of the shelter of the stack of planks and crossed the puddle, wetting his shoes and socks. The cold shock nearly stopped his heart. He passed the coal tender, reached the sliding door, and tried to move it. Too heavy. Too heavy. It was a massive wooden door, and he could not budge it.

'Damn.' He was out of breath, freezing cold, and

powerless. 'Damn. Damn. Damn.' The men's voices were not getting closer, were they? Was something jamming the door? Hurry, hurry. These things were on bearings that should move to a touch, one man's touch. He was one man. He was Edmund Eben. He repeated the name to himself, moved his hand in the rail channel, just a foot of rail channel, and found it.

A chock. It was a wooden block, dirty with oil, used to wedge the sliding door open just a foot. But it also stopped it from sliding properly. Gathering wits, breath, and guts, he squatted on his haunches and waited another two or three minutes. What was that? He started. A large creature, a rat, scampered so close to him he thought he heard it pant. It darted away, into the darkness. Then there was another. And another.

Breathless, anxious, nervous. He stood to his full height, forced his shoulder against the wooden door, pulled at the chock, and moved it. The door slid back on its own weight. It made a rumbling, grinding noise.

He held his breath again, waited another three minutes. Had anyone heard that? Perhaps not. Now all he had to do was haul himself up and in. Flexing both arms, with the fabric bag hanging from a shoulder, he leapt up, engaging knees with the rail channel. No.

Try again. He threw the bag into the car, and got one knee up. It hurt, but he gritted his teeth and hauled, up, up, up. In seconds he stood on the board and side-stepped behind the door. Rolling. Heavy. Rolling it almost shut again.

It had taken twelve seconds. Perhaps twenty. He made sure the door was open a crack, like before. He restored the chock. It was pitch dark inside the boxcar. But it was packed with sacks and crates. Something that smelled dusty and full of soil. An earthy smell that choked him. A familiar stink he could not place. Too nervous. Slow down. Slow down. Breathe easy.

'Arghh.' The breath, the life, all thought, everything was knocked out of him at once. Someone hit him hard, on the back of the head. 'Argh!'

It was not hard enough to knock him out, but enough to make him turn to face the aggressor, with one arm up to shield his face. It was not enough to protect him. A fist came out of the dark and hit him in the eye.

'Arrgh!' He hit back, as hard as he could, into the dark. Jab, jab. His bare fist encountered something. Something hairy, bristly, something that moved away quickly, and just as silently.

Whoever it was knew about the wooden chock. He heard it clatter to the floor of the car when the man removed it, and then there was a thump when he jumped out, half falling to the sodden ground, and then scampering noisily away. Another rat, that's all he was. Larger, but still a rat. Would he return? Moses did not know, he was immobile. His head rang. He had to risk staying there.

He caught his breath, swore, touched the back of his sore head, and felt around for the chock on the floor of the boxcar, which took a while. He stopped to listen. His ears rang and hissed, and pain started to edge its way behind his eyes. What was that? A thrumming sound squeezed around the pain.

What was that?

Rain, rain on the roof of the car, rain pocking puddles outside. The rumble and hiss of a distant truck. He restored the chock once more and squeezed through stacks of sacks to the far side, dizzy and unsure on his feet. He moved to where there was just enough room to move. This was where that man must have lain. He had disturbed a vagrant, that was all.

Now it was a matter of making room to lie back, to pull off those cold wet socks, and to wait until the train started to move. He touched his face gingerly, it stung on the cheekbone, under his eye. He had nothing to hold to it but a clean pair of underpants, but no. It was not bad. All he had to do was let it scab, which it would. All he had to do was lie back and wait for movement, for the train to roll. To roll towards Bremen. He finally sat back, exhausted.

Why was he doing this? To find Acker Bilk? To find a woman in a soft woollen shawl? To get to America? To get some sleep? Sleep. Sleep. His rough breathing slowed after a while.

He was woken by something. The choking smell of soil? A blinding slant of sunlight coming in through the crack at the door across the car? It was movement. Someone had kicked his foot. The train had started to roll along, and he was wide awake, or nearly. Gazing at the khaki legs of someone standing over him. Towering high, up, up, up, to a capped head and a face that glared.

He stopped breathing. Sleep still dulled his head. This was the end – was it the end? Was this the man from last night? No – a soldier. A military policeman? A soldier? It *was* the end. Whoever it was dropped to his haunches, squatted so that their faces were almost level.

'So?'

The only noise after the monosyllable was creaking and hissing from the train's movement. They were travelling at speed.

'So, *mladík!*'

The new Edmund Eben rubbed his eyes, rubbed his nose, touched the place on his cheek which was raised and swollen, and sat up.

'So, youngster. Someone got you good, there.' The

soldier reached out, pointed at Edmund's face. Came just short of touching him. Then his hand dipped into Edmund's breast pocket. He took the two cigarettes and looked at them, placed them both between his lips, and lit them with an efficient lighter, which he snapped shut and put back in his pocket. Then he flipped one of the cigarettes, and handed it to Edmund, while inhaling deeply on the one still between his lips.

This reminded Edmund so much of Uršula he had to swallow and fight back words, tears, sharp breaths. He took the cigarette, and inhaled smoke, which struck him, filled him immediately with the dull sensation of hunger, deep inside. His head boomed with audible pain.

'Travelling, eh? Off to join the circus.'

'No, no.'

'No? Not travelling … on a moving train?' The man rocked on bent legs, nearly lost his footing, stood up straight.

Nothing showed in the eyes clearer than lies, Uršula would say. 'I have no idea where I am,' Edmund said, looking up. That, if nothing else, was the plain truth.

The soldier lurched, turned, slid his back down against a pile of hessian sacks, sat, and threw off the peaked brown cap. Something – a gun or truncheon or baton – clattered at his side as he sat back, stretching long legs out before him. 'I do. I have an idea where I am. And you. In deep shit, is where we are.' He took three deep breaths, then turned to look at Edmund's astonished face; Edmund's fear-filled eyes, and grinned. 'Someone rearranged your face, boy. Or half of it, anyway. Do you have anything to eat?'

Paralysed vocal chords, immobile tongue. Seized throat.

'What's in that fancy bag of yours?'

Edmund remembered the clutch of klobasniky he had taken from the dish on the stove. It felt as long ago as a year. They would have shrivelled, dried up, mouldered, in all that time. Was it really only yesterday morning? He patted the bag, and heard the rustle of greaseproof paper. He said one word. 'Klobasniky.'

'My lucky day. Hand them over. You know what? *Your* lucky day, too.'

There were only two left. The soldier unwrapped them slowly, put them under his nose, took a deep breath. 'She could cook, whoever you left behind.'

Edmund swallowed. Then he nodded.

'You will most likely never see her again, you know that?'

He nodded again.

'What? That's it? Don't resign yourself to what I say. Don't just *nod* at me. Say something! Assert yourself, boy.' The soldier took one of the rolls and nipped off an end with buck teeth. 'Mm?'

Edmund shook his head.

'Are you hungry?'

At last he could say another word. 'Yes.'

'Do you know where this train is headed?'

'Bremen.'

The soldier laughed, the back of his head resting against the sacks behind him. 'Man. Man – these potatoes are not going to Bremen. These sacks are not going to Germany. I would not be on this train if it were rolling on to Bremen.'

Edmund shuddered. He could not understand why this soldier was on the train, alone, with him, in a boxcar crammed full of potatoes. The smell in his head, in his nose and mouth, was now recognizable. Unmistakeable. Nothing smelled like a rotten potato, nothing. And there were bound to be a couple of rotten ones in that car crammed with sacks. Potatoes. Still dirty, caked with the soil they grew in. 'Where then?'

'Do you know what I am? I am a man in trouble. And here I am, on a moving potato train, eating klobasniky out of a fabric bag. In the company of a boy who thinks we're going to Bremen.' His laugh was far from funny. He looked at Edmund. 'Do you have a name? I'm Ludvik.'

'Ed... Mo – '

'Edmo, they will shoot me on sight if they find me, you know?' He finished the pastry, wiped his mouth on the back of his hand and patted his side. Once more, he lit two cigarettes, this time from his pack, and passed one over, after flipping it backward. Then he bit half off the other filled roll and passed it over as well.

Edmund took both. Cigarette in one hand, roll in the other, he did not want to try and make head or tail of the soldier's words.

'They will shoot me on sight, understand?'

Nodding at a soldier. At a deserter, a defector? Nodding, nodding and eating the rest of Uršula's klobasniky. Thinking he would never taste her cooking again. Emotion, surprise, shock and distress froze his chest. Pain froze his face.

'You'll be black and blue tomorrow, Edmo.'

It was an hour before Edmund could speak, an hour of watching the soldier nod off, nod, nod, shake himself awake again, smoke another cigarette and nod off again. He could not sleep. How did one sleep, travelling at speed inside a lurching boxcar of potatoes, with a face that felt it was going to explode, in the company of a soldier – deserter or not?

'Where are we bound, then? Do you know?'

'Ah! He speaks!'

'Do you know?'

The soldier shrugged.

'There was a yellow card that said Bremen.' Edmund told him what he saw.

'I think yellow means in-bound. I think red is out-bound.'

Edmund bit his lip. 'Was there a red card?'

'Antwerp. It said Antwerp. Big black letters on red card. That end of train. Stuck to another boxcar. So full of crates, it was, that other car, of glass bottles or something, that there was no room ... no room for even one man to stand.'

'Glass bottles!'

'Fancy ones. Fancy-work. Decanters, you might call them – there was a printed label on one crate, with a picture. From Bohemia to the world. Crystal decanters!'

Edmund did not tell him the irony, the fluke of travelling on the same train as decanters from his factory, if that was the case. It was a coincidence that no one would believe.

'We're on the way to Antwerp.'

'Antwerp.' Repetition. Safety in repeating things.

'In Belgium. The Low Countries. Near Holland. You know.'

Edmund Eben nodded. He took a deep breath. He was on the way to Belgium.

'But when we get there, you disappear, you hear? No hanging around me like a burr. I'm getting rid of this uniform, and I'm ... look, I'm taller than you, but I need your jacket. And your hat.'

'No! Not my klobouk.'

'I need it.'

'Not my klobouk.'

'Hah. You need it to cover that bright hair. Your jacket, then. And when we jump off the train, it's every man for himself, understand?'

'*Jump* off?'

The soldier laughed again. 'Jump. What? You think I'm going to wait politely until the train reaches a complete stop?' He imitated an announcer's intonation. 'I won't *mind my step*, sir. I'll be out the instant the train slows to a roll that won't kill me when I hit the ground outside. You do what the hell you like.'

'And ...'

'And you never saw me. You've been all alone since you left Zábřeh. All alone. Never, ever mention a word of this to a soul. Don't be stupid. They'll detain *you* if you speak of soldiers. Soldiers on trains. A soldier on his own on a train. No.'

'Do they detain people in ... in Antwerp?'

He shrugged. 'How do I know?' I have never crossed the Czech border before in *my life*.'

Neither had Edmund. And he would not know exactly when that would happen, when the train went over the border, in this dark boxcar.

The soldier did what he said he would, and jumped off the train, wearing Edmund's jacket, leaving behind his own, without a backward glance. The train had slowed, but it was still a stupid thing to do. Edmund pushed his head out of the crack in the sliding door and looked back. Ludvik had rolled down a grass embankment, and was rising awkwardly to his feet. The train reached a slight bend and Edmund lost sight of him. He knew he would never see him again. Rolling the door back and sticking the chock in was not easy with the train rolling and weaving so much. It gained speed once more, and it was a good hour before he heard the whistle. It slowed once more, and there were shouts. Was that sound he heard a ship's foghorn? He had no idea.

There was the brackish smell of water. He looked

through the opening once more. The sky was bluer here. And birds flew about. He saw a line of angular metal cranes.

Seven

A is for apple

'*Een engel bij de haren heeft je opgetild.*'

The voice startled him out of his mind. Out of deep deep sleep. Out of a sense of safety, inside a narrow space; cramped but dry. Ah – stiff, cramped, uncomfortable. 'Wha- what?'

'An angel has lifted you by that red hair of yours.' The man beckoned. He nodded and beckoned. He opened cracked grey hands, palms upward, and nodded and beckoned again. Then he smiled. Two missing teeth and a silver molar.

What was he? Who was he? Moses ... no – *Edmund*, Edmund Eben, did not understand a word the man said. He was disoriented. Hungry. He had no cigarettes. It had rained for a whole day and all through the night, so he sheltered underneath a gangway. He had the sense it led on board a vessel of some sort, but could not see well enough in the rain. Hungry. All he saw was a wall of green painted metal. Then he saw a parked truck, some distance away. For an hour or so – how did he know how long? – he sheltered underneath its high chassis, not daring to sleep, in case someone drove it and crushed him to death. His feet were wet and clammy. He shivered and shook. Hungry. When there was a break in the weather, he tried the passenger door, and climbed inside.

Such a relief, such a relief to get out of the rain, that constant heavy drizzle, so all he thought to do was take off his soaked jacket – the long khaki jacket left in place of his old one by the errant soldier – to kick off his shoes, pull off his hat, and lie back. Hungry. And sore. He sat up again and looked at what he could of his face in the rear-view mirror. His left eye was swollen shut, a purple shiny slit. His cheekbone was scabbed and fiery red. There was nothing he could do about it. It was starting to throb. He stretched out along both seats. The gear lever stuck uncomfortably into his side, but with his hat as a pillow, was instantly asleep.

'An angel lifted you from your hair.'

What did he mean? Edmund touched the top of his spiky hair, imitating what the old man did, and looked at the man's bald head. He should have locked the truck doors from the inside before he fell asleep. Too late. He was discovered now, half asleep at the Antwerp river docks, inside a truck, where he had no business to be. He shook his head. What could he say to this old dock worker that would not get him arrested, or taken away, or returned to Prague in deeper trouble than he was before?

The man made eating and drinking gestures. He smiled. He said a number of words, of which he understood none. Then he heard, among the gabble, something that sounded like coffee.

Edmund nodded. 'Káva.'

The man smiled. 'Coffee?'

He nodded again.

'Bread? Bread?'

'*Chléb*?'

'Bread.' The old man made eating gestures and sounds again.

'Edmund nodded and smiled. '*Chléb. Chléb.*' There

were some words that were impossible not to grasp, no matter the language.

Edmund handed him his soaked jacket, slipped on the unlaced shoes, and clambered down from the truck. When he stood, the man was about a foot taller than he was. He looked up into his eyes, and wondered whether he could trust this early-morning soul. The entire dock was still deserted.

'You fortunate boy. Haha! You unlucky so-and-so, also.'

'What?'

The man pointed at his own eye and grimaced. He meant Edmund's face looked awful. He beckoned.

What could Edmund say to make him understand? 'America. I want to go to America. On a ship.' He looked and pointed at the vessels behind them.

The man launched into a barrage of words, interspersed by little funny elfin good-spirited laughs that negated his lofty frame. 'Ha ha. Ha ha ha. Ha!' He gestured that Edmund should follow him, so they traversed the dock together, and soon they passed through a gate and crossed a quiet street, where a line of parked cars and shut doorways were not so different from the ones he had last seen in Prague.

They turned a corner, and walked past a row of identical brown doors. The man seized him by the shoulders, turned him around, and pointed at the distant group of lofty metal cranes they had just left behind on the wharf. '*Antwerpen!*'

Edmund looked, unable to grasp what the man meant.

'My docks. My Antwerpen!'

Edmund nodded.

The man made eating gestures and sounds again. His empty mouth munched. '*Hongerig?*'

'*Hladový. Hladový.*'

It was not so different. It meant what it meant. He was hungry, and the man understood that much.

They walked together. The streets started to come alive with people, cars. Bobbing umbrellas sprouted wherever Edmund looked. After a few minutes, the old man ducked in a doorway and he followed. The heavy door slammed behind them. There was a woman, who frowned and shouted at the old man, but banged a tall blue enamel coffeepot on a stove and gestured Edmund towards a chair.

'America, eh?'

Edmund nodded. 'America.'

'English? You speak English? *Engels*? Eh?'

Edmund shook his head.

She understood. 'You won't get to America without any English. What happened to your face?'

'What?'

The woman shouted at the old man from the stove. 'Ask him!'

'Eh?'

'Ask what happened to his face.'

'He's been through a hard time. He is from the Eastern bloc – look at the jacket – a uniform, and obviously the wrong size. He's a fugitive, and it's a wonder he has a face at all.'

'Poor devil.'

He was given a plate and a cup, which he placed in front of Edmund. He was also given a small enamel basin in which some hot water and a flannel swam. It was for his face.

He wrung out the flannel, placed the hot wad to his eye and winced aloud. The old man pointed at his cheek and waggled his head. What followed was a breakfast of sorts. Some bread, a lot of butter, a plate of what looked like herring, and a whole scalding coffeepot of the best coffee he had ever drunk in his life. It was so good he only thought to add sugar and milk after his second cup. The milk was thick, with globules of cream on top. The old couple sat across the table, staring at him.

Their conversation seemed angry, impatient, but there was the occasional toothless grin from the woman. The occasional nod. She disappeared, wiping her hands on a voluminous white apron. On her way out, she turned a switch on a radio, high up on a small shelf on that clean kitchen wall.

Edmund stopped with the cup at his lip. He gripped the table edge. Music filled the kitchen. Guitars, drums, young men singing at the tops of their voices. The old man grinned. 'Rolling Stones, eh? Beatles?'

'Beatles.'

'Hah ha! Beatles, de Beatles. *Can't buy me love.*'

'*Can't buy me love.*'

The old woman returned, placed two tiny pills on the table. 'Aspirin. Swallow them.'

Edmund swallowed, swallowed, using the last of the coffee.

Then she threw a small stack of books on the table, and put the pot on again. Children's books. Board books. From the look on her face Edmund saw she had done this before. Well-thumbed books. Old books. Sitting next to him, she turned the pages of the first one. It was an alphabet. An English alphabet book with words and pictures.

'*Engels.*' Her mouth formed the words. 'English! A is for apple.'

'*Jablko.*'

She shook her head. 'No. No – apple. Say it.' She filled the cup with coffee again, rose, pushed the stack of books towards him and nodded. '*Engels.* Learn

English before you do anything else. *Then* you might get to America. You fortunate young man. If anyone else but Gerrit had found you, you'd be on the way to the station right now, you know. And look at your face.'

Edmund had no way of deciphering her gabble. He drank coffee, sat back, and leafed through the books. Leafing, leafing, through the whole stack of board books.

Eight

Flour and facets

He counted fifty-seven dry days in the whole twenty months he spent in Antwerp. It rained almost every day, sometimes for a few minutes, sometimes the day long. Edmund could not say he hated it. It was sometimes warmer than it was back in Prague. He was finally in the west, the longed-for west. And he still had to experience the sense of liberty he thought would be here.

Work at the mill was backbreaking, but it rendered him anonymous, and that was what he wanted at first. Getting work was vital, and he was told how to do it by the old man. Using hand signs, winks, nudges and his strange elfin laugh, he got Edmund to understand that he had to look for work right away.

'Papers? You have no papers, right? Where is your little book?'

He showed the man his yellow Czech registration card, which contained his life story: movements, employment history, and vaccination records.

'Good, good. You need ... you need work. Wait, wait wait. This isn't your name. You said your name is Edmund, not Moses.'

'What?'

'This not your name? Look – I'll take you.'

'What?'

'Where. Where. Not what. I'll take you to where my

sons used to work.'

He was pushed into a line of waiting men in front of a big square building by the river. Soon, they were herded inside, where they filed to a woman at a table. Edmund listened, listened hard, trying to understand. When it was his turn, he gave his new name. She wrote it down, looked up at his face and winced. Then she said something to a man standing behind her, something like '*Moedig.*'

The man leaned down and whispered to her. Whispered, whispered. They both looked up into Edmund's face. '*Een moedig vluchteling.*' The woman's eyes held something like compassion. 'A brave fugitive. With unusual red hair!' She looked him in the eye, in the eye, asked for *papers* in a number of tongues.

'*Papíry,*' he repeated, but could tell them little else except shake his head. '*Ne.*' He pulled out his pockets to explain he had none. His yellow card, showing his old name, was useless to him now. He had hidden it at the bottom of his checked bag. '*Ne.*' It was exactly what the old man Gerrit had shown him to do. He had to do this to start again. To gain purchase. To take on a name.

The woman quickly filled in a form, after getting him to repeat his name. Edmund, then a pause, then Eben. She folded it in half, and gave it to him. The man behind her waved him onward into the passage and a flight of stairs at the back. Everything was covered in a fine layer of white dust.

Weeks later, he learned that it was his bruised and cut face that got him the job at the flourmill. It was his face that elicited compassion from the old man. He found out Gerrit and his wife were known as the 'Dock Angels'. They took pity on fugitives from the Eastern bloc, those who did not speak Dutch or German, and if they were disabled or injured in some way, were more likely to offer their help.

He was placed at the end of a conveyor belt, where heavy paper sacks of flour came, regularly, spaced closely together, arriving in a never-ending stream. He had to place them on a flat barrow, in a kind of pyramid, and a boy would cart them away. Fast, he had to work quickly, or the sacks would tumble forward off the belt and burst on the floor. It was obvious after he missed one, and it exploded in a cloud of white dust. Before it settled, he had the next, and the next, and the next, and the next on the barrow.

'*Ja!*' someone shouted to someone else high in the roof of the place, which probably meant he could cope with the pace, and they left him to it.

He lost only two sacks in his first week, and the second one only because someone spoke to him while he worked. The skin on his hands eroded with the fine flour he constantly handled. His palms became shiny and soft. There was a powdering of flour on everything, including his own clothes and skin after a while. To gain purchase and grip on the bags, he was given a pair of light blue rubber gloves, a size too small. It worked if he soaked them from time to time.

With a piece of paper – his name, his new name, correctly spelled on it, EDMUND EBEN – safe in his pocket, and some money coming in, he could consider leaving the home of the old man and his grumpy but hospitable wife. They were wonderful. They were generous and good, but he could not keep going from one refuge to another, from Uršula to Gerrit, and from there, to who knew where.

'Strike out on your own,' the old man said through his terrible teeth.

'Hm?'

It took a while, and a mixture of English, Flemish,

hand signs and facial grimaces, for Gerrit to get his meaning across. 'Row your own boat. Live your own life.'

Edmund agreed, and nodded.

'And find a woman who thinks the world of you, no matter how many of your teeth fall out of your head.' He grinned. 'We fight. She bangs that coffeepot on the stove like some judge with a gavel, but we are lost without each other.'

Teeth, coffeepot, judge ... what did the man mean?

More gestures.

'Ah!' Edmund understood the gist of it. The exact meanings of some words still escaped him. The when, where, *how* of things people said still confused him to frustration.

Gerrit moved up to his wife, who was ironing things by the big black stove, and placed a hand on her shoulder. 'Eh? *Zonder elkaar zijn we verloren.* Eh? Nothing without each other, we are. Nothing.'

She growled, but her nod and slow smile confirmed what the old man said.

'See? See? Now go out into the world and get that, if you can. He he heh!'

The old man was right. Edmund did not know about finding the right woman, but that piece of paper from the factory would be the saving of him. It would be his passport – he could get identification, and it would open doors.

He could leave the stiff camp bed they had given him, squashed under the steep stairs, close to the stove downstairs.

'Nothing wrong with it. Both our sons slept here at some time.'

He liked the spot, despite its lack of privacy, because it was close to where the radio stood, on its shelf, and it was the first thing the woman turned on when she came down, early each morning. He had memorized all the vocabulary in the alphabet books, and wanted to learn more. He knew all the words of the most popular songs.

He was diligent, a workhorse in that mill, even though he had never had such strenuous labour in the glass factory back in Prague. People started to notice him.

'Get Edmund to do it.'

'Send Edmund.'

'Edmund will do that well for you.'

And yet, he was never one of them. They smoked together, standing inside, out of the rain in the courtyard. They liked him. He liked them, but he would be a stranger for as long as he worked there, until his hair turned white and his teeth, like Gerrit joked, fell out of his head.

He needed to learn more. He needed to find his feet. He needed English. Everything he saw around him, he could name in in Flemish now, and in *English*. Flour, sacks, white, barrow, boy, conveyor belt, roof, floor, flour, flour, flour. *Meel, meel, meel*. Flour – it was everywhere. In every breath he took.

Old man Gerrit found a friend who found another friend, who found him a room in an attic, not too far away from the mill, and showed him the way to the closest library, where he could look at books in English. There was also a cinema, where Edmund spent a lot of time, mouthing phrases with the stars. *Psycho, Lawrence of Arabia, Westside Story*, and *The Graduate* were films he watched more than twice each, learning as he went.

His favourite line was *And what am I? Cut glass?* Edmund said it over and over to himself, chuckling at the connection to his past at the crystal factory, walking, walking the Antwerp streets, starting to understand his freedom, starting to breathe deeply, taking in his good fortune. His damp klobouk was discarded in favour of another, more western, hat; a rainproof Belgian cap with a back flap and the badge of a local brewery on the front. He grew his hair over his collar, and wore a new kind of smile that was less cautious and full of fear, less carved with the suspicion of the Eastern bloc.

It was almost inevitable that he should gravitate to the most popular quarter, frequented by the youthful crowd. It came from drinking all sorts of different beers in small brown pubs, watching people, practising his English whenever he could.

'Do you speak English?'

Many did. He would listen for the right kind of music in the right kind of pub, walk in, and find someone on whom to practise his phrases.

'Do you speak English?'

Sometimes it was a forlorn girl, who smoked hand-rolled cigarettes and complained about men, money, the weather, her parents. Sometimes it was a group of students, whose brand of socialism made him laugh. They knew nothing of real socialism; socialism that kept people prisoners, that put listening devices in corridors and halls, that made them buy oil in rinsed-out vodka bottles, that turned the heating on and off in sub-zero temperatures. Sometimes it was an older man in jacket, tie and all, having a quick beer before heading home to his family and slippers, who smiled about some things, and moaned about the bureaucracy.

'Speak English?'

They would talk of trains, towns, the cinema, life, cigarettes, women. They got used to him. And yet he never felt really part of the scene. It was as if he watched himself, from high above the bar, behind those bright light bulbs, over those slightly swinging glass lampshades.

'D'you speak English?'

A young man, with big gloves and a huge brimmed hat lying on the brown pub table nodded and made room.

'I'm learning English.'

It did not seem like a silly thing to be learning English in the middle of a sprawling Belgian city. The sixties were opening up the whole world with easier travel, youthful exuberance, pop music, t-shirts with slogans printed on them in English, the hippy culture, and a kind of freedom Edmund was only starting to taste and appreciate, no matter how alien it all felt. He told this young man his intentions, choosing his words, finding the right intonation. He told him a bit of what he had done so far.

'If you used to design crystal vases, what are you doing in a flourmill?'

Edmund had never asked himself the question. It confused him. Where he came from, you kept to the work you could get. Choices were not commonplace. Options were few and rare. He looked at the hat on the table. He looked out of the pub door at the rain. He looked at the row of light bulbs over the mirror behind the bar.

The man spoke. 'Liège.'

'Sorry, what?'

'Liège. You must get on a train to Liège, and find work at the glass factory there.'

'There is a glass factory!' His eyes lit up.

The young man put the enormous brimmed hat on his head. 'It's either that or polishing diamonds. And I doubt anyone will employ you to do that. It's more or less a closed shop, all family-owned and run. But...'

'But?'

'But anything's better than work in a mill. It will break your back.'

'It has.'

'You know what? I'll take you to Anshel. You're very lucky – he's thinking of travelling to Liège himself, in a week, I think. He's a bit of a rebel, with a suffocating family, but don't tell him that, okay? He will suggest something.' He turned and paused. 'If he likes you, okay? Only if he likes you.'

Anshel was Jewish, with light grey eyes. He asked the same question, with a crooked smile that only used half his face. 'Why do you work with flour sacks, when you can ... what did you say?' He looked at his friend, who broke into Flemish, or Yiddish – how could Edmund tell? They went too fast. 'What did he say?' They discussed him for a while, nodding heads and using their hands in mirrored gesticulation. Wave, wave, point.

'Yes – come with me. Come on the train. What's your name – Edmund? Come with me, Edmund. Both looking for new work in a new town, we will be. Eh – eh. The glass factory would be great. We'll see what happens at Val Saint Lambert, shall we?'

Edmund looked at the thin lopsided young man, with questions of his own. 'Why are you going?'

'Do you mean when? Do you only speak English?'

'And very little Flemish. And Czech. And I do mean *why*.'

'Ah – English then. I'm going because I have three brothers, and my father's diamond-cutting business is getting crowded!' He grimaced. 'And they have found me a *nice Jewish girl* to marry. And I don't want to marry. You want the story of my life? Besides, I'm left-handed, and all I want to do is design, not polish, polish, polish.'

'Design vases, yes.' The hope in Edmund's heart started to grow. 'Design bowls.'

'*Bowls* – say it properly. And chandeliers!'

Edmund laughed. 'Yes, chandeliers! Anshel – when do we leave?'

'Tomorrow. Meet me at Antwerpen Centraal, at eight, and we shall be on our way.'

It was neither easy nor difficult. Neither awkward nor smooth. But when they got there, Edmund realized Liège was not like Antwerp. Everyone spoke French. Another problem. Another hurdle. Edmund looked at Anshel. They had already started to understand each other, using English and a kind of stuttered '*eh-eh-eh*' Anshel used, to punctuate his sentences.

'Do you understand them?'

'Not always, Edmund. Every fourth word or so is a problem. But that means only a quarter is undecipherable. We'll work on the other three-quarters, eh-eh-eh.' Anshel's optimism would prove to be their deliverance. 'First, we look for a room. Do you mind sharing a room with a Jew?'

'Not unless you mind sharing with a Gentile.'

'There we are, then. Eh-eh-eh ... let's look for a district called Seraing. That's where the factory is. And let's eat. I eat everything, you too?' Another lop-sided smile.

They found a room under the roof of a tall narrow house not far from where the factory was indicated to them. It was tiny, and had hardly enough room for them to stand in. They sat on the ends of two narrow beds on either side of a high narrow window cloaked with a heavy tapestry curtain, and ate kippers and bread they had bought on the way.

'It's expensive.'

'If we get work it will be find.'

'Fine. *Fine*.'

'*Fine*, fine!' If Anshel corrected his language like that all the time, he might lose his patience; he would be tied in knots of frustration. He would explode like a flour sack. But he would also soon be word perfect.

The man at the factory laughed so hard he came close to toppling out of the tall chair behind the counter. 'Sure! Yes! Not a problem at all! *Oui, oui!* Haw-haw! Come and listen to this, Jean ...' He turned to another man behind a door. 'Jean! Come and see these two young Antwerpers. They want design work. Design work ... haw-haw-haw-haw!' He broke into a cough and wiped real tears from his eyes. 'Ooooh. I love my job sometimes. Laughing makes me digest my lunch, you know? This is good.' He slapped a thigh. 'This is rich. Haw. Rich. Haw!'

The other man, Jean, did not even smile. His face barely moved. 'You can put them in the *Salle d'Exposition*, I suppose.'

'Oooh! Whoa-haw-haw-haw – no. No! Let's make them *designers*, so that this establishment, this big success since eighteen twenty-six, will immediately run into the ground. Will suddenly get into financial trouble and close down. *Pouff!* Designers! Haw! You don't also want to cut the blanks, do you? You don't want to work on the abrasive wheel, as well, do you? Whoa-haw!'

'I cannot work on the wheel – that is specialized and artistic – but I can mark blanks.' Edmund stepped forward.

'Flemish I can handle, young man. But ... what's this, *English* now?'

Anshel spoke for him in his poor French, telling the

stupefied man what Edmund had said, and was met with guffaws and snorts.

Poker-faced Jean came forward. 'Enough with this laughter. What did you say?'

'He can mark blanks. From designs – that's what he said.'

What followed was a kind of verbal test. *What colour is the pigment? What does this mark mean? And this ... and that?* There was a silence, in which the two factory men nodded at each other and disappeared behind the door. Re-emerging with a tall woman, they pointed at Anshel and Edmund. Waiting, waiting, while they were looked up and down.

'Which one knows about blanks and marking?'

'That one, with the *Trappist* hat. But not a *word* of French, he has.'

They were bidden to follow her, and soon were filling in light green forms.

'Papers please!' The woman looked at what they had. 'Hm. Edmund Eben, all you have is a flourmill form here,' she said in French.

Edmund stared at her glowering at his precious piece of paper. He had no idea what she said, no idea what to do. No idea whether this was one of the stupidest things he had ever done.

'A paper from the mill,' he repeated, first in Flemish, then in English.

'*Mill*, say it properly.'

He wished that Anshel would shut up about his pronunciation.

'But it says your name clearly enough.' She looked at him over a pair of wire-rimmed glasses. 'Do you have an *identiteitskaart?* You lived in Antwerp all your life and do not have one? Impossible. And please speak in French!"

'But I … Not … I mean, not all my life. No.'

Anshel kicked Edmund in the heel.

He stopped talking.

She wrote something in a book, muttered *political refugee*, looked up, looked to the left, and then the right, lowered her voice, and continued in Flemish. 'Look – we need workers. All of a sudden we need people. I'll put you in the *Salle*, and you,' she turned to Anshel. 'You work in the *Seconde Salle*, and if you are any good … Look, you must do this. You must familiarize yourself with our products, with everything we make.'

'Oh, yes.'

'And then?' Anshel was still unsure.

'Then ask questions. Find out about the whole process, from furnace to exhibition. From blowing to sale. From sand to … to chandelier.'

'*Van zand uit kroonlucter.*'

'And then?'

'And then we'll see.' She looked back and forth again.

'And …'

'And the shifts are long, and you better appear on time. Hear? On time.' She pointed awkwardly at the clock behind her, and at the punch machine that took the work cards. Then she shoved pieces of paper at them both. 'Start Friday. There will be a card to punch, in and out, for each of you. Show these slips to the Salle supervisor. Wear stout boots. Hm – those are fine. We give you an apron. Don't lose it, all right? I hope neither of you is ham-fisted.'

'We are both right-handed.' Anshel beamed.

'No, no, no – *he* is, but you are a leftie. I noticed when you were writing. That's another thing. Tell the truth or they'll find you out.' She took Anshel's big hat off the counter and handed it to him. 'Edmund – is it true you can mark up from design plans?'

'Yes, Madame, it is.'

'Hm. We'll see. Start Friday. Get here early. That's all.' She dismissed them with an arch look through thick lenses. 'You might last longer than a week, if you try.'

'A week... a week? Is that all? I thought...'

'No, stupid. She meant we must *try* to last longer than a week.'

Edmund hated being called stupid. He glared at Anshel, whose lopsided face was starting to grate on him.' All right. All *right*.'

But he was optimistic, and patient. His untidiness was only a small problem in that tiny room, because neither of them had much to leave lying around.

Edmund wondered if any room-mate in the world was perfect. He thought back to his months with Uršula. Now she was far from perfect. And he still missed her.

Nine

Frustration and freckles

Disaster. It was a disaster from the start, and almost to the finish. Almost. Not a huge disaster, perhaps, but a disappointment, at best. He dithered between thinking it could not be worse, to accepting he would make the best of it given time. It was frustrating and upsetting. And it had something to do with Anshel, although not everything. And it had something to do with his own restlessness, although not always. Anshel contributed to Edmund's unease, to his self-doubt. To the sense of always being an alien, even though he was now in the 'free world'. Would he ever learn English properly? Was he stuck in Belgium, in that heavy drizzle, under those leaden skies, forever?

Even the Jewish youth's optimism grated on his ears. 'Well, Anshel, no – we might *not* learn to like it in time.'

'Of course we will.'

The factory was nothing like the one in Prague. To start with, it was more modern, and much more of the process was automated. The girls were shrill and brazen, the men were tired and had jowly faces and bloodshot eyes. Or so they seemed to Edmund, who – after more than two months in the place – was getting sick of memorizing styles and model numbers, names and dimensions.

'Hand Mr Claeys a number sixty-seven, will you?' No *please*. No *thank you*.

'The twenty-five centimetre platter with fern etching and bevelled edges?'

'Edmund, for heaven's sake, do not ask each time. Yes, yes. It's that one.'

'All right, Johanna.'

'Miss Verhoeven, please.'

It was too formal. Too exact, too stilted. It grated on his nerves. The money was not bad, and he was managing to save quite a lot of it, unlike Anshel who, having escaped the strictures of his orthodox family, was sowing wild oats all over Liège.

'But Johanna. Johanna – we have just had lunch together. Under a tree. You ate one of my pickles. I ate one of your beignets.'

'Two, you ate. But hush. This is business now.'

The bureaucracy was overwhelming. He had never seen anything like it. The old Prague factory was casual and confused, unsystematic; a state-run organization that was a shambles compared to this private enterprise. There were ledgers, report books, lists of this and lists of that. Boxes had to be ticked, inventories verified, stock accounted for, entries checked and double-checked. Inspections happened regularly. Rows of sales figures and amounts of money needed adding up. Edmund spent his entire work-day, sometimes, pushing a pen. If he saw a ledger, his stomach would come close to a heave now. He was not good at paperwork.

The artefacts were beautiful, He did not doubt the craftsmanship that went into their making. He admired the way everyone observed the rules, and called each other mister and miss, and how everyone clocked in and out so punctually. He did it himself, but he was stultified. Bored rigid. He was lonely. A stranger, and fed up. He hated, hated, detested rows of figures.

'I never thought I'd be bored in a glass factory.'

'Edmund – do you know what's wrong with you?'

'Yes, I can't add or subtract in my head. I can never remember which one is model seven-seven-four. And my pronunciation's all wrong.'

Anshel laughed. He laughed so loudly someone on the floor below would soon stand on a chair and bang on their ceiling with the end of a broom handle. 'You need something. Do something jolly. Look on the bright side. Come out, come to a pub or a café ...'

'Is there music?'

'Of *course* there's music.'

Over a greasy paper bag of too-sweet *smoutebollen*, large beers, and a pack of cigarettes in yet another brown pub, Anshel tested Edmund's English vocabulary. His mouth ringed with doughnut sugar, the little beard he was growing shone, crystalline and shiny in the pub light. The Jewish youth glimmered and growled. '*Salmon* – say it properly.'

Edmund sighed loudly and sat back. 'Oh, I am *so sick* of this!'

'Yes, good! You said that very nicely.'

'I am going mad very nicely, too.'

A voice at his shoulder. 'How can you go mad nicely?' A female voice, belonging to an angelic face. A face covered in freckles. A curly blonde, she was, with drooping eyelids and a light blue hairband that matched her eyes. Her t-shirt too was blue, unevenly tie-dyed, one big asymmetrical splotch obviously done at home. 'But I suppose you do *everything* nicely. Are you buying me a nice beer then?'

'Edmund – are you buying this young lady a beer?'

'Anshel, I'm off home. Sorry, miss. Perhaps another time?'

She laughed. The dusting of freckles over her nose

creased and crinkled. 'Another time I'll be far away in England.'

'England!' The whole world immediately expanded, grew, widened to include this young woman's country. *England. Westminster Cathedral. Queen Elizabeth. The Beatles. The Black and White Minstrels. Cilla Black. Cliff Richard.*

'Just through the way, over the water, across the channel!' She sat across from Edmund and rested her chin in one hand. 'How I finished up in Liège I really do *not* know. All I know is that it was in a yellow Volkswagen combie, with some French-speaking fellow.' A deep sigh came out of her pretty mouth.

He sat right back on the brown bench, forgetting his resolution to trudge back home on his own. 'But surely you...'

'Don't take her literally, Edmund.' Anshel turned to her. 'Edmund will now practise his English on you.'

'His English what?' She paused and burst into loud laughter. 'Oh, his *English*.' She extended a finger and poked Edmund in the chest. 'I'm sure you don't have to practise *anything*. You're perfect as you are.'

Now he saw she was quite drunk, or drugged, or both. Another woman who would never dream of wearing a soft woollen shawl, she was.

Anshel whispered, 'Do you think she is high?'

'As a kite, my darling.' Her voice was low and sweet, and she addressed only Edmund.

He wanted to know whether whoever she travelled with was still there, with her. 'Volkswagen combie. Yellow.' There was safety in repetition.

'Hm?' Her dreamy eyes fixed, fixed on his face. 'He keeps calling you Edmund. I'll call you Edmund too, if you buy me a beer.' She deliberately ignored Anshel, who got up, flapped his arms uselessly up and down, turned round and departed in a huff. 'Well, see you two later.'

He made a straight-backed exit that told Edmund he would not be in their room that evening, but off to talk and drink with the employees of a leather factory, where they tooled calf and goat skins for book binding. Most of them were Jewish, so Anshel fitted in perfectly.

'He will be all right later.'

'Who?' She looked at his fingers.

He understood her game. 'What is your name?' His English was going to come to good use.

'You have nice oval nails. Long fingers.'

'What's your name?'

'Amanda. But don't let that get in the way.'

In the way. In the way? He shook his head and smiled vaguely.

When his beers arrived, Amanda took hers up in a mock toast. 'Here's to us, Edmund. See – I do what I promise!'

She promised him the moon, and gave him what seemed like everything then, but some days later felt like nothing. Except perhaps dozens of English words he tried to commit to memory. Months, months later, one of her sentences, one of the seeds she had sown, grew into a desire.

He remembered the encounter with a wry smile, on the very day he was summoned from the Salle d'Exposition at the glass factory, to a small room whose walls were half glazed, so one could see the bent heads of workers inside, as they transcribed, copied, and printed designs and plans.

What triggered the memory of his night with Amanda, and how they were burst upon by Anshel at dawn, when he returned from his own exploits on the other side of the ancient city, were the sparse freckles on the nose of the man who took him across the factory. They were more probably due to age than sun-filled youth, but Amanda's face danced in Edmund's head.

'Are you listening? We want you to observe what happens in this design room for about a week, because Menheer Verbeke ...'

He was impressed. 'Mister Verbeke?'

'Yes - he needs someone in the marking room.'

'I think I know what happens in the design room. I used to work in one. And a marking room.'

'Do you doubt Mister Verbeke's decision?'

Edmund kept silent after that, and his promotion went on to take him to a large marking room, where he spent months placing grey and blue marks on glass blanks, mostly large platters and stemmed glasses. He had expected to inhale the pungent red-lead and turpentine smell, but in this place, the marking fluid was composed of different chemicals, and smelled rather sweet.

'We give you three pairs of white gloves, which you must keep laundered. You mustn't ask for more gloves before the year is up. Do you understand? *Compris?*'

They were excellent gloves, which made gripping the glass objects easy. But it was far from easy keeping them white and clean, not losing them, and remembering to clip them together in pairs. He found the best way was to use three wooden clothes pegs, and a cloth bag to keep them in, which reminded him of the brown checked bags Uršula used to have around her apartment, in which she kept her things. Stockings, gloves, loose buttons, small change, jar lids, tin spoons, hair kerchiefs, shop coupons, clothes pegs, hair curlers, keys, bottle tops and corks, clean glass jars.

Was he taking on habits to remind him of her? He still missed Uršula. He still felt an outsider in this place.

Compris? Compris? All they ever asked was if he understood. Never if he was all right. Never if he was comfortable. Never if he had enough money. Never if he was happy. Happy? Happy? Never.

Disaster. Disappointment. Disillusionment. He should never have come to Liège. But he could not have stood a week longer in Prague. He had yearned for freedom, and now that he was free, he felt imprisoned, caught under glass. Literally. Literally, caught under glass in that factory where he was alone, where he would never be anything but an alien.

Anshel had been summoned back to Antwerp. Bribed would be a better word, but he never said the word to him. Not because it did not enter his mind, but because he did not know how to say *bribery* either in Flemish, English, or French.

Edmund's mind reeled with it; *úplatkářství.* Bribery, bribery, bribery. *Anshel, Anshel, you fool.* Bribed by the young man's own father, who promised him a fantastical sum of francs to return to the diamond-polishing Anshel abhorred. All was forgiven, and he would not be forced into marriage to the daughter of a jewellery retailer. Well, that hopeless optimist might be happy. How could Edmund know?

Alone, alone; more alone than ever after Anshel left. He could afford to keep the room on his own, on what he made as a marker of glass blanks, which was a blessed luxury. But there was a battle royal to persuade the woman who let him the room to take down the other bed, so he could have space for a table.

Arms akimbo, mouth straight, eyebrows raised, cheeks reddening. '*Non!* I am not going to take on the expense of a table, or a chair! *Compris?*' Her explosion, in French, was half-expected.

He was not stupid. Of course he understood.

Edmund had enough French by then, enough patience, enough resilience, enough pacifying skills, to calm her down. 'All I need is space. I will obtain the table. I will get a chair.'

'You don't want a *mirror*, too, do you, to look at that ... that copper-coloured hair? And what will you do with a *table*?' Unthinkable; ridiculous, absurd. It was inconceivable that he might want to do anything as lofty as write or draw.

It was Amanda who had given him the urge, with casual, throw-away words. If only she knew how close she was to his desire. Pretty, pretty. Blonde and pretty, and quite stupefied on whatever she had smoked. Standing between the beds in nothing but what she called *knickers*, that single night, she had made him laugh twice. Once at the funny name she had for underwear, and once for what she suggested.

'You could paint me – I'm beautiful enough, darling!' And she struck an unselfconscious pose. Arms, her arms everywhere, in the air, down her sides, fingers splayed like daisies. She meant it as a sexual come-on, and it had proved quite effective. Her hands went everywhere, and she was as different from Uršula as she could possibly be. Edmund was perplexed at first, then cheered, then joyous. They had used both beds, and her boisterous intimacy managed to quell Edmund's loneliness for a while. She chattered and exclaimed the whole time.

'Amanda! You are so talkative!'

'You're so unusual! So *gentle*.'

So Uršula was right.

Months afterwards, all that the memory did to Edmund was make him think about differences, differences ... women were so bewildering. Brown hair, blonde hair, smiles, frowns, fluttering hands, downcast eyelashes, and not only that.

He was filled, more than anything else, with a yearning to draw, to paint. His blue and grey marks on those glass artefacts were even more persuasive. His fingers moved as if of their own accord, creating desire. He remembered his own designs. The ones he had painted in red-lead pigment. The ones from his own musings and wild ideas. He would not dare pull such a stunt here. Val Saint Lambert was not such a place; it was a shrine, this factory. It was a shrine to delicate, shiny, fragile objects. Everything happened precisely, to an exact plan. He could not pass off his own designs, not even to assert a small rebellion.

No. Mister Verbeke's temperament was not to be provoked in that way. Edmund kept to the factory plans, and marked, marked, marked for the duration of his interminable shifts. But he thought of landscapes, of still lifes, of portraits, of shapes, shapes. Flowers and birds and the sky streaked with red hues on cold mornings. Light, light, streaking and slanting into a room through a window too small, too narrow, to contain it. Up walls, over windowsills, lining walls, defining ceiling cornices.

He remembered how it was in Prague, waking in the dark to windowpanes icing on the inside, where the light was too grey to enter rooms; but here, how could he think about light? He needed to remember practical things. Remember the gloves, remember to clock on, remember the brushes, remember the stands, remember the plans, remember the time, the time, the time.

Ten

An owl's curved back

Brushes, brushes, small tubes of paint, more brushes. Small boards covered in canvas, ready to be coated in gesso. Linseed oil, turpentine – ah, that smell – and a couple of small knives. And more tubes of paint. Rose madder. Indian yellow. Purple lake. Viridian. Oxide of chromium. Phthalo green. Raw Sienna. Brown ochre. Raw umber. Charcoal grey. Indigo. Manganese blue. Venetian red. Zinc white. A block palette of sheets of oiled paper. A small wooden palette. A small easel? This will cost the earth, the earth.

'I don't think I can buy the easel.' He spoke to himself, a strange thing. Stranger was that he said the words in Flemish. He no longer knew who he was, or what he was. Words in his head tumbled, roared, wheeled in three languages.

She looked at him, the woman in the shop. She narrowed wrinkled eyes and looked at him. Her fingers held up a cigarette to her lips, a vee of indecision. Then she slapped her other hand down on a thick stack of pink wrapping paper on the counter. Slap. Slap. Thump.

'Take that pencil.' In Flemish. Flemish, not French.

He stared.

'You have a name?'

'Edmund.'

'Take the pencil, Edmund. Draw me a bird – on the

wrapping paper. Here.' She exhaled in round puffs.

'What kind?'

'Where are you from?'

So his accent was detected. 'Prague.'

'Prague! A barn owl, then. A Czech owl, hm? When I come back, we'll talk money.' Out through the door behind the counter, she went, old as Methuselah, short and straight as an exclamation mark.

It was a fine, fine pencil. A luxury. A combination of generous black and resilient sharpness. A sliver of paradise twenty centimetres long, with a square eraser on the end.

A small owl, on a roof. A roof with an icicle. And a hint of sheen, moisture. And a moon rising out of the corner of pink paper. Detail for the owl, moon sheen on feathers, and a tiny mouse – cross-hatched fur – caught between those claws, shaded, shaded some more ... she was back.

He did not stop. He heard her breathing but did not stop. A torn neck, a lacerated neck, for the mouse. He licked the pencil. He rubbed the paper with a knuckle. A tail, a long tail almost twitching with the last of life.

'All right. Stop.' Her hand fell flat on the paper and she turned it. Swish. Turn, peer.

She angled her face so their eyes met. 'Do you always do what you're told?'

He swallowed. He peered at the gold letters on the pencil flank. The pleasure of that brief time, all it took to sketch the bird; that pleasure was boundless. He sighed. 'But this ...' He sighed.

She heard it.

'This is such a ... a good pencil.'

'You might put it in the bag too. Good for drawing birds, I suppose – it's a Blackwing!' She smiled at last.

'I'm eighty-two. In two weeks, I close this shop for good.' Her cigarette, smoked down to the orange filter, was crushed to a tiny crimpled stub in a large glass ashtray. She exhaled and cocked her head at him. 'Come on, come upstairs and meet Gust.' She tore what he had drawn off the large sheet and held it at arm's length. 'He's sick, but he likes visitors.' With the sketch dangling from her hand, she tilted her head from side to side. 'He likes birds.' She mumbled to herself. 'I say draw a bird, and he draws a bird! Hah!' Then to Edmund. 'Turn the shop sign, will you? Closed! Closed for the day! Closed for the evening.'

Edmund did as she asked. He had not experienced any kind of hospitality since Gerrit and his grumpy wife. Perhaps this old woman had coffee. Or soup. And *smoulebollen*. Perhaps. He left behind, propped against the bottom of the counter, his bag. All that he thought he could afford, he had crammed into that checked brown shopping bag of Uršula's.

Ah. Uršula. She had never seen him like this, standing in an art supply shop, buying things to fulfil a hankering he felt now more than ever. A thirst for something ... for what? He wanted to create, to create, to fulfil a feeling. He wanted to draw, paint what he had left behind. The factory, looking like a gulag in the snow. The bridge at ... no, no, he could not think of that.

Homesickness had him by the throat. Lonely for the crude camaraderie of the squats. Sick for the warmth of that heavy checked quilt. Longing for the companionship of standing in line – with strangers who became regulars, everyone in the same predicament – for whatever provisions were available that week. None of that here. What did he want – to be alone, or with others? What did he want? To be free? This was free?

He had no idea what freedom meant any more.

Up, up, up into the rooms, the storeys over that shop. Past a warm kitchen, past several cupboards let into the thick wall. Past a radio playing softly. Past the smell of yellow soap, past a flowered curtain. Into a room where he saw the back of a dark red velvet armchair, huge, and the top of a white head.

'Here he is, Gust. You have company.'

A hand emerged and waved them forward.

'Look – he made you a bird. And his name is Edmund.'

The bushiest, whitest eyebrows in the world. 'Just Edmund?'

'Eben. I am Edmund Eben.'

'Oh – look at this. You can draw. You have the right idea. You crosshatch neatly. To make the side of a bird look rounded with life, curved, you need ... hand me that pencil!'

Edmund looked down at his own hand, where the pencil still hung. 'Ah – here you are.'

The old man scraped a few lines and dashes, and the bird's back became magically rounded. It jumped off the paper, alive. 'See what I did? Have you ever had instruction? Can we have some ...' He looked at the old woman. 'Shall we ask him to supper, Therese?' He looked up at Edmund. 'Sit down so I don't have to break my neck to look at you. Stay to supper, and ... you know, Therese always cooks enough to feed the entire population of Liège. Have you ever taken drawing lessons? Painting?'

'No. I ...'

'An autodidact. So are you staying to supper?'

'Thank you ... yes.'

'So let me tell you something about drawing birds. It's all in the posture, all right? There are several possible angles for the tail in relation to the head, and then the legs ... see?' He drew lines and circles on the back of Edmund's drawing. 'But you should be doing architectural stuff, look at that! Look at the line of the roof you drew. I'm the one who likes birds, but you – you can do more. You know, the weather has been strange today. More umbrellas up and down the street today. Depending on its mood or state of attention, a bird's legs ... are you wondering what's for supper? Because I am. I think I smell *stoofvlees*. You see we still do things the Antwerp way. We have been here for decades, but eating is eating. Now, see how the legs are pushed forward like this when the bird is at rest? Have you ever drawn buildings, interiors?' Chattering, talking, babbling happily and changing subjects every few seconds.

Edmund was charmed and fascinated. He pulled a stool over and sat near the old man, who never stopped talking.

'We are lonely now that Marguerite, from across the road, is dead and her sons have all moved away.'

'That was nearly two years ago, Gust.' Therese appeared and jangled cutlery, tinkled glasses.

The old man rose and pulled himself to table, cruising along by holding onto one piece of furniture after another. Chair back, sofa arm, sideboard. It was as if they had been placed there strategically so he could get around. He spoke the whole time, without drawing breath, leaping from drawing to painting, from neighbours who had died to the weather in Antwerp, from closing the shop to Therese's people in Liège, from ageing to investing in shares. It did not stop, until his wife brought in a large tray on which were two steaming serving bowls.

'Meat stew and mashed potatoes. You cannot get

more Antwerp than this. I am so glad you joined us on the evening I made it fresh. See? I make *stoofvlees*, and we receive a guest.' She served her husband first – a great plate of meat and potatoes, and went back to the kitchen, to return with an enormous bowl of very hot peas.

'Ah – good, peas, peas. Now serve yourself and eat. Eat, Edmund!' Those were the last words the old man said for a good half-hour. He tucked in to a big dinner, concentrating on the food, chewing each mouthful with great appreciation.

Therese winked at Edmund and smiled. 'See? All I have to do to stop him talking is prepare a nice dinner and we have peace for an hour or so. Hm!'

They never spoke about money. Edmund left what he thought was the right sum on the counter on his way out that first night, for the supplies he took away, and from the look on the old woman's face the next time he arrived, he knew it was acceptable.

Never – he could not weigh or measure what he learned from Gust Baert. Never; incalculable. He knew it would take some time before the garbling of words, words, words and topics took some hold of his mind, sink into memory, prove useful. The man could talk. The drawing they did, at that wide oval mahogany table was precious.

'Don't just disappear. Come again on Wednesday.' The white eyebrows waggled. He drew promises from Edmund, assurance he would return. They craved his company. They waited from visit to visit.

'Ah! There you are.' A hand motioning him forward. 'Listen to this.'

The music was sublime.

'Let me tell you about Bernstein. He is quite clever despite his popular appeal, you know.' Gust Baert had a big grey record player, and a drawer full of boxed collections. Jazz, opera, symphonies, and popular music theatre, and film sound tracks. Edmund looked at it with wide eyes.

'You choose. Put something on, go on.'

He was made to select background music on each visit, handling the large black records with gentle reverence, until he did not know what he looked forward to most – music, music, music or the drawing lessons. Then there were politics, philosophy, literature, avian anatomy, religion, art, history, and social theory. They were brought up, discussed, debated; jumbled and convoluted, but fascinating. Not only for the content, but the ease with which they tumbled from the old man's mouth.

Weeks went by, months. Edmund sketched well, gaining approval from the old man and his wife, whose grasp of art history, whose memory, was phenomenal. Wishing, wishing, wishing he would age in this way, with the lives and works of the expressionists, the impressionists, the Pre-Raphaelites, lodged neatly in his head. No, in his heart. Therese's knowledge did not seem to flow from her brain. It erupted, with some passion, from her heart, but she made no undue fuss. She would light a cigarette, hold it in the erect vee of her fingers, squint against the smoke, and softly, slowly, present her precise, neat facts.

'I don't know if I have it right, now,' she always started.

Edmund had no doubt she did.

Gust Baert nodded and smiled. Not in awe of his wife, but gravely, simply acknowledging her mastery of the art theory at whose practice he excelled.

People knew who he was. Edmund dropped the old man's name around Liège and it was recognized. His work hung in a number of galleries. He had a large painting on permanent exhibition at the Musée Curtius. Signed in tiny letters on the right-hand bottom corner. Augustus H Baert.

Although Therese treated him like an invalid, Edmund could see nothing gravely wrong with the old man, except perhaps the need for him to steady himself as he cruised armchair to sideboard, sofa to table. Perhaps it was a weak heart. A heart that was certainly deeply and emotionally submerged in his art, and in the books that were the mainstay of his youth.

'Read Conrad, of course, and then think of the life of Lou Andres Salome, and read the poems of Rilke, and then – you have English? Good, you know English – then you must read John Fowles. Let me tell you about Fowles. He is writing some interesting ... and don't forget we are having some nice *waterzooi* tonight so you must stay, because Therese will be offended if you do not taste her wonderful soup. Marguerite's boys are gone. We had none of our own, you see. And read Hugo Claus ... perhaps there is an English translation of his poems, or you can read them as they are. Now where you come from is curious, remarkable. Many churches and things.'

'Most are now ...'

'Yes, yes. The Communist thing is lamentable. But really, you must go to the New World, because that's where you will be safe from ... they are saying the world is heating up. Hah! The greenhouse effect, they call it. Now when I was young, I grew tomatoes – yes, tomatoes in the middle of Antwerp, under a glass dome that someone ... you said you work in a glass factory. Of course – Val Saint Lambert. Now that is nothing, nothing like drawing birds and oh! Water – let me tell you the theory of drawing and painting water. You see,

Leonardo created this great folio where ... ah! Here's dinner. What did I tell you? Waterzooi! But study Leonardo's architectural things ... and look at the work of Peter Ilsted. Ah – good soup, this.'

Then there was silence, broken only by sighs of contentment and polite slurps from his pursed mouth. And his lowered eyes all but hidden under those remarkable eyebrows. Very nearly half an hour of silence, during which the beautiful chicken soup, with whole sections of fowl, tender and very very hot, were eaten together with irregularly chopped carrot, turnip, celery, marrow, potato, translucent onion, the occasional sliver of lemon peel, and streaks of beaten egg like strands of sunshine that resisted the attack of spoon, fork, or knife, all slippery in a golden broth that must have simmered for hours inside the kitchen where Edmund had never been.

'Some people beat the egg right in so the broth thickens. But we like to see where it is.' Therese wielded a spoon with delicate little movements, herself a bird. 'And you say you are bound for America, Edmund. Not too soon, I hope.' With her shop below now closed, Therese craved his company. 'You think we are important to you, because you are learning and gaining friends in an alien place, like you said. It must be like time-travel for you, coming out of all those shortages and deprivation into the nineteen-sixties!'

'Nineteen-seventies, soon! Just a few years.'

'Yes, yes – but we ... we feel you are important to *us*.'

She had heaped what was left of art supplies in a box, jammed at the bottom of those narrow stairs, in their *maison et boutique*, and often gave him something on his way out. A tube of paint, a precious pencil, a stack of handmade papers, a bendable human model made of teak, a long thin brush.

'Let me tell you about America, son.' Gust cruised over to his big red armchair via the sideboard, sofa arm, chair back and table. 'Ah!' An enormous sigh as he gentled his body into the hollowed out form of his body the armchair provided. 'Let me tell you why it's completely the wrong place for you. Now – that dinner was delicious, and it's because Therese orders meat and chicken straight from the farm, where they feed livestock some secret kind ... Yes, domestic fowl ... infinitely interesting and easy to draw. Feathers, you see, are forgiving. You can add a dozen pencil strokes to correct an angle – remember angles when drawing birds – and everything adjusts under your own nose. But rooms – buildings ... aha, not so easy. Faces, not so easy.'

'But why should I not go to America?'

'America? All wrong for you. Coffee? Shall we have a coffee now?' He looked at his old but sprightly wife. 'I can hear noise from the street. It's not Christmas already, is it?'

Edmund shook his head and waited, knowing it would come out, this man's advice, in its own time, between the weather, seasons, recipes, death notices, quotes from poems and classic works, bits of biographies, histories, and local gossip. Between ruing their lack of children, rejoicing over some football win, lamenting the lack of flavour in some beers, or wondering where his old black jacket had ended up.

'That jacket was threadbare, Gust.'

'So you gave it away.'

'No, I did not.' Therese was adamant. But she was truthful. 'It went in the bin. No elbows to speak of, it had.'

'America is all wrong for you, because of what I

think. I think a lot, about you, about Michelangelo's church ceilings, and how the mezzotint is probably the highest of the arts. I also think of how you must find it so boring placing marks on vases and bowls when you really should be either playing the organ or painting portraits. How's this for a profile?' The old man angled his face. 'Ha ah ha! Marguerite's youngest son tried, but he had no idea that faces are like buildings – not forgiving at all. Distances ... and I do not mean the distance between Liège and Antwerp, mind you ... have we had anything for a snack yet? Perhaps a nice coffee and a slice of tarte framboise? Or am I just wishful thinking?'

Therese came in with a tray. 'Dessert, gentlemen?'

He smiled. 'See? This is a terrific woman, and you have noticed that already. So you must find one soon, but not here, not here. Find one in Australia.'

'Australia!'

Therese handed him a plate with a generous slice of raspberry tart on it. 'We talk about you when you are gone, you know. We will miss you, son, but you must go to Australia. There you will be able to paint.'

The old man gazed at his plate. 'I know you are thinking you can paint anywhere. It is not so. Not here, not here. You see this place is wonderful, it's like a big brown pub, the whole of Belgium. Did I tell you I think the King will abdicate? Now that is a face to paint. But it's been done. Stamps and portraits, the vehicles for kings. And this is a very good tart, so eat it.'

While he ate, Edmund wondered why they suggested Australia. It had never entered his head. The world took on a wider aspect, just as it did when he met Amanda. He remembered her and her freckles, thinking there must be many freckled girls in Australia.

'Mm.' Gust wiped his mouth on a voluminous

napkin, and rolled it over itself, many times, his skeletal hands mobile and impatient. 'Go to England. Get in line, ask them to include you in their ten-pound program.'

Therese nodded, looking at Edmund's dumbfounded face. 'In that way, you will not be regarded as a refugee. Never say the word refugee, you understand? It's the best way to land in some godforsaken, distant, forgotten camp.'

'Getting to England is a matter of going to Ostend, and taking the ferry. Now Ostend has a very nice gothic cathedral dedicated to Saints Peter and ... I have painted it many times. Therese ...'

Edmund took a deep breath. The old man turned to face him. 'Sit closer so I don't have to crane my neck to see you. In Australia they will welcome you, because they need to populate that vast land, and you will be able to paint. The climate is ... and their *birds*, their birds! It rained all day today. I have been thinking of taking a stroll, but Therese won't hear of it. I have a book about their famous painters somewhere. Very innovative, they are, those Australians, because they hanker for a history, see? But you will take yours with you ... ha ha! Not only history, I mean, but your paints and things and you can paint on the ship as you go over. Three months, it takes. Practise your English.'

Eleven

A novel packed with banknotes

England, England. England. *Ten-pound program.* Edmund did not know what that was or whether he could ever be included. The only papers he had were a form, from the glass factory, bearing his new name. And his old Czech identity card. Instead of puzzling over the decision of whether to listen to the old couple over the closed art shop, or to resume his old plan of trying to get to America, he painted.

He coated canvas cards in gesso. Card after card after card, propped up all over his tiny room. They took an interminable time to dry, in that small damp space at the top of the house. Leaving the window open was a mistake. The rain slanted in and wet his pillow. The smell of linseed oil and turpentine excited him, though, and he tried to understand why Gust told him to paint interiors. He was not that good at perspective, but he did not allow frustration to slow or stop him.

He painted his room from all angles, and the rooftops across the way. His bed, the angle near the ceiling, with his coat hanging from a hook.

He spoke to Johanna at the factory. He took her out for a drink. He wondered whether her sculpted angular face was what Gust meant. 'I could paint you one day,' he said. Vague, vague, but he was starting to want youthful female company. She was attractive in her own way. 'You could come up to my room, and I could paint you.'

Johanna took the large globe of a glass and sipped her Kriek beer. 'I suppose.'

On the way to her house, she slipped her hand under his elbow. It was promising. At her door, he kissed her cheek.

'Oh!'

'Johanna, next Friday, perhaps we shall do this again.'

They did, and she sat and sipped her Kriek Lambic in exactly the same way, so it was hard to think a whole week had gone by in which he had marked several hundred rectangular cake platters with scavos and stipple after stipple after stipple, swags of pinch-notches and vees.

'We can go to my room and I can make a small sketch of you, perhaps. Head and shoulders. What do you think, Johanna?' Edmund had tidied the room, stretched the bedclothes tightly over the narrow bed in the corner and put away all his clothes in preparation for her visit. He was thinking of more than just a sketch. Perhaps she would spend the night with him and they would squeeze into that small bed.

She looked at him in a straight unflinching gaze. 'Edmund, I don't think it's quite the right thing for me to do. I asked my mother, and she said as a Catholic girl I really cannot risk either my reputation, or for things to get out of hand, before we are married. *Ça ne se fait pas.* It's not nice.'

'*Married!*'

Her face went a deep red, then her lips went white. Her hand was halfway to her mouth with the beer glass but she set it down, down again very deliberately. Slowly. 'Edmund.'

'What?'

'So mother was right when she said your intentions might not be serious.'

No idea. No idea what to say.

'Say something. You can't lead a girl on like that and then ask her to your room on a pretext. It's not nice.'

Speechless. Did she really think he considered marriage? Just like that?

'Johanna ... we are ... it's ... these are the nineteen-sixties. People aren't as – '

'Please take me home. It's insulting to think you were only thinking of taking advantage of me. Sketch ... portrait ... head and shoulders! It's not *nice*.'

From then on, they addressed each other formally, and only if necessary, at the factory. She never again allowed their eyes to meet. Still, Edmund remembered her well, because in one of their conversations, she did confirm that what the Baerts had told him was true.

'My sister's husband is English,' she had said one day, long before he had asked her out to have a drink at a pub. They sat under a tree having lunch during a factory break. 'It's quite remarkable – they have a ten-pound scheme. English people can sail to Australia to settle, very cheaply. They are not refugees, they are emigrants.' Her words were prim, but the information, when he remembered it, was useful.

Eventually, it was the IOM that gained him access to England, and then onto a liner bound for Fremantle, in Western Australia. The whole operation cost him a great deal more than ten pounds, which was only the price for his passage over, but it was not money he paid reluctantly. After all, saving, squirrelling, stashing, hoarding money was second nature to him. In a sock, in an old envelope, in an old tobacco tin, inside the leaves of a paperback novel in English, folded into Uršula's old checked shopping bag, he divided and sorted his money from the glass factory until something told him it was time. The novel grew so thick with packed banknotes it could hardly close.

Leaving the Baerts was not easy, and he came away in tears, as he left them, clutching a small table easel, the last thing the tiny old woman thrust into his hands as they walked through the old closed and vacant shop below their house.

'Now we await your letters, from anywhere you land. Do not forget us. Gust is getting weaker, as you know, and he will now live for your words. English, Dutch, French ... any language you care to write in. We'll be waiting.' Her cheeks were far from dry.

Edmund could not speak past the knot in his throat, which welled more the further he walked from that closed shop. They had liked him, valued him, for who he was. Orphan or not, displaced or not, Czech or not. Would he ever find that again? He could hardly swallow. Throat aching, aching. Breath shallow until he turned the corner at the chocolate shop. He might never turn that corner again.

There was excitement in his heart too, a flurry, a loose shingle of hope and exhilarated anticipation. The next afternoon, he was due to stand in line for the ferry at Ostend.

'You are a displaced Balt.'

Edmund looked at the man behind the counter, fighting the desire to respond. He won the internal battle against defending what he was to himself. *I am a travelling artist*, he wanted to say. *I am a citizen of the world. I am free.* They were words he could have used, as he learned very well from listening to youthful travellers in Belgian pubs.

But he held his tongue. As he also did in England. *'Ah, a displaced Balt.'* They all said it. They read it from their lists, their manifests, their big books of names.

He held his head high and did not nod, but tacit acceptance was acceptance nevertheless, and he received a stamped certificate, which was nothing but a glorified receipt for his ten pounds.

'You are a displaced Balt. Four hundred of you on this ship alone, fifty of which are Czech. Enjoy your assisted passage to Australia.'

The piece of paper to add to his little stash of identification documents showed he was in book 291, number 87, published by the Commonwealth of Australia, and the name on the dotted line was scrawled so badly as to be illegible. Only the capital Es of his name could be made out.

'And what is that thing?'

'My bags, and this is an easel.' These were words he had practised many times.

'Ah – your English is quite good. Well done. But that is not a camera easel.'

'No – a painting easel. For canvases.'

'Wood will need fumigating when you arrive in Fremantle. Welcome aboard the *Australis*. There are eighteen hundred other emigrants going on today. Please put your luggage on the rack.'

Many of those eighteen hundred people were under twelve, he took note, with occasional annoyance about the noise, mess, and continual running about on deck. Children were more prone to seasickness than some adults, which made the interminable voyage less than completely comfortable. Besides, sharing a tiny cabin – several of which had obviously had been partitioned off from a larger stateroom – with three other single men, made it cramped and smelly.

But they all spoke like Amanda. He listened to them speak to each other, and smiled, smiled, broke into laughter when he remembered her say *knickers*, and *darling*, and *perfect*, and *you're so gentle!* And he saw a few blonde women, and light blue eyes, and perfect teeth. And rosy cheeks on prattling youngsters.

'The ship is entirely packed with noisy, sick children,' he said to himself in English, one sunny afternoon, after being bumped on the shins by a little girl racing about on deck, as he was stretching his legs. Leaning, rubbing, rubbing his bruised leg, swearing in three languages under his breath. 'And it is getting too hot.' Leaning, leaning, struggling out of his brown jacket.

'Of course it's hot.' A young man at his elbow pointed out to sea. 'That's Capetown. See that line of land on the horizon? South Africa. Some days ago, I cannot recall how many, we crossed the Equator ...'

'The noise was unbelievable.'

'Yes – people celebrate the crossing, it's only natural.'

Edmund smiled. Although there was nothing natural about crossing a notional line on the globe, he could see now that he could either make the rest of the voyage as miserable as the beginning had been, or he could cheer up and talk to some fellow passengers, such as this young Englishman. 'Are you English?'

'We'll all soon be Australians, I suppose. I am a British subject, yes, born in Malta. Maltese, Maltese. I'm joining my uncle in Melbourne. Do you have a sponsor?'

'I have papers to introduce me to an employer in Melbourne. Assigned to me by the IOM. I'm a displaced person. That's what they all keep calling me. That's as close as I could get to being sponsored.'

The man nodded. 'Melbourne! That's exceptional

luck. Most are shunted to the country. See that man in the yellow shirt? His destination is the Queensland hinterland.'

It meant absolutely nothing to Edmund.

'He'll have to endure many more days' travel after he gets off the ship in Fremantle. And then he'll cut sugar cane for the rest of his days. What happens to you in Fremantle?'

'Just a train to Melbourne, to face my new employer.'

'Employers are sometimes better than kin. More useful, at any rate. My uncle's not very friendly ... barely civil. He's made me promise to pay for my keep, despite what the forms and papers say. Over a barrel, that man has me. As dour and stingy as his brother, my dear departed father.' This was sarcasm Edmund had not heard since Prague. Recognizable, familiar, identifiable.

'I understand,' he said. Candid. Open. 'I do understand. He must be a man who has faced hardship.'

The Maltese man tilted his head from side to side, and then nodded. 'Haven't we all? What do you think I'm doing here, on this crowded ship?'

Edmund looked around, seeing now similar stories on all the men's faces, and twice that on the troubled faces of the women. None of them on that ship was sailing away from happiness or good fortune, and none could predict what they were sailing onto. The pall of anxiety was palpable; a cloud of hope hovered over all their heads. 'We're all sailing towards a kind of freedom we cannot even pronounce.'

The young man seemed surprised. 'You are Polish? Hungarian?'

'Czech, but I have lived in Belgium for nearly five years.'

'So you speak French? Much use that'll be in

Australia!'

'French and Flemish ...'

'Flemish?'

'Very similar to Dutch ... and English, English, English.' Edmund buried his neck in shoulders warming from the sun. Elbows on railing, he peered out to sea, with a tear-inducing fresh breeze in his face. He would never forget the roll of the swell, the smell of choppy sea, the scudding clouds ahead of them, the occasional streaks in the water he was told were dolphins. Dolphins! Sometimes it rained, diagonal rain which was sharp and fast, and stinging, unlike the soft heavy Belgian drizzle that greyed his days there. Sometimes there were rain and sunshine together, sunshine and rain, and often, the moon and sun in the sky at once.

'Is that a normal thing?'

'I have no idea.'

No one knew much – they were all in the same predicament, but it was so different from standing in line for food rations in Prague.

They reached a point in the voyage – a magical point, he felt it – when they went from being a departing crowd, a crowd that had left a world behind, to a crowd that was on the way; arriving somewhere. The change was noticeable. In one night, regret, longing and distress transmuted into anticipation. They no longer moved away from, but toward something.

He thought of Anshel, of Amanda, of the Baerts, of old Gerrit and his dour wife. And of Uršula, Uršula. He had left them all behind. Even Ludvik, the soldier on the train, who had a strong belief in liberty. Ahead was real freedom, perhaps, such as he had never felt since leaving Prague. He sailed towards everything that was new, armed with nothing but paint brushes and hope.

He said so much to people at table.

'You have languages, which is the main thing.'

There were three sittings for dinner, and he always sat next to someone different, grateful that the four hundred or so children had a dinner sitting all to themselves, and it was possible to eat in comparative peace.

He ate sausages that were nothing like the sawdust-tasting ones in Prague, bread that was nothing like the delicious bread of Belgium, fried eggs that tasted metallic, boiled vegetables that seemed too limp, and bland sauces and puddings he could not identify.

'What is this?'

'Sponge pudding and custard. Delicious!'

'Pudding.' He remembered, *P is for pudding* in the English alphabet books of Gerrit's wife. So this was what that strange bowl-shaped thing was. Pudding. His spoon sank into the sponge and he tasted it. Sweet, sweet, warm and comforting. 'Pudding. I like it. *Vynikající.*'

'Beg your pardon?'

'Delicious.'

'How many languages can you speak?'

He always smiled at that question. 'Just enough to get me through, around, and past.'

They always laughed.

He had languages, but he felt as if big parts of him were being left in each place he visited. Broken off, scraped, lacerated. A leg in Liège, an arm in Antwerp, his stomach at the station in Zábřeh, skin off his face on the train to Belgium. His drawing fingers on the mahogany table of Gust Baert. His scalp on the low bulkhead of his shared cabin. His heart, his heart, at the glass factory, where Uršula was still marking blanks with that abominable red stuff. Blowing funnels of grey smoke during her break, at the leaden sky over the factory. Did she think of him? Perhaps. Perhaps she did now.

Twelve

Rabbit fur

Melbourne was a revelation, from the traffic and well-mannered crowds, to its mish-mash architecture. Australians spoke an English that did not sing to Edmund's heart. It took a good month before his ears could take in whatever was said to him without some repetition, explanation, reprise, clarification. He was perplexed often by more than just the language. Somehow, he was expecting something like American pop culture, which he had seen in so many films while he was in Belgium; with very large cars like aeroplanes, and an ice-cream parlour on every corner. It was nothing like that. Nothing like that at all.

A few days, sparse waking hours, a flash in his mind was England before his voyage, but he had also imagined Australia was to be like that; very similar, with small quaint shops, red pillar boxes, and a population made up of descendants of English convicts. The last was hardly true anymore, he was to find. There were complexions and features from all over the world, from dark swarthy skin of Sicilians and Greeks, to high cheekbones very similar to his own. Perhaps he would fit in. He and his red hair would disappear into the crowd.

Here, cars drove on the left, and traffic signs were universal, he supposed, but everything else was surprising, new, and different from the shipboard dreams his head had conjured for him on the way. Vastly different from anything anyone had said, even the English officers on board the *Australis*, when they were asked, frequently and stridently, by many of the emigrants. 'What's it like? What's it like?'

His assigned employer, a milliner, was out in the sprawling suburbs, not in Brunswick as it said on his letter of introduction. He rode on a bus as far from the city centre as one could get. And then, without notice, after just a few days' work, and boarding at the local hotel with several other immigrants, who worked picking fruit, he was sent on a train even further, to settle in a country town.

'You're a hat maker, aren't you, young fellow? So make hats you shall.'

'I shall?' He had hardly worked a week at the milliner's shop, taking in the startling variety of hat styles. 'Here,' the milliner had said, before he was sent off. He threw a large pamphlet at Edmund. 'Here's an old catalogue you might like, Ed. All the hat styles are in there. You look the bookish sort! Read it.'

It was a very old catalogue, but interesting, after having spent a short time in that shop. The names were peculiar. The materials strange, the fashions enduring.

'Plenty of rabbit pelts out in the country, let me tell you. Can't cull the creatures fast enough.' The person telling him this wrote out a letter for him on a large rectangle of yellow paper and put him on a bus.

'Rabbits?'

'That's what some hats are made of. Felt – it's made of rabbit fur.'

'But I ...'

'You can't work in a shop that's closed, mate. That's for sure. Wangaratta will be lovely for a man who's used to European villages.'

He reeled, stumbled, blinked in the white sunlight when he got off the train. It was nothing like what the man promised. No central square. No old men in cloth caps playing chess in dim cafés. This was no village.

'As similar to a Czech or Belgian village as chalk is to cheese. Is that what you're saying?' That was what he was told when he exclaimed about the difference.

'Chalk and cheese?'

'That's an Aussie expression mate – when things are very different, they're like chalk and cheese, okay?'

It tickled his humour. A distinct liking for Australian informality, humour, and notions of equality rose inside Edmund Eben. It was a sentiment he had never thought he would feel.

'You might be a newcomer, mate, but you look pretty much like a common Joe Blow, and everyone can say your name, which is a start! No Imski-Omski with you. That ginger hair will get you places.'

'Ginger. *Ginger.* Places?'

'Anywhere you like, mate.'

But it was rough in the hat factory, where he was put on the steamers, stacking hat cones as they came out of the presses. The rabbit fur was fused by steam, and pressed into conical shapes, which turned orange with the heat, all heavy and blistering hot with steam.

'Hotter than boiling water!'

'What?'

'Don't put your hands or face in the way of that steam, Ginger.'

He was glad of the warning. The cones left him in piled stacks, still searing and cloudy with steam, on their way to the blocks, where they were shaped into hats, cooled, and stacked once more.

Then they disappeared, down a long passage to the

women on sewing machines, where bands were sewn on, inside and out. Trimming and buffing further down, and then tissue paper wrapping and packing was done before boxing.

Dizzy, dizzy with heat and finding it hard to breathe, he was shown the entire process. He never once dreamed he would find himself stripped to the waist in an oven of a tin shed, stacking cone after cone after cone after cone. Hot, hot hands, hot chest, hot feet in boots he longed to kick off.

'What do you mean you're off?'

'Off?'

'Ya can't *leave* yet, mate! We were promised by the agency or whatever they call themselves that you'd work out the year.'

'But it's only August. And it's too hot.'

'It's the middle of *winter*, ya drongo.'

'Drongo?'

'You nutcase. You idiot. You madman. You clod. You nincompoop. You ignoramus. Just wait till it's summer and this place fairly *boils*.'

Edmund turned away. Turning, turning, turning back when he heard the man call another one names, possibly more colourful than the ones he had addressed to him.

'This isn't where you leave those dockets, Pete, ya dodo. You bloody wombat, you ugly mug, you sucked mango. You lousy bastard. I feel sorry for you, hah hah hah! You'll get this right, one day. Or perhaps you won't, ya dag. Ya drongo.'

They both laughed, both, both – the insulter and the insulted, slapping each other on the back.

Edmund turned, turned back. Stared at them. Looked from one to the other. They stared back. It dawned on him, in a vague way. You smiled if they insulted you, and you turned it into a friendly gesture. A game, perhaps. 'So I can leave?'

Both laughing men waggled heads at him. 'Work another month, mate, and Charlie over there in the nice dry cool office will sign your docket, and you can head back to Melbourne, out of this heat. It'll take you a while to get that the further north you go, the hotter it gets. Not like home, eh? Not like Poland or wherever you're from.'

'Prague.'

'Prague, Poland – same difference. Ha ha ha!'

'Where's he from?' A third man joined them. Red singlet sweat-pasted onto his torso like paint. Corrugated forehead grimed with sweat and grit. 'What did he say?'

Edmund smiled at him and followed suit. 'Prague, ya drongo.'

'Ha ha ha! You're quick on the uptake, for sure. Stop with us at the pub later, and we'll drink your pay away, ay?'

'Piss it down the gutter, we will.'

'Yes, piss it down the gutter, you lousy bastards.' Edmund found a linguistic way into a left-handed kind of friendliness.

'Hah ha ha ha!'

He had two more months to work before he could get back on the coach away from the hat factory and the "village" that was Wangaratta. It was nothing like a European village, populated with mainly wool workers from all parts of the globe, and not one Czech person. Not that he hankered for company of that nature, now that he understood what it took to become Australian.

He carried his easel out sometimes and painted *en plein air*, trying to capture the landscape on canvas. With a brush in hand, the words of Gust Baert came to him sharply, and he understood why the old man thought he should paint architectural things, large things. Sheds, sheds, warehouses. He was starting to love this land, too. It was land the like of which he had never seen, with a million different greens, rounded hills, and outcrops of rock whose greys were impossible to replicate. Gun metal, charcoal, steel.

The air was so clean and clear visibility carried for miles into the distance, so trees were one inch tall, but perfectly visible, their outline perfect, their features flattened. The light was intoxicating. He woke thinking he could paint it. 'I can paint light.'

'Yeah – pull the other one, mate.'

'No really – look. And ... no, really, look, look at that.' He pointed. 'That's a trick of the light. The landscapes look painted. The land looks like someone *painted* it onto the distance.' Edmund pointed outward, to where rounded hills pocked with strange vegetation rose like waves, like rounded swell he had seen on the ocean. The light captured it, sent the hills back, brought them forward, flattened them.

People came to look over his shoulder, but never more so than when he painted inside some shearing shed, warehouse, or store. He liked beams, rafters, warped floors whose planks were grey with age. 'Look at that! Look how he does the light.'

He heard their praise, their surprise.

'You should be in the city, Ed. Get to the city and paint things there. You'll get noticed, I reckon.'

Thirteen

St Kilda

Perhaps Edmund Eben was doomed to missing. Missing. Longing. Craving. Yearning. Aching for something he could not name. Missing the rough fellows he drank with in Wangaratta now. Blokes, they called themselves, blokes who drank themselves silly, insulted each other gleefully, and smoked their throats hoarse. He fitted in and stood out. All at once.

He was the redhead who could paint, the ginger one they called "Blue", the one with the weird accent, the one destined to leave for the city. So they saw him off, still teasing and joshing on the platform at the station. 'Sure we'll give you a lift. Can't wait to see the back of ya. Ha ha ha! Where's your gear?' One of them hauled his big bag.

'No more steaming hats, no more bloody rabbit pelts for you, ay, Blue? Get down to the city and show them what's what, you cheerful bastard. Show 'em, Ed. Paint your heart out – make a few more pictures like you made of the public bar ... all browns and what not.'

'What not.'

'Ha ha ha. And go on giving as good as you get.'

'It's never enough, you sod!' Edmund knew what to say now, and his vowels shortened and lengthened as the weeks went past. 'You fellas always get me. I'm ... stumped!'

'Too brainy for yer own good, ya galah!'

They punched his arms, teased him about the amount of luggage he carted off, and waved until the train was out of sight and he could haul himself in from leaning out to the waist.

He had looked hard at the landscape and figured this brown, grey and green place, this place of a hundred browns, was not a country for pretty pictures. No climate for sweet pinks and blues. Watching the landscape whip sideways outside the train window, under the scorching sun, the details blurred but the colours remained; sun baked, sun dried, sun bleached, sun drenched, sun masked. Brown, orange, ochre red, dark yellow, dun, beige, gold, taupe. His palette, his palette, his colours. His paints. His Australian colours. He sat back on the uncomfortable seat and thought, thought, imagined a big palette daubed with beige and brown, brown and ochre, ochre and tawney red.

They had warned him to seek another employer before he jumped on the train, something to go to when he arrived, but he could not possibly endure another week in that hot steaming hat factory. Besides, talking on the phone was something he had learned to hate. He would find something in Melbourne, surely. He would stumble upon someone in need of help. He had to take the risk, even though he had less money than he thought he would, due to the drinking he did with the fellows.

'Your turn to shout, Blue!'

And his shout would cost him quite a few dollars. Cheerfully, cheerfully was the only way to take it. Cheerfully. Gleefully. Optimistically, like he learned from Anshel. He was learning. Learning to look on the positive side of it all. He was becoming Australian. This was the only way to take it all on. An exercise in assimilation. One he found challenging. One he found daunting. One he could do. This was where he would stay. The small print at the bottom of one of the pamphlets he was given said it all. It was a matter of twenty months, perhaps, before he could confirm his commitment, become an Australian citizen, and he had every intention of doing so. So. So. So he would be the person he wanted to be. Edmund Eben, artist. Edmund Eben, *Australian*.

And he would do it in Melbourne. His first impression, when he had got off the train months ago, was a good one, and it was not negated when he stepped off the Wangaratta train on his return. Certainly not Prague, but there was a feel around the town he liked, something he could not describe in words.

'Righty-oh, the work office ... Straight down Collins, and second left, and watch for the trams, mate.'

He loved the trams, and rode them willingly, but often got lost, which merely improved his English, through asking for directions and chatting with pedestrians. It familiarized him with the way people spoke. It taught him how to speak, how to intone his sentences, how to modify his drawl. He knew his letter of introduction to the first milliner's shop would still open doors. The receipt from the shipping office would still do the trick.

He spoke about looking for work everywhere he went.

'What's your line of work?'

'I've just left a hat factory. In Wangaratta.'

'The best place for you ... do you know the best place for you?' An effeminate young man turned to him in a delicatessen, which Melbourne people called a *milk-bar*, a place where the smells of ice cream, milk, confectionery, cheese, bread, and ham mingled with the dry dusty scents of cigarettes and newspapers. The youth spoke to him sideways, eyes cautious, when he heard Edmund talking about finding work.

Edmund waited for his suggestion, waiting, waiting and looking at how the white street light, the unique watery muted Melbourne light slanted into the shop, staining floor, counter, wall, and shopkeeper, with yellow, white, yellow, faun. He turned, turned, following the light, committing the colours and angles to memory, examining the strange youth, whose hair appeared dyed, and whose eyelashes bore faint traces of some sort of make-up.

'I'm Les. I'm down at St Kilda. There's a great hat shop just behind where I live. And I bet you the fellow who runs it could do with a bit of a hand.'

'A *bit* of a hand?'

'Some help.'

'Will you go with me part of the way?'

The youth looked surprised. 'Sure. The tram goes along the seafront, and we get off near Fitzroy Gardens. Then we'll get up the hill, and down again a bit. I'll be home then, but I'll show you where to go.'

'Where do you work?'

'At the Prince of Wales. And um ... at the Ritz.'

'A hotel? And I cannot find work there?' Edmund wondered if he could be a porter or something similar.

'I don't think so, somehow. You're a bit too straight.'

'Straight?'

'You'll figure it all out, soon enough.'

Edmund enjoyed his tram ride to that part of town, which immediately gave him a familiar sense, a feeling of déjà vu. Smells, smells, sights and sounds that did not quite ring with good taste, that ran just short of seedy, that gave him a shiver of doubt, but which threw him back to Prague, some Prague back streets, which came alive only at night. At the milliner's, a big man who looked hale and robust, and somewhere in his forties, perhaps, was arranging hats in the window.

'Harry – give this man a job, darling.'

'Ha ha – get out of here, Les. Not another of your girls.'

'Not this one, my dear. This one's for real. Cheerio!'

Alone, alone with Harry the hat man in his hat shop.

'I have no work for you, young fellow.' An accent, an accent recognized.

Edmund broke into Czech. *'Dobrý den, pane.'*

Harry's face was a picture of surprise. 'This is Melbourne – we speak English, I suppose, but .. but ... *vítejte, příteľ!'*

'Thank you. Thank you for the welcome. I seek work. And a proper place to stay. The men's lodge in the city is ...'

'Awful. Yes. Well, there are rooms right above this shop, and the one next door. I'll give Clare a ring. She'll come down and speak to you. But work... so tell me, how long have you been in Australia?'

The story of his journey, including the long voyage, tumbled out, peppered with Czech words and phrases. As he spoke, Edmund noticed how he dwelled on the good parts, the positive aspects, the encouragement he had found, the optimism and confidence he had gained since the dawning of how things worked in this country came to him. 'I think I like it here.'

'You look like you do, you sound like you do, most certainly.' Harry dialled a phone and soon a young woman joined them.

'Clare will rent you a room.'

'How about a little place of your own?' She was petite and alert, with arched painted-on eyebrows.

'I might not afford it. I need work. I was in Wangaratta, and ...'

'Oh my! Working in the wool mill!'

'In the hat factory.'

'Hear that, Harry?'

The shopkeeper ducked behind the counter, invisible, invisible for a long moment.

Evading the question, perhaps, avoiding having to explain why he would not offer Edmund a job. A long moment, when Edmund looked at the young woman, Clare, in her twinset and pearls, her tweed skirt, her patent leather shoes. She must be English. He had seen women dressed in that way on his way to the wharf. He should ask her where she was from. Everyone did that to open conversations. He liked her short bobbed hair, held back on either side by clips with pearls to match her necklace.

'Are you ...' Interrupted. Stopped. Halted by Harry's arm that emerged, shooting up, long and brown, from behind the counter. Just an arm, holding aloft a hat, which twirled, like in a circus act.

'Harry!' Clare laughed.

It went on, a twirling, twisting, weaving hat on an arm.

Edmund understood. 'Homburg!'

The hat and arm disappeared; replaced, replaced in a flash by another. Spinning, spinning in the fingers of that long brown arm.

'Trilby!'

Quickly, rapidly, replaced by another.

'Pork pie!'

And another.

'Panama!'

And still another.

'Fedora!'

And another.

'Cap, cap – um ... eight-point cap.'

And another.

'Boater!'

And another.

'Beaver top hat!'

And Harry's head, beaming, wearing a deer stalker. 'I wish I could employ you full time, but I can only afford ... three days a week, perhaps. Now listen, you are *impressive*. They don't make all these hats up there at Wangaratta – they make broad-rimmed felt hats for countrymen. Cattleman hats for drovers, they make, farmers... how do you...?'

Edmund looked at his shoes. 'It's not special. I do what everyone does. I make sure I know as much as I can about anything I do, or work at.'

'Oh, it's special, believe me. It's special. Well done. I can pay you by the hour, all right? You work, you get paid. You don't work ... well – then you don't earn. Start on Monday, next week. And soon maybe, perhaps, maybe I can take a holiday.'

'A holiday!' Clare's eyes widened. 'That'll be a first, Harry. You never budge from this shop.' She moved closer to the hatter. 'And you'll trust a blow-in with your shop?'

'Three days, I'll take, for my sister's wedding. Besides, he is Czech.'

'Australian, soon.' Edmund let him know he heard.

'That's right. And you'll live over the shop.'

'And I will help you. And treat it like my own. And paint on the days I do not work.'

'Paint? Walls?'

'And roofs, and churches, and birds, and trees, hills,

landscapes, crags, horizons.'

He moved into a massive room, complete with wash hand basin, closed off toilet, and kitchenette. It was floored in garish linoleum, bumpy and cracked in places, but swept and clean. The windows soared to the ceiling, which was made of ornate pressed metal sheets, painted yellow and peeling in the corners. The bed seemed enormous, bare except for a flowered bedspread.

'You'll use the shower on the floor below yours. And you'll have to get your own Manchester.'

'My own what?'

'Sheets and blankets and towels and all that. *Linen.*'

'Manchester.' He had learned a new colloquialism. Committing things to memory was becoming a daily necessity.

Learning, selling hats, buying sheets for his new bed; learning. Learning to make friends. Walking into small milk bars and listening to conversations; something taught to him by Uršula, who was so far away. Who never answered his letters. Perhaps she never got them. Perhaps she had no time. Perhaps she destroyed them, because they were written words. Perhaps he was replaced now, underneath that big quilt, by some other lost soul from the glass factory. But he did what she taught him. Saving money. Keeping his things neat. Collecting words. Collecting little bits of information. Assembling a life, assembling meaning.

There was no standing in long lines here, like he did for Uršula. The abundance of food was at first staggering. The supermarkets made him stand and stare. More than six brands of butter. Five different kinds of oil. Large packs of lard. Cartons and cartons of eggs. Sides of mutton. A whole aisle of confectionery and chocolate. Fruit juice in large bottles. Trays of sausages. Boxes of tropical fruits, stands of bananas.

Observing, noting, remembering combinations of customs and habits, all rolled into an Australian blend. He saw it in Harry; that familiar old-fashioned Czech prudence, coupled with Australian humour, which tested Edmund on his feet about hats, without humiliating him. He would never forget that. Like he would never forget his first sight of a wall of fruits of all colours, which went almost to the ceiling of one shop.

He saw it every day, all around St Kilda, in its strange narrow streets, its splendid foreshore, its long long jetty that did not seem to serve any purpose. There were buildings that looked like old-fashioned halls, almost like European or colonial hotels and banks. There were cake shops the like of which he had only seen in Antwerp. And a motley crowd of people from everywhere, including Jews in big hats.

'A melting pot, this is.' Someone replied to his observation about it. It was one of a group of young men, in to get a trilby each for 'the show'.

'What show?'

'Where have you been, mate? There are only two things you need to know about Melbourne.'

'Yeah – the Melbourne Cup and the Melbourne Show! Come along for the ride. C'mon!'

Edmund had no idea at first what they were talking about, but remembered information he found in newspapers under the counter, read at the time Harry took his three days away.

'Read all about it, Edmund.' He had advised. 'You'll find people come in for hats around that time. Spring, spring – our best selling season. Men will want something to throw in the air when their horse comes in.'

'Horse!'

'At the Melbourne Cup. Big race. Spring carnival.'

'And the ladies?'

'They go to the city, and spend a fortune on confections they might only bring out once.'

'Confections.'

'Elaborate head gear!'

The young men in the shop for 'fancy trilbies' were right, it was busy in Spring, and groups and gaggles of them rode about in chunky square cars. Many boasted about the power of their Holdens, and the EH was a model he learned to spot. Light blue, khaki, yellow, or aquamarine, with that noticeable white white roof, it was a car he would not have minded driving himself.

It might add to his sense of freedom, to his sense of belonging, to his sense of having arrived, if he could drive an Australian car.

'I would like an EH Holden.'

'Hah! Edmund, get real. You simply can't afford it.' Harry had a realistic practical bent, one Edmund could not afford to ignore.

'Ok, Harry – I won't go and blow everything I've got on an EH.'

'Didn't think you would, but stranger things have happened. I thought you were going hooning with a bunch of fellows.'

'Hooning?'

'All right, not hooning exactly – go to the show and have a wonderful time. Meet some sheilas and enjoy yourself. Don't get too drunk, y'hear?'

He did get drunk. So drunk he was sick, sick, sick all over the back tyre of just such a car, in the car park at the show, abandoned by the rest, burnt by the sun, head banging with the noise, the heat, and the press of the crowd.

The last straw was a ride on the ferris wheel, or

perhaps it was the dodgems that finally brought the contents of his stomach – hotdogs with too much mustard and potato chips fried in oil – to his throat.

'Arggh.'

'Not on my car, you sick bastard!' Jerry the driver swore, but handed him a nicely laundered handkerchief. 'Ya'll have to hose it down later, ya dodo.'

He had executed some rite or other, a rite of passage that put him in with that crowd. It went on for months. Cinemas, dances, and a rowdy, raucous, hilarious visit to the Les Girls show at the Ritz, right around the corner from where he worked in Harry's hat shop.

After the show, his eyes wide from the spectacle, something he had never before experienced, Edmund was made to accompany the crowd to the stage door.

'Did you get it, Ed?'

'Get what?'

'You did get that they're men, right?'

'What – all *men*?'

'Yeah. The girls are all blokes, din'tcha notice?'

It was impossible to notice. They were brilliant, sparkling, completely convincing. There were whistles and cat calls, right there on the narrow back street where the steps of the stage entrance was.

'Ooooh – I remember you! Hello, Edmund!'

How could she ... he ... she possibly know him? Confusion assailed Edmund, and he scanned the transvestite showgirl's face. Still in plumes and fishnet and not much else, she preened and bent knees, turned this way and that. When she winked, the thick make-up and false eyelashes, the bright red lipstick on the wide mouth struck a chord, a sliver, a thread of memory.

'Did you like the show, my pet?'

'Yes, yes.'

'Hey! Edmund knows the showgirls! Hurray! You dark horse, Edmund.'

Where did she know him?

'I'm Les, darling – got you to Harry's shop that day. Remember?'

He remembered. He remembered. Of course he remembered. His timid smile was cheered by all, and grew to a grin.

There was a lot to remember. Edmund committed it all to memory, living very nearly a double life. Selling hats, painting, and driving around Melbourne during the night with a bunch of fellows who would have drunk his pay away if he let them.

'Your shout, you stingy bastard!'

He learned how to take insults as well as the best of them. And give as good as he got. 'Put your money on the counter, ya drongo!'

It was a cry he learned to make, authentic and loud. They were of Italian, Portuguese, Croatian, Maltese, Greek, Dutch, and Sicilian stock, and they all rolled their customs and habits into the Australian mix that was St Kilda.

Fourteen

Cakes

'Is that Hermelìn? Hermelìn cheese?'

'No, young fellow. It's camembert. How much do you want?' She held a big knife over the wheel of flat white cheese.

It looked so much like the cheese from his childhood, from the long refectory table at the orphanage. Ah, the nuns would cut slivers of it, and place each one on a buttered piece of bread, each slice passed down the table until all white plates were laden with bread. They would then bow their heads for grace. *Bless us, O Lord, and these thy gifts ...*

'Are you going to stand there praying, or do you want to buy cheese?'

Had he said the words aloud? Talking to himself was becoming a habit. 'Hermelìn is Czech cheese.'

'And camembert is French, I suppose, but this one's made here, out in the ... where do they make this, Millie?'

'I don't know. Somewhere up the country. I do know its price. Do I? It's ...' A sigh of frustration from the older woman behind the counter. 'A dollar and ... and some cents! I still can't get my head around this new money. Or the new weights.'

'You never will, then. Hardly new, Millie! It's been months and months now. Years even.'

'It could be years. I still miss my pounds, shillings, and pence. I still miss my pounds and ounces.'

'A small piece, please.' Shopping on Acland Street was enjoyable. Edmund took cheese, pickles, salami, pastries, cakes, and deep-fried fish to his room over the hat shop and ate at the same large round table where he sketched and drew plans for his paintings. Light sliced into the room from across the way, over the rooftops straight into his window, drawing yellow lines across the lino floor. Making a visual puzzle of his tabletop easel.

He loaded a palette with yellows, fauns, greens, browns and greys. He used golds and beiges and painted an interior, taking a corner of his room, with that slice of bright light, and wished he could show it to Gust Baert. He *would* show it to Gust Baert. But it had to dry properly first.

I have been here a long time, he wrote in Flemish, hoping he would not mangle too many of the words. *I am now an Australian citizen, and I understand dollars much better than some of the residents who have had more than four years to get used to them. I am painting, and working in a hat shop, with a Czech called Harry. And this interior, which is an exercise in light, is for you and Therese.'*

He did not write that Harry had taken to leaving him in the shop, trusting him with his livelihood, his huge investment, his precious boxes of expensive hats. Harry was seeking a wife.

'I am settling down, at last. If I could be like you, Edmund, I would build a life … a good life.'

'Like me? Harry!'

'*Optimistický.* You look on the positive side of everything that happens. Even the bad things that happen. Like that cut.'

'Oh this. It was nothing.'

'It'll mark your face for life.'

Edmund touched his cheek. 'It's nothing.'

'It was something. Something bad. You get into the wrong crowd. You get into drunken scrapes. It's not real fun when young blokes get into fights, and their heads are cracked on the footpath.'

'Oh Harry – it's not that bad.'

'See? Optimistický. One thing, though.'

Edmund sensed what was coming. He looked at his shoes.

'You drink too much. You're hanging around with a crazy crowd. You spend too much money on cigarettes and booze and ... look, are those new shoes again? And new trousers? And a real leather belt?' Harry rolled his eyes. 'Okay. All right. The real leather belt I understand. But those awful shoes, and those flared trousers!'

'Harry, I know ...'

'You know a lot. You think you do. But one thing you've still to learn. You'll fall in with some crazy young woman, and she'll strip you of every cent you have. That's the next thing that will happen to you.' Hand on counter, eyes to the ceiling. 'And Clare – what's wrong with Clare? She likes you. She has her own business, renting rooms. She would make a nice wife. Pity she doesn't like me in that way, so much.'

'She's at least three years older than me. And ... what's the word? Prim. A little staid. Very ... I don't think she understands um ... music.'

'So? All the better. Look at me, I'm nearing forty, and I have still to find a woman – a nice European woman – who will cook and clean and iron my shirts like she should.'

'You mean a housekeeper.'

'I mean a wife, Edmund.'

'These are the nineteen-*seventies*, Harry. People don't think like that anymore.'

'*You* sure don't think like that. I can see it. Some young Australian woman will clean you out. She will flutter eyelashes at you ... call you *darling* and *love* and *sweet* and *honey* ...'

And turn his head, and be willing and fast and loose in the back of a Holden. Yes, he had met many girls like that, in mini-skirts, wearing eye make-up not so very different from the transvestites at the Ritz.

'They'll get you, Edmund.' Harry nodded his round head at him, telegraphed his own fear with rolling eyes. 'They'll ruin you. Make one of them pregnant, you mark my words, make one of them pregnant, which can happen, and your life is over. Over. You hear? Over!'

Edmund smiled through the warning. He had had such an encounter the previous night, with a plump willing dark-haired girl who seemed eager, as eager as he was, to neck and spoon and carry on in the back of Wilf's car ... or whatever the words were that glossed over what really happened. She had surprised him, but he was not about to hold back. Not after the beer he had drunk and the laughter in that club, and the beat and rhythm of the music which contributed to the whole feeling, the entire throb of the night. He was not about to tell Harry what happened. And that it would happen again tonight when he met her near the garages behind the club. The Galveston Avenue, that crazy club, which, for some reason he could not fathom, they all called *Fred's*. There was no Fred. But who cared?

'So you watch yourself, young man. Don't throw all caution to the wind ... to the sea breeze that comes in over Port Phillip Bay ... don't be a dumb galah!'

'But ...'

'I know, I know. You're thinking you don't want to

be as cautious and wary and suspicious as I am, either. That's what you're thinking. Well – my hard work, my struggle ... I will not waste it all on some uncaring, ungrateful woman, see?'

The conversation was curtailed when a customer walked in to buy a panama hat, but the words rang in Edmund's head long after.

She disappeared after that, the brunette whose name he could hardly remember. He never saw her again. He gave her a hat shop card that night, proudly and self-importantly, he thought now. He had watched her walk away without a backward glance, straightening her mini-skirt, tucking in her blouse, and patting her fringe and ponytail. She disappeared into deep angular shadows thrown by buildings. He wondered about her, but he never saw her again.

Was Harry right? Or was the truth somewhere in between the hatter's extreme caution and old-fashioned views about what women were really like and what a wife was really for; and the devil-may-care views of the blokes he moved with? *They* hardly knew. Could hardly express an opinion. All they cared about was drink and smoke and deep-fried food and thumping music and sex. There was no one in between. No one from whom to seek a differing opinion, a more moderate opinion.

Uršula – ah, Uršula did not differ greatly in her views from Harry. What if he could ask her now? What if he could once more trudge up those concrete stairs and knock on that brown door? What if she once more lifted the side of that quilt for him to *come to bed*? *Are you going to stand there and freeze?*

He never saw that Australian brunette again. And did not bother with others for a while. He sought the truth that lay somewhere between her and Harry's ideal. He sought something, someone. He feared loneliness, so he painted. Rooftops, for their lines, remembering what Gust Baert had said, wishing he could once more climb up to that home above the art supplies shop and draw with him at the table. Gust's letters, written sometimes on that pink wrapping paper, were full of little margin sketches. He waited for them. There were corners filled with light. Little portraits of Therese, sketches of his own wrinkled hands, and birds, birds. Whole sheets of paper covered in Flemish words and birds.

He held back. He saved his money.

'What's with ya, Ed? Lost your taste for fun, mate?' The Holden boys asked, knocked on his door, tempted him with their rollicking stories and escapades.

'I'm working on a big picture. I need to finish this painting, that's all.' And he never resumed the blistering pace of before. Never again went on two-day benders of hazy, forgotten sprees down and up the back streets of St Kilda, getting into fights and risking getting his skull broken on the edge of some kerb. Never again spewed his guts into the walled-off toilet in his huge upstairs room over the shop, where the bumpy lino was striped with morning light, which barrelled, streaked, and crackled into his hangover like lightening.

Lightening, lightening. It threw split-second shadows of objects he hardly knew were there. The winter embraced Melbourne and shivered the binge he had revelled and rolled in right off him. He had revelled and rolled for nearly a year. And nothing to show for it but a pot belly. *Edmund Eben, shape up.* He spoke to himself. *Edmund Eben, listen to Harry.* He counted his dollars again, and squirrelled away his money, this time in a bank account, rather than a sock, a metal hinged box that used to contain lozenges or tobacco, or a novel whose pages bulged with notes. A bank account. A real place to keep his money.

Lightening and rain, rain, rain, dribbling and drizzling, pouring and spouting over his windowpanes, keeping him inside, sketching.

'I'm freezing.' They were words he never thought he would say, in a place like Australia.

Clare smiled. 'Freezing? Here – take this up. You'll have to fill it with oil yourself, but.'

It was a cylindrical kerosene heater, with a wick that glowed blue, which showed through the metal grill at the bottom. It smelled, it made his eyes water at first, until he learned to regulate the oil flow and leave a window open a crack. But it took the worst off the chill in his room.

The big round table was covered in work. Work, he called it. His work on pages and pages of plain white paper he walked all the way to Acland Street for. He drew like one demented, scribbling, drafting, sketching, and scribbling some more. It was at times irrational and at others considered, careful, exact, with perspective improving, vanishing point correctly calculated, all lines satisfying.

He tamed his craving for alcohol with sugar. He devoured cakes and pastries, and walked off the energy on the foreshore, St Kilda to Elwood and back, and back, and back. St Kilda to Brighton. St Kilda to Elsternwick. St Kilda to Caulfield.

'To Caulfield – are you crazy? That's miles!'

'I'm crazy, Clare. I'm crazy.'

He tried all the cake and pastry varieties in the brilliant shops on Acland Street. *Sacher Torte*, Polish cheesecake, chocolate *kugelhopf*, lemon tart, poppy seed cake, *millefeuilles*, vanilla slice, éclairs, and oh, oh the brilliant plum lattice that whipped him back, if he closed his eyes, to the orphanage kitchen.

It was not as rich with butter in his childhood as it was here – divine, divine – because of the strictures and austerity of those times, the deprived times of his childhood. But he had recently read Proust, and yes, yes; the taste had triggered a memory of sitting at a long refectory table, and occasionally being treated to a small piece of plum cake with glistening sugar granules on top.

Post-war scarcities and severity meant his childhood was bereft of abundance and luxury the like of which he saw here in Melbourne, but some things rang a loud bell, tugged at memory cords in his head and heart. Oh, that plum cake.

Almond macaroons, marzipan sticks. He ate them all, clutching paper bags stuffed with the sweets and walking, walking off his desire for beer, for cider, for anything to make his head spin. Spin, or steady? After a while it was a stretch for him to recreate the feeling. Spin, or steady, or sick? The sugar, flour, butter, and fruit in the cakes he ate made him better.

'You're looking nice and plump, Edmund!'

'Too plump, Harry.' He might be putting on weight, but he sold many many hats to a dwindling market, and swore he ran the danger of wearing one himself soon, if he was not careful.

'You would look nice in a homburg.'

'Don't push it, Harry. I see you're wearing one yourself.'

It was to hide his bald spot, of course. 'Lorena likes it.'

Lorena was everything Harry had sought so avidly for years. Her people were Portuguese and traditionally inclined to habits and customs the hatter recognized and in which he found refuge.

Edmund figured the man felt safe. Safe in the arms

of a woman whose domestic skills were superior to his own ability to analyse, to figure what she sought for herself. But it did not matter, after all. Romantic love, ideal love, was only a fairy tale, to be found only on a flickering screen at the cinema, or on television.

They were married without undue haste, and now lived in a newly-built house in Bentleigh, where they grew tomatoes and eggplant at the back of their block, and where soon the sound of little voices would drown the sounds of work; digging, drilling, hammering, of new houses rising all around them.

'It pays to wait, Edmund.'

'Does it?'

'It pays to wait.'

Edmund waited for the pull of alcohol to pass. He ate his way out of the craving, becoming an addict of sugar instead. 'Lemon tart, Harry. Kugelhopf with plenty of chocolate icing, eh? That's all I want.'

'Then come tonight and have a nice piece of *bolo rei.*'

'Is it the one stuffed with preserved fruit?'

'And nuts, yes. And coated in a shower, like snow, of confectioner's sugar. That is Lorena's specialty.'

The doughy texture of *bolo rei* tasted vaguely like the *smoulebollen* he had eaten in Belgium. 'Yes, thank you – that I cannot resist.'

Life threatened, however, to be filled with nothing but eating and selling hats. Only painting lifted him from the brink of abject boredom. On some evenings, listening to the rain thrum on the roof, the cars hissing past up and down the street, the occasional shout from a group of young men hell bent on stupefaction, Edmund would sink into a haze of sadness, of nostalgia, of craving for something familiar ... a checked quilt, a bowl of steaming *waterzooi* in the company of an old

Belgian couple, an alphabet book in English. The search for a soft woollen shawl around the head and shoulders of a shadowy woman. A woman to cherish. To adore.

He was lonely again.

Fifteen

Out of nothing

February, 1974. The seventeenth of February, the seventeenth; he remembered it well. The day his whole life changed. The hottest day he ever endured. Forty-two degrees in the shade, and he was not about to stand in it. Not in the St Kilda streets, where the bitumen turned soft, the tram rails glimmered hotly, ready to buckle, and the sky went white with it. He would not have gone out in that, had it not been his craving for something sweet. Something cold and sweet, like the cream filling of an éclair kept in a cool glass case.

Or ice cream. That was what Edmund wanted. A large tub of ice cream he would devour in one sitting, filling his stomach with cold, cold, cold. Cold solid frozen cream, freezing, gelid, glacial. He braved the deserted suburb, and walked down to Acland Street. Everyone must be 'down the beach', all gathering on the torrid sand, standing in the waves, up to their waists, talking, shading their eyes, plunging in the water every now and then to cool their core. Standing in water, swimming, watching his fingers turn pink and wrinkly. No, no. It was never his thing. Besides, the sand ... it got into everything.

His core was hot, so hot he felt he would go mad with it soon. Perspiration stood out on his forehead in beads. The belt around his waist felt like a brand that would cut him in half.

The cake shops. The line of cake shops, a deserted footpath. Not a soul to admire the cakes. There was usually a crowd outside, looking at the cakes like they were pictures at a gallery, or some television show, or cinema screening, or stage presentation of something alive and entertaining.

A voice behind him. 'No one here today.'

He saw her, reflected in the shop window, among the cakes, the glorious little cakes, all in perfect lines, on perfect trays. She too looked perfect. He turned. 'Well, Clare. Just you and I.'

'Too darned hot.'

He laughed. 'I'm after some ice cream. A huge tub. That will cool me down.'

'Not a bad idea. Look – I'll send up an electric fan on a stand to your room. I'm sure you could do with it.'

'That is so kind and thoughtful.'

'You're a good tenant, Edmund. I've never had someone who paid on the dot, each month. It's fabulous – I don't have to fuss or worry.'

'Really?'

'Really. Now I could do with some ice cream.'

'What are we standing here for, then? This is shocking weather.' He looked at her prim checked sundress, whose straps were narrow, to match the strappy sandals on her narrow feet. There were little plastic shells sewn onto her straw handbag, which had faux cane handles. Two clips with shells on them held back her hair.

'I'm meeting a friend.' She looked at her reflection in the shopwindow.

'A mad dog, or an Englishman. Can't be anything else, eh?'

She laughed. 'Look, come along, why don't you? We

can have an ice cream down the road. You'll like Giovanna.'

Giovanna. She was not someone he had seen in St Kilda before, but Edmund recognized her. He had never met her before, but he recognized her. Her spirit. Her charm. Her tacit melancholy. Determined, though – he saw it in how she held her head. A determined young woman, small, petite, with bright eyes and a Roman nose, but with character that filled rooms.

'This is Edmund, the Edmund I mentioned.' Clare kissed her on the cheek, and seemed to vanish. She was there, she did not move away, but she vanished.

Giovanna's smile filled the café, the St Kilda street. The world. Silent, pensive, but smiling, she nodded at Edmund. 'How nice to meet you,' she said. Absentminded. Absent. Her mind was elsewhere. He felt she wanted to be alone. So why was she braving the hot streets, the company of a friend, if all she wanted was her own company ... but how could he make such an assumption?

Out of politeness, she smiled. Did she notice Edmund, take note of his name? He slid down in the hot metal chair, observed her dark wavy hair, full lips, and sad, sad dark eyes. Heard her accent.

The best way to open a conversation. 'So where are you from, Giovanna?'

'Down the road – Elwood.'

He was taken aback.

Her sad eyes smiled. She knew what he meant. 'My family is Sicilian. Dad is Sicilian. We're from the southernmost point of Sicily – Ragusa. I was born there. And my mother pretends she's Sicilian too, but she's really Maltese. She's not well now, though.' Concerned. Exotic. Little. Petite, unusual.

'I'm sorry.'

Captivating, that sad smile. Captivating.

'What about *your* mother?' An unusual voice, too.

Edmund lowered his eyes. What about his mother? 'She ... she's ...' He leaned on the table, forearms on the edge. Then he gripped that edge, knowing what he said might either damn or save him. Forever. 'In my mind, my mother wears a soft woollen shawl, Giovanna. I can't see her face. I can't. She wrapped me in that shawl. It was after the end of the war. The Soviet armies descended on Prague and it was difficult, it was impossible. So to save me, she wrapped me in her soft shawl and left me on the steps of an orphanage, in an apple basket.'

Her eyes were wide. Abruptly. Unexpectedly. Her hands, together, flew to her cheeks. 'Oh my goodness.'

'I ... I cannot remember her face. I was a week old.' It did not seem humiliating any longer. It was just the truth. His truth.

'Oh – suddenly I feel blessed. My mother's sick, but I am blessed to have enjoyed her so long.'

For an hour they ate ice cream and talked, talked. Clare watched them, bemused. Amused. She sat back, better to watch what was taking place at her table. Ate ice cream and knew she watched something momentous. Giovanna took up and set down her spoon a thousand times, animated.

'Call me Vanna. Call me Vanna – everyone at home does.'

Edmund gripped the table edge and leaned forward, as if worried he might lose eye contact with her. The history and geography of Europe unravelled at that table, in a narration that was more than just personal. It was paving the way.

'Look, you two...'

Giovanna and Edmund looked up, silenced,

surprised, almost surprised to find Clare there. They both surfaced from somewhere deep, to catch their breaths, to gulp for air.

'Look ...' Her smile was happy, awed by what she witnessed. 'I must catch the tram ... that way. But don't let me break up the party. Carry on.' She smiled again.

They needed no second bidding.

His first phone call to her after that was nervous. Uncertain. Unsure how she would respond. 'Hello, Giovanna...'

A few words. Cutting. Cutting him short. Rapidly changing his mood, his intentions, his rehearsed phrases. 'My mother just died. Sorry. Sorry, Edmund. Sorry.'

Sad. Agonizing. Tearing at him. Heart rending, distressful, that the first formal event Edmund attended with Giovanna was her mother's funeral. On a brilliant cloudless day, numbed by the collective emotion of two devastated families, he was overcome by grief to see Giovanna floundering with hers. Ah, she looked distraught.

As soon as he could he left them to their private grieving, astonished by their cohesion, envious of their oneness, their family spirit; saddened almost as much as they were.

He walked away anesthetized by something he could not name.

'It's almost as if my own mother died, just now. Whereas I lost mine decades ago.'

'But did you ever grieve?' Harry knocked knuckles on the hat shop counter. 'Did you grieve?'

'How do I remember? Probably not. I was a week old when ... How do I know?'

The hatter took a homburg and smoothed its brim with the forearm of his shirt. He held it up to the light streaming in from the street. 'You've grieved now. Now you can go through a new phase.'

What did Harry know about all this? What did he know about Edmund? What did he know about an orphan who had come through so many changes? All he wanted to talk about was Giovanna. She existed among a crowd of relatives, in his mind, lost among cousins and siblings and a huge crowd of uncles and aunts. A sea of black clothing, a wave of dark hair. A galaxy of sad eyes.

'Are you seeing her again?'

How did Harry know? He just went with Clare to the funeral, and it was only by chance he got to stand by Giovanna for a short time. Only through determination that he told her he would phone her. How did he know?

'I should phone her.'

'Look – bring her round to meet Lorena. Sounds like they'll get on. After a suitable period, I mean, *samozřejmě. Naturally ...*'

'*Samozřejmě*. Of course. Thank you.'

A week, a month – an eon – before he saw her again. A frenzied search for something to give her, to relieve her of grief. To distract himself from the question, the question.

'Harry – I just don't know whether she will even remember me. I can't pose the question. *Do you remember me?* It's stupid.'

The older man paused. Turned. Tilted his head. Reached for a soft hat brush and balanced it on a forefinger. Looked at Edmund without a word.

'Seriously, Harry. All I can do ...'

' ... is think of her, you lovesick loon. You madman. I wish, I wish I was twenty-six.' He put down the brush. 'She remembers you. You went to her mother's funeral, Edmund. You are a permanent *značka* in her mind. An indelible mark. You and your orange hair.'

'How do you know?'

Harry had no idea, but he had to reassure Edmund if he was ever to serve another customer. 'I just know. Now come back to earth and see if that gentleman would like to pay for the panama hat he has been trying on for fifteen minutes, will you?'

There it was. He found it. At last. At the Melbourne central city shops, in the window of an establishment that seemed created exclusively for a wealthy clientele. Customers to whom money was no object. There it was, draped over a stand; beautiful, stylish. Perfect. Perfect. Faultless. Just as he had imagined, all his years. Imported from Europe. Made of the softest cashmere. It looked deliciously soft even behind plate glass. Grey – the perfect grey; one of the most difficult hues for an artist to create, one of the most elusive on his palette.

He loved the shawl and its woven pattern, floral, in a kind of silver tone, shot through with threads of a darker charcoal hue. And subtle black tonings. A good design, an arrangement he could visualize on a crystal bowl. Unbelievably expensive, almost out of reach. An insane purchase, which he asked to be gift wrapped. Wrapped, wrapped, folded between expensive tissue, every fold a sweeping gesture. Ah. Perhaps it was worth every cent. Perhaps this shawl was his most foolish purchase ever.

'I thought you would never call me.' She was breathless on the phone, as if she had run to pick it up. 'I thought I'd never hear from you again.'

Words that sang, sang, replayed, rang in Edmund's ears. For several days afterwards. Even when they met. Even after several meetings. On the foreshore, at a bus stop. Outside a cinema. *I thought I'd never hear from you again.*

She talked a lot, skipping over the ends of her own sentences to start others. She made him laugh, cynical and perceptive, analytical and clever, hilarious and absurd, all at once. His mind leapt and scurried, to keep up with her lines of perspective.

'How wonderful that you paint. How wonderful that you can do that.'

'Really? Really, Vanna?' Pleasure, pleasure. A wave of pleasure he barely understood.

'Oh – of course *really*. It must be awful to have to work at something else to be able to do your art. You should really be painting all the time. You must find a gallery to show your work. Perhaps an agent. Let's talk to Uncle Mario.'

Let's – she always said *let's*. It was always *us, we*.

Astonished, continually, by her immersion into his life.

Clare translated it all into words he could take in. 'She thinks you're wonderful, Edmund. What's not to understand? She's never met anyone like you.'

Harry too, after meeting Giovanna, offered explanations. 'This is so new to you? That someone thinks you're perfect? Ha ha. Look – you're not perfect. No one is. Not even me! But you're perfect to her, see? You're perfect for *her*, she thinks.'

Perfect. Perfect. Just right. Ideal. She was ideal for him. She was what he sought. For so long. Not ideally beautiful, perhaps. But such willingness to bend around his notions, his ambitions. Her willingness blended with his own desire; to make her happy, to like what she liked.

'Have you given her that gift you talked about? Did she like the shawl?'

Edmund looked away. 'No, Harry. Is it a good time to give her a gift? Will she think it's presumptuous?'

'What? Have you had it upstairs in your room all this these weeks? Edmund – what is *wrong* with you?'

'I can't do calculations in my head, my pronunciation's all wrong, all I want to do is paint, and I have no idea where I stand with Giovanna.'

Harry slapped the counter. Slap. Slap. Drum, drum, with impatient fingers. 'I give up. I give up with you. First, you turn St Kilda over with your juvenile antics. Then you mooch around for months wondering whether you'll ever find "her". Then, when you do, you mooch around wondering what to do *about* her.' Drum. Drum. Deserted shop. Sharp sunlight streaming in a slant up to the counter. Up the wall. Across the ceiling to the fluorescent light strung on two chains.

He could paint that. Angular light. Browns, browns and dun, beige, gold, fawn, taupe, ochre, burnt sienna. He could paint it, and Giovanna would say he should exhibit it. Wonderful, she would say. Wonderful.

'Listen to me, young man. Don't make a big deal of it. Just take her out, buy her a lemonade, slip the parcel across the table. Then sit back and enjoy her ... what you call them ... exclamations. Women do that. *Oooh. Ahh.*'

Across a table. Across the table between them, at a small restaurant in Elsternwick, where every few minutes, he could hear a train trundle past, where a huge sign, *Velvet Soap*, hanging across the street, stuck in his mind. Where he noted her pale pink nail polish, and that she had a new haircut, which made her look all the more attractive, vivacious, talkative. So talkative. Like him. They often spoke at once. Laughing, laughing.

'You know, I would have been plunged into depths of despair when Mamma died, if it were not for you.'

'For me?'

'Clare said you were a distraction, but I think it's

something else. You're *interesting*, that's what.' She nodded in a way he understood.

Sliding the parcel across. Without a word. Looking at her face. Her eyes.

'Oh! For me? It isn't even my birthday. How wonderful.' And unwrapping it, hastily, curiously, full of excitement. 'Oh. Oh, how *lovely*. Oh, this is very special.' She took up the shawl. Exclaiming, holding it up. 'So soft, so special. And grey – I can wear it right away. Right now. Right now!' Draped, arranged, swathed around her head and shoulders.

Edmund was enchanted, surprised to see it was just as he imagined. Just as he dreamed. Just as he desired it to be. 'Beautiful. You look beautiful, Vanna.'

'Because I'm happy, Ed*mundo*. Happy, happy.' She smiled and tilted her head. 'Thank you. This is lovely, I shall treasure it always.'

He saw she understood the meaningfulness of it. He felt she knew how important the shawl was. It was one of the moments he would never forget. How she turned his name into a special name. Her own name for him; Edmundo, Mundo. *Mundo*.

Out of nothing he had sculpted an imaginary persona, such a long, long time ago. And now this young woman saw him, believed him; made it all real.

If you enjoyed this novel, try another work of fiction from this author.
Find this ghost historical on Amazon.

The White Lady of Marsaxlokk

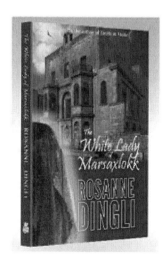

Based on local anecdotes and landmarks, *The White Lady of Marsaxlokk* is a melancholic story of the melding of history into present day. It takes the reader on a engaging journey through time, to a captivating house which still attracts attention, on a feasible excursion that is enchanting and just a little bit eerie.

29214134R00170

Printed in Great Britain
by Amazon